What happens when the metaphysical rules no longer apply?

An allegorical story of personal discovery and growth ... and perhaps angels, too.

The Mirror of Gabriel Street

The Mirror of Gabriel Street

By
Farley Dunn

THE MIRROR OF GABRIEL STREET

Farley Dunn

1st Ed.

Minneapolis, forgive me for taking liberties.
This is a work of fiction after all.

ISBN: 978-1-957173-53-5

Table of Contents

Part One

The Bright Beginning

1

An Old Mirror

ALEX MORTON woke up to his phone vibrating against the nightstand and the comforting knowledge of not being late—yet.

6:23 AM. Not early enough to impress anyone, but not late enough to cure his exhaustion.

He reached toward his phone and tapped it before rolling to his back and blinking his eyes. Minneapolis summer sunlight filtered through half-closed blinds, turning the dust in his apartment into slow-motion glitter. He lay still for a moment, watching light spill in thin horizontal bands between the blinds. The dust motes caught the light the way the birchwood on his long-ago trips with his father had once caught the sunrise: thousands of quiet galaxies spinning in his apartment air.

He smiled at the thought, then immediately scolded himself. Romanticism before coffee, Morton? Rookie mistake.

The city outside was already living faster than he felt capable of following. Streetcars hissed. Someone down the hall thumped an early treadmill. He forced his legs out of the bedding and muttered his first prayer of the day—not to any deity his father would recognize, just to momentum.

He pushed back the bedding and sat up, rubbing his hands over his face and forcing his hair out of his eyes. With a deep breath, he pushed the night away, forever gone, a video reel in the can with the set already broken down to be repurposed for other scenarios. As he stood, he took in the shape of himself still in the rumpled bedding, the pillows crushed as he tossed during the night, and the vague aroma of sleeping man that filled the room.

A normal morning. Alex's life as always. No different than usual, and he adjusted the elastic beltline of his sleeping pants before taking a final look around his bedroom and heading through the open bathroom door.

The mirror over the sink ran the full length of the bathroom and was his first stop. He needed the toilet—normal, he conceded, after a full night's sleep—but it was never his first action each morning. After his dreams, the ones "in the can," he needed to assess who he really was, that his identity was uncompromised, and the world had returned to the reality of twenty-four-year-old Alex in his trendy apartment jutting into the outstanding and hip skyline of modern-day Minneapolis. Only when he caught the confident smile in his bathroom mirror did his heart truly settle. The thick shock of sandy blond hair, the full lips, the strong chin that was the only one he knew ... yeah, he was there, real and just like always. The image in the mirror pointed two fingers at him and, with a mock-swagger, whispered, "Own the day." The slogan was one he'd downloaded from one too many motivational videos.

That didn't mean he believed it. It was closer to superstition for him. Repeat it, and when the day ran smoothly, he knew the reason. If he missed his slogan, and the elevator was late or he spilled coffee on his freshly pressed shirt, then that was the reality of it. So, in a nutshell, he didn't entirely believe it but repeated it anyway.

"Own the day, yourself," he said with a grin, wishing the man in the mirror an equal dose of good luck. He always did that, repeating back what the man said to him, an inside-joke between two friends who were closer even than twins. Because the man in the mirror was himself, through and through, even though they'd never met.

He cut his eyes to the shower door and the towel draped over the top. A quick touch told him it was damp from the night before but not too damp to use as he shaved. With the towel beside the sink, he pulled his shaving kit from underneath and opened it on the counter. The morning had grown long, and the toilet suddenly took precedence. He flipped up the seat and anticipated letting go of the final remnants of the night. He glanced up to find his doppelgänger doing the same. The image looked up just as Alex did, catching his eye, and Alex looked away, oddly embarrassed. It was just a reflection, he told himself. There was no one there. The vaguely clean-cut man who copied every motion that Alex made consisted of light, no more than photons and energy, and no more real than his dreams.

There was always that half-second, though—the flicker in the mirror when he looked too long. Just the hint that his reflection's eyes seemed sharper than his own, saw something Alex didn't, even into Alex's soul and into the heart of who he was.

He laughed it off as he completed his absolutions and flushed. He put a broad hand to his face and rubbed sleep from his stubble as he stepped back to the sink and dashed a dollop of shaving cream into his palm. He worked it over his chin, pulled out his razor, and began to scrape it along his neck, leaving smooth skin behind. With a quick rinse of his face and his razor, everything was quickly stowed, and he grabbed a clean white shirt from the laundry chair. His phone vibrated again from his nightstand. He buttoned up his shirt, pulled slacks from the back of the chair, and slipped his legs inside. With a tuck and a buckle, he walked into the bedroom for his waiting socks and shoes.

No more time for metaphysical pondering. The world was coming to life. There were spreadsheets to build and clients to charm.

He slipped his phone into his pocket, but before leaving the room, he glanced back at the bed. The shape of him. And the shape of the man in the mirror. Which one slept there last night? Or did the man in the mirror have his own bed on his side of the glass?

Alex laughed as he headed towards his front door. Just before leaving the apartment, he paused at a small mirror by the door and snapped his tie in place. When he smiled, the reflection returned it half a beat late.

Old mirror, he told himself.

Still, he paused. Somewhere in that put-together stranger he kept noticing traces of a boy crouched in wet leaves, freeing a frightened bird before anyone could call him brave. The memory gnawed sometimes, gentle but persistent, like water through wood.

He chuckled and brushed off the feeling. He hoped the other him on the other side of the glass found time to straighten his bed. And if he did, maybe he'd straighten Alex's, too.

2

The Illusion of Numbers

THE ELEVATORS in the Kane & Sutter Consulting Tower glided up to the twenty-second floor so quietly they might as well have been thought-powered. Frosted glass, "open culture," and an espresso machine built like cathedral machinery. Alex was early, of course. He always was. Associates who wanted to be partners before thirty practically lived on caffeine and optimism.

He merged seamlessly into the swirl: polished shoes, crisp badge on a lanyard, small talk that sounded spontaneous but wasn't. After two years, it had become second nature, calling to people he knew, answering well-meaning jabs lanced from associates' desks.

He paused at the reception desk. Stacie Laughton worked the morning shift, and she was dressed to the nines today.

"Something special we don't know about?"

"Oh, what do you mean, Mr. Morton?" She winked at him.

"Oh, so I asked the wrong question. Is there *some-one* special we don't know about?" Stacie was easy to tease with. She never appeared to have a bone to pick with anyone, and she seemed to really enjoy the people around her.

"Don't you get me going, Alex. You know you're the only man in my life." She blew him a kiss. "Now off with you. I clocked in twenty minutes ago, and I can't waste the company's time on you."

"Ha!" Alex rapped the top of her desk. "Morning to you, too, Stacie."

He let himself be swept further into the building, nodding and greeting people he'd seen only yesterday.

"Morning, Morton!" shouted Rick from Accounting.

Alex turned to see Rick Calloway leaning against his desk with a cup of steaming coffee in his hand. It was the man's calling card, especially before they were on the clock. Alex chuckled and lifted an arm to wave.

"Hey, Rick. First coffee or third?"

"Third's for quitters." Rick lifted his steaming brew in a mock salute to the small talk going on around him.

"Then I'm up for it!" This time Alex laughed. He enjoyed Rick's company. Would they ever really become friends, outside-of-work friends? They were working on it. Above Rick, a giant clock pulsed on the wall, telling everyone in the building that time to clock in was on the way.

As the minute hand clicked over once more, Alex was reminded: *They like you because you're easy. Don't complicate your life with too much trust.* He wondered at the small voice inside that seemed to take the world around him and translate it into something *else.* Sometimes he thought he'd become exactly what his father admired: results walking upright. He wondered whether that counted as success or surrender.

"Morton," called his boss, Eliot Kane, emerging from his office with the grin of someone who knew he could ruin or rewrite any career with fifty words. "Got a sec?"

"Always for you, Eliot." Alex's voice managed that perfect tone between eagerness and self-respect. He prided himself on it, like a gymnast balancing between enthusiasm and dignity.

Eliot clapped him on the shoulder. "You've got presence, kid. Clients like you. Keep it up, and you'll be front-lining presentations before Q4."

Alex feigned modesty. "Thank you, sir."

"Okay, head out. We've got a day to slip under our belt."

Alex moved towards his desk with its granite top, sleek desk pad, and three colors of pencils with neatly turned erasers in their matching container. He even had a window, which was more than Rick could say. The inbox on his desk held a file folder. Paper was still a thing, even in their digital world. He tapped it with his knuckles and pulled the corner up to reveal the Coomer file. He knew it and knew it would consume his morning.

Before he was halfway through the folder, mid-morning sunlight had begun to bounce off the cubicle glass, scattering miniature halos across his desk. He tracked one as it slid toward his keyboard, then recalled his father cleaning fish on cold aluminum, with sunlight flashing on fish scales in much the same pattern.

The memory stung in a way he couldn't name.

"Stop it," he whispered, half aloud.

Several people glanced his way. Shaunika, sitting at the desk next to his, looked up from her keyboard and asked, "Did you need something, Alex?"

He'd forgotten how sharp her hearing was, either that or she was hyper aware of the people around her. She always noticed whenever Alex talked to himself. He covered with, "Running numbers, Shaunika. Sorry."

Numbers—the safest illusion of control he knew.

What made him think of his father? He had a pretty good idea. At twelve, his father took him fishing on Lake Mendota. "A man needs focus," the elder Morton said, baiting the hook with mechanical patience. "You think too much about people. Think about results."

Alex nodded, not totally understanding the cutting remark but also determined not to make too much of it. He and his father were fishing together, and he wanted that to be enough. So, he kept watching the way sunlight flickered in perfect lines across the lake's surface, tiny fractures of radiance linking everything, and wondered if light hurt itself coming through the waves.

He caught a single perch that morning. His father cleaned it in silence, the very act praising Alex's efficiency. There was no kindness in his father's world, only efficiency and performance. Alex learned to speak performance fluently after that trip.

He was drawn back into the room. Eliot. The Coomer file. Q4.

And the clients liked him. That was straight from Eliot's lips, so it was good as gold. Wasn't it?

What he didn't say, didn't want to even think: that

every compliment from Eliot came laced with invisible shackles. Each “keep it up” meant one more hour of unpaid time, one more forgotten weekend.

Still, he felt alive moving among the city’s towers of glass. He loved the pulse and the polish. He could almost believe that the momentum that came with each closed deal provided the purpose that carried him forward each day.

3

Coffee with Complications

DESPITE ALEX'S devotion to the corporate deity, once eleven-thirty clicked over on Rick's clock, and the scale-like sparkles had departed his desk for the harsher shadows of the overhead spotlights, completing the Coomer file began to pale against his desire to be away from his desk. There were only so many Coomer rabbit trails he could run before even he needed to chase something else.

At a quarter of, his phone vibrated.

REN: Noon—our table. Bring your existential crisis; extra napkins provided.

Alex grinned. Renee Delgado, good friend and sounding board for those times he wanted to burst the glass walls of corporate. He was his dad's son, but at times ... well, at times, he had to let go of that boy who had felt the pain of the fracturing sunlight, and it wasn't always easy.

At noon, he met Renee at their usual spot, grateful for the break. The café, Foodz, tried too hard to look accidental, with a rusted tin overhang and mismatched chairs. Even the counter for ordering looked temporary, just two long timbers on galvanized pipe legs. Posters delivered a laissez faire air of bohemian afterthought. However, even the mismatched chairs matched if you saw the pattern. And the posters were clearly curated, with their bohemian theme.

It was the smell of beans and burnt optimism that peeled back the onion skin of respectability, that and the students staring into cluttered laptop screens overflowing with half-finished futures.

Renee was mid-rhyme, humming something into her phone's memo app. She lifted her head from the screen.

"You're late," she said as he approached. "I wrote a verse about punctuality. It's very judgmental."

Alex smiled. "Sorry. Corporate worship service ran long."

"Praise be to PowerPoint," she intoned, crossing herself dramatically. "You do know that self-sabotage gets you nowhere in my storyline."

He laughed gratefully as he pulled out a chair at her table. A glance at the wall-hung menu was a reflex. It was burned into his brain. The trouble was that he was undecided. The memory of his father hadn't fully evaporated.

"You look tense. Spreadsheet haunting you?"

"Deadlines piling up," he said. He didn't say anything about his father. Who dredged up memories from half a lifetime ago and let them haunt half their day?

"Isn't that their nature? Piling? Like snow with email attachments?"

"At least the snow is pretty, until you walk in it for a week." He grinned to show he meant nothing by it.

Renee had this spark—half sunlight, half mischief—that reminded him of how humor could keep a person alive in a world that monetized souls by the hour. She had the rare gift of disarming him without pity. Her guitar case leaned against the table. Stickers on it read Love Wrecks Gently and Coffee Is a Sacrament.

"How's the music?" he asked.

"Unprofitable. Therefore authentic."

He watched her stir foam into small cyclones and thought briefly how unsupervised joy looked: ordinary things attended to carefully. Renee was unselfconsciously casual and easy to be with, even when stirring her coffee. He envied that.

The talk turned to dreams. Renee believed they were subconscious postcards; Alex preferred to call them neurological spam.

"And what did your brain-mail deliver last night?" she asked.

He hesitated but slipped back into trust. "I was walking on frozen water again."

"So," she said, sipping foam. "Dreams still weird?"

He tried to hide a flicker of disquiet. "Weird's a strong word." It was the very word he'd thought to himself, and he'd been trying to push it aside all morning.

"Symbolism alert! Your subconscious says you're too comfortable on thin ice." She tapped the side of her musical case where the sticker read, Coffee Is a Sacrament. "I can order you a cup."

"I'm thinking on it." He glanced at the girl behind the counter. She was wiping the sturdy boards with a rough, damp cloth, as if waiting on him to approach.

"So, no thin ice?" Renee tapped the tabletop, pressing him.

"Perhaps. Or too cold to feel it." A shiver ran down his back, catching him by surprise, almost as if someone were standing behind him, not quite touching but almost. A warm breath of ... concern? Protection? If so, he hoped someone had his back.

"You told me you were flying over a lake with a guy who looked like you."

"I was probably sleep-scrolling Instagram."

"Uh-huh. Self-obsessed even in your REM cycle." She stood. "I'm getting you coffee. And a sausage roll? That's what I'm having. You can repay me later."

He nodded as he let her jab land. It was easier to let Renee turn things into jokes. It kept the edges soft. But her song lyrics often rang truer than his dreams. What would today's sound like? He was surprised when she left her phone on the table with the screen still on. She tapped next to it to draw his attention and walked away. Even upside down he could read her lyrics from earlier.

Alex on the sand / At his back an unseen hand / Where will a good man land?

He smiled, the tension broken. The banter—both verbal and written—helped him push aside the warmth at his back. It was there increasingly often, especially whenever he let his guard down for too long.

As Renee returned with their lunch, she studied the area behind him, her brow knitting as she took her chair.

"Who was that?" She nodded over his shoulder.

"I don't—" He turned and no one was there. He shrugged and laughed it off. "My guardian angel?"

"Now, that's a song I could create. Probably

unprofitable, but man would it sound authentic."

They both laughed and focused the rest of their attention on their sausage rolls.

4

A Light in the Hallway

THAT EVENING, Alex waited in the hallway for Eliot to finish a call. Evenings were his exercise in false calm. He would often run spreadsheets until the numbers turned decorative, then walk home through streets salted white with the glow from the streetlamps. Tonight, the glass walls of the office tower reflected pale blue from the city lights, something that must have always been there, yet something he didn't recall. Nothing else seemed different, from the soft whir of the building's air conditioning to the aroma of nothingness that emanated from the polished floors and gleaming handrails that ran alongside the escalators. Well, not nothingness, he gradually realized, but the aroma of high-quality polish and wax.

He noticed, surprisingly, a soft brilliance at the corridor's edge near the emergency exit—like moonlight refracted through water. The water at the lake when he was twelve seemed to overlay the scene for a moment before Alex blinked the memory away. That was twice today. He shook his head to clear his thoughts.

Someone must've left a lamp on in the stairwell. It wasn't a big issue, but company policy stressed environmental accountability, and that meant that all lights were off when employees left a room, stairwells included. He turned his head to investigate, but the light disappeared and was gone. He frowned, certain he had seen it, then gave credit to whoever was in the stairwell. After all, the portion he could see formed both a beginning and an end. The employee could easily have been heading away from Alex, and he wouldn't know.

The issue was the late hour. When he worked this late, he sometimes saw things, which was likely due to low blood sugar. His last meal was the sausage roll from lunch, and it was gone hours ago.

Moments later, Eliot appeared, his phone pressed against his shoulder. He waved towards Alex to indicate that he saw him and paused before shutting down his call and dropping his phone into a pocket. He thumbed toward the exit, a quick and strategic move to show his time was important and that Alex mustn't shave off too much.

"Quick update—new client, huge opportunity. She's in Omaha for a three-week training session with one of our teams there, then she's headed in this direction. Sophie Verden, mid-west development fund. Smart, strategic, and exactly the type of connection you want. Thought you might like a heads up so you can oil the valves and be running on all cylinders." Eliot laughed. "Or something like that."

"Of course. You know you can count on me."

"Right. I'm off." Eliot smiled and bumped his shoulder with a loose fist then wagged a finger in his direction as he walked away. "Oil, Alex. Oil."

Eliot's enthusiasm seemed company focused,

and his smile harmless enough. But for the briefest instant, Alex thought he saw something else in the man's eyes: a gleam too sharp for friendliness, like a reflection glinting off a blade. Overhead, something buzzed, and for a moment, the world closed in, darker, more ominous, as if the light was being sucked away. Then, when Eliot turned his back and headed towards the exit, the fluorescent lights hummed back to life, and the world felt ordinary again.

"Wow, what was that?" The question was real, although it wasn't the first time. Yet, falling on the heels of the stairway incident ... put the two together, and it was weirder than even his dream from the night before.

Outside the building, the summer evening simmered with the final dregs of the day's warmth.

Somewhere near the Nicollet Bridge he always slowed, watching the reflection of the city's nighttime skyline play across the river's black skin. During the day it was bright and cheerful, often with kids throwing Frisbees along the banks, perhaps dogs chasing bones or sticks, with mothers walking babies in gleaming strollers. Those times showcased the good parts of Minneapolis.

At night? Under the cover of moonlight? With the stairwell and Eliot sucking the lights out of the sockets, well this wasn't the gleaming tourist draw that drove the city's financial officers to hire more travel agents. The view of the black water and the undulating reflection of the buildings' lights reminded him of something lost—maybe the simple symmetry of childhood certainty.

Had his childhood ever been certain? His needs

were certainly met, with a big house and a pool, summers on Long Island, and sleep-away camps in Vermont. Yet he'd desperately desired something from his father that the old man hadn't known he needed and had never provided.

Alex hadn't known he needed it, either, but now he did, and sometimes he felt the hollow space inside.

At moments like this, he focused on the world as he lived in it and told himself: You're doing fine. You pay your rent. You don't hurt anyone.

But deeper inside, another part of him sometimes clambered to the top and demanded to be acknowledged: So what? That's maintenance, not meaning. Your father maintained life, but you went without. You wanted more, and look at you now. Always hungry. Always searching. You know there's more to life than big houses and sleep-away camps.

Alex did, even if he hadn't known it at the time.

He took his time across the bridge, considered the advantages of catching an Uber next time, and decided that winter was soon enough to be lazy. Summer was for walking under the star-studded sky.

As soon as he opened his door, he remembered the Alex-shaped space in his bedding. It was too late to correct it, and he could only vow to do better in the morning. Less metaphysical pondering and more real-world tidying. His stomach growled in anticipation, and he headed to the kitchen half of his living area. There was no dining room, but the island was a ten-foot granite overhang that accommodated four stools just fine. He cooked without ceremony: eggs, toast, and a glass of juice. While at the cooktop, he used the remote to click on the television and chose a podcast to fill the silence. He didn't have to keep his eyes on the screen and could still follow along. He spoke back to them sometimes, testing opinions under his breath the way a singer tests a note's key, even though it's a song they don't actually intend to sing.

When he'd polished his plate with the last bite of toast, he slipped the dishes into the washer, poured himself a glass of water, and made his way into the living area. Outside, darkness had settled across the surrounding buildings. As he stood by the window, he saw several lights go dark, a sign that it was about time to hit the showers and the sheets.

As he turned away, the city lights twisted his glass of water into a shimmering aurora. The world felt dangerously transparent—and good.

He worked his phone from his pocket and tried calling his father. The emptiness of the night, he supposed, and wanting it filled with something familiar.

Voicemail. Again. Always.

Results, Alex, his father's remembered voice still lectured. Not moods. Not stories. Not an empty city skyline that mirrors the empty life you lead.

He imagined the man's neat desk and was reminded of the Kane & Sutter lobby. He wondered if loneliness smelled like lemon polish and neat solutions.

He felt the hairs lift on his neck, caught a shimmer in the glass, and remembered Renee at lunch. A shiver prompted him to look behind him, but of course he was alone. Then, the door was locked, and his apartment had only three rooms. Where was there for anyone to hide?

He kicked off his shoes and began unbuttoning his

shirt as he headed to the bathroom, certain he could make it all the way into the shower without looking in the mirror once.

Metaphysical pondering. Not on this night. All he wanted was sleep.

5

Coffee at Two

ALEX WORKED HIS head against his pillow. The day's warmth had evaporated in the small hours of the morning, and he was warmly cocooned in his bedding ... but still he couldn't sleep. He glanced at his nightstand. The glow of the clock on his phone read well past midnight.

"Thank you, phone," he muttered.

It wasn't the machine's fault he tossed and turned, but the numbers were his reminder that he had a busy schedule the next day. Dancing only worked if you were alert enough to keep up with the music and not step on your partner's toes.

He studied the ceiling, his eyes tracing the lines where it met the walls. Clean, sharp, and just visible as dark against darker in the slivers of light from the streetlamp outside. Many times, he'd imagined the ceiling ripped away, leaving the empty sky overhead. Would he sleep better with the stars for companions? He didn't know. How would it impact on his three private rules for sanity? He ran through them.

1. Say thank you, even to machines. As in, *Thank you, clock.* He smiled in the darkness. Grace practiced becomes reflex, something his father

had never shown.

2. Notice one good thing before heading to bed—any size. Being thankful for small things encouraged him to be aware that life wasn't all bad.
3. Never let cynicism finish a sentence for you. Trust was a better option, even if it sometimes burned you. Have faith in the impossible, and the impossible will find you.

Most nights rule #2 kept him alive. "Today's good thing," he would whisper, "Renee's foam galaxies." Or "Marcus didn't tease me about my shoes." Sometimes, "A child laughed on the train—proof of civilization."

They were small lights in the shadows that dogged him. He guarded them like smuggled contraband.

His breathing slowed, and his body became limp. He was drifting off. He could always tell when the room around him started closing in on itself. Later, he would remember the time on the clock, 1:47 AM when the dream returned.

He saw himself standing on ice. He knew the location, with Lake of the Isles frozen beneath his feet. Ice meant winter, and he noticed dry snow whipping in the wind. He wasn't cold, and that was odd. But as in dreams, he noted it, didn't find it disconcerting, and accepted it as it was. A man stood beside him—again unusual, as Alex rarely visited the lake with friends—dressed in clothes so simple they seemed ancient: gray trousers, white shirt, open at the throat.

Another oddity, one that Alex noted and accepted in the dream: The man's face was familiar. Too familiar.

"You're back," Alex said in the dream. He had the prescience to think, back? That meant they knew one another, perhaps had met in a previous dream. Or was this someone from his life in the real world that his brain was pulling from memory?

He once again felt the oddity of Renee's question: *Who was that?*

And his reply: *My guardian angel, perhaps?*

Who was this oddly familiar man to him? Just the remnants of a conversation with a friend?

A few moments passed, with the wind-driven snow swirling across the ice. In an especially strong gust, the man's white shirt vibrated against his chest, more undulating light than solid fabric. Not talking didn't seem odd, just considerate. Waiting on an answer, the quietness giving the companionship a familiarity that wrapped itself around Alex.

"I never left," the man replied.

His words weren't whispered, but neither did they fight with the wind. Alex heard them as though the man was whispering directly in his ear, with the warmth of his breath against his neck. A shiver traced a finger down Alex's back and was comforting rather than disquieting. The man focused his attention on Alex's face, and his expression was as calm as the snowfall Alex just realized was drifting from the sky.

"You look like me." Alex was puzzled he hadn't noticed snow collecting on the man's eyebrows and lashes. When he blinked, he realized his own were also snow covered.

"I *am* you." A smile danced at one corner of his lips. "The part you ignore in daylight."

"Me." Alex's thoughts erupted into a kaleidoscope

of fractured memories.

The glow over his shoulder, the light in the stairwell ... those weren't him. *The part you ignore in daylight.* Renee's question and brushing it off. How many times a day did he do that? The words stitched a thread through a hundred examples that flashed through Alex's thoughts, and they became a spiderweb of awareness that sent a shiver through him.

Suddenly the cold was real. The ice under his feet, the blustery bite of the air. His breath misted as he shivered. Above, the night sky swirled with colors that did not belong to any weather report ever given during a Minneapolis summer. The air burned with a thousand brushstrokes of aurora green.

The man reached toward him and placed a firm hand on Alex's shoulder and squeezed. "You asked for clarity. But clarity burns."

And then the ice cracked beneath Alex's feet.

He woke with a shout that startled even himself. The light from the streetlamp outside his apartment flickered at that exact moment, as if in response.

"Talk about weird. Renee, you should write a song about this dream."

He tossed the bedding back, noted the slivers of streetlight across his bed turning his legs into dark and light, and swung them to the floor. As he stood, he wiped his face and muttered, "No one has actual angels in their rescue plans."

The man hadn't worn wings, had he? If so, the dream-memory had erased them. If they met again, he would have to look for them, maybe ask him if he really was an angel.

Then, he'd clearly met him before in his dreams,

and he'd never thought to ask him then. Or tonight. What made him think he would remember next time?

Two in the morning. Make the bed? Likely he would return to it, so no. However, coffee might put his thoughts back in his head.

In the kitchen, he clicked on the machine and leaned against the counter with his arms crossed while it hissed and burbled. His hand found the shoulder the man had squeezed, and he fought unexpected tears remembering a long-ago longing for a hug from his father. Was that the reason for the dream, resolving his memories of the sunlight on the lake? That fishing trip had been the shift from boyhood longing to determined achievement. Which was better? He caressed the shoulder, still feeling the man's fingers pressing into his skin. Then the coffee machine buzzed and pulled his attention back to the kitchen.

Coffee at two in the morning, because what else does a rational adult do after encountering a glowing doppelgänger in a dream?

He did make it back to bed, leaving a half empty cup on the coffee table and the imprint of his forehead on the sliding door as the dream churned inside him.

6

Breakfast Banter

THE NEXT MORNING was the first time the mirror truly hesitated.

Alex was brushing his teeth, half-asleep from his early morning meeting with his coffee maker and humming a tune he didn't recall knowing. In the mirror, his reflection blinked a fraction late. Alex blinked again, and his toothbrush froze in mid-air. He could see the towel from the night before hung on the shower door as always, not as neat as he wished but straight enough. His shoulders were bare, one relaxed and positioned low; and the other tightened with the toothbrush he held at his mouth. He was about to shrug it off, when behind him a pale flare shimmered, like striking a match, a quick burst of light that faded almost before he could define what he had seen.

He turned his head toward the empty space and looked the other way into the bedroom to see a partially open blind. Could something have reflected through them? He set the toothbrush down, spit out the toothpaste, and moved to the window and peered through.

Nothing. At least not now. No traffic, just people going about their early-morning business grabbing a bagel, stopping for coffee at the shop, or picking up donuts for breakfast. A normal summer morning in Minneapolis.

"Did you see that?" he asked the empty apartment.

The lights hummed, polite and mute. His phone on the nightstand blinked steadily as if reminding him that time marched on, so get back to the sink and to business. The day wasn't going to forgive him any wasted time, and he had company arriving for breakfast.

At the bathroom sink, when he leaned closer, his reflection shifted and then aligned perfectly, as if it forgave his disbelief. Alex blinked, and the reflection mirrored his action exactly, asking if he really thought he had seen something or if it was his rough night.

He laughed softly. "Too much caffeine, buddy. You're hallucinating decency."

He rinsed his mouth and stored his essentials away. Today was about comfort, and he rummaged in his closet for lightweight running pants and a coordinating pocket tee.

The doorbell rang just before seven, and he called, "It's open."

It would be Marcus Havel, a fellow employee at Kane & Sutter who was an old college roommate. He was an IT consultant with the company, but what bonded the two men was Marcus' love of philosophy podcasts. His strict Lutheran upbringing had tumbled aside with his college experiences, leaving him spiritually skeptical, but as Marcus joked, that didn't mean he couldn't also be curious. He was also quick to prick Alex's ego when it got out of hand. There had never been anything romantic between them, but Alex sometimes thought Marcus leaned that way. Whichever, Marcus had become a rock in his life when he needed a friend most.

Marcus smiled warmly, pulled out an earbud, and grasped Alex's hand. He pulled him in for a chest bump before laughing. "You heading out for a run? I didn't bring my buddy-up gear. Think my boxers will serve as running shorts? Or will people think we're a couple if I do?"

"Morning, Socrates. We live in the same building. You don't have to jog in your boxers."

"Oh, but I do. How else will I find a beautiful woman who will put up with me?"

"You're out of luck. There aren't enough of those in Minneapolis for both of us. Come in, you jerk." Alex stepped aside to give him room to enter.

"Then I guess it's just me and you today. Breakfast ready?"

"Have you cooked it?" Alex was in the kitchen, and he broke out a half carton of eggs and a slab of bacon. The bread was already on the counter. "What were you listening to?"

"Listening to?" Marcus glanced at the television. He frowned, then noticed the earbud dangling at his chest. He always wore corded ones, saying that at least the battery never ran down before his phone went dead. "Oh, these. No podcast this morning, just catching up on phone messages. None of importance, but now that you bring it up, I'll finish while you cook."

He flopped on the couch, kicked off his shoes, and curled his legs under him. With his earbud back inside, Alex knew he'd lost him for a time, and he pulled down a bowl and began cracking eggs.

The noise of the plates on the granite counter attracted Marcus' attention, and he joined Alex over toast. He touched an earbud, pulled it free, and said, "This time a philosophy podcast. He's almost finished." Alex could hear the voice through the earbud.

Alex shook his head and lifted a slice of toast from the machine and set it on his plate. The memory with his toothbrush darkened the room, and he let himself slide into what it might mean.

Marcus pulled one earbud out. "You look haunted. Bad dream? Or client calls again?"

"Both." He tore off part of the toast and dipped it into the runny egg yoke before pushing it into his mouth.

"Did dream-Alex finally get that corner office?"

Alex buttered a second slice of toast aggressively. "Dream-Alex fell through a frozen lake while *talking* to himself."

Marcus raised an eyebrow. "So ... classic Minnesotan networking event."

That drew a reluctant laugh out of Alex, which was half the reason he kept Marcus around: humor as survival tool.

Marcus eyed him more seriously, though. "You've been twitchy for weeks. You sure you're not overdoing it?"

"I'm fine. Just tired."

Marcus nodded slowly. "Sure. Just know that even angels need PTO."

Alex blinked. "What?"

"Figure of speech, man. Don't get mystical. Hey,

hand me the butter knife. My toast is growing cold." Marcus carved a dollop and began buttering.

"Right," Alex said, almost to himself. "Your church upbringing."

"You got that right. I might meet a real angel someday. I'm on the lookout, after all."

Alex smiled, yet he felt something twist inside him. Angels. That word again. A soft feeling of warmth brushed the back of his neck. No wind. No heater vent. Just warmth, inexplicable and intimate, like invisible sunlight.

That night he dreamed he was back in the birchwood, and the same shimmer waited beside a fallen branch—but this time the creature that flew free wasn't a bird. It was him, and he was haloed in sunlight.

He jerked awake, his hands digging into the bedding, whispering, "A dream's just the night remembering it can speak."

His whisper hovered in the darkness, as though deciding on whether to answer or not, an echo in the dark. Perhaps he imagined it—or maybe he didn't.

A single beam from the streetlamp traced a line down the wall, sealing the darkness in the room with a whisper of light.

7

The Client

THE GOOD WEATHER wasn't to last. Where Minneapolis had basked in the glow of a late summer through the middle of September, an early Canadian Clipper was forecast on all the weather podcasts. Marcus was the first bearer of the news.

"Maybe this is good for you, Alex."

"What?" Alex and Marcus were at the park, and Alex chucked a Frisbee at his friend. "And miss out on this? How is an early winter something good for me?"

"Cool your jets." Marcus leapt and snagged the plastic disc just before it blotted out the sun's orange disk hovering just over the trees. "There's got to be a reason that overheated brain of yours keeps glitching with those dreams of yours. I vote too much sun during that picnic on the summer solstice. I knew we shouldn't have invited Renee. She brought so much food that we had to have two meals just to finish it." He twisted his torso with the Frisbee held low, and as his body unwound, he released it hard. The disc hit the tight grass and arced into the sky

"Not fair!" Alex's legs thrust him into a sprint toward the trees, and he caught it but also tumbled into a roll. Surprisingly, he came up uninjured, without even grass stains for his trouble. He did notice that one side of his collar was flipped to the inside, and he straightened it before pushing his thick hair from his face.

"Good move. How did you manage that?" Marcus appeared at his side. He dropped forward with his hands on his knees and panted.

"The same as you." Alex was pleased, though he was equally surprised to have survived the ordeal with so little damage.

"Nah. It's like the gods of infinity helped you catch that."

"Who's having weird dreams now?"

"No, man. It's like you floated through that. You never touched the ground. You were glowing. I want to learn that move."

"Yah, it's called tripping. Even you can do it." Alex teased but his friend's words were like a pin into a cushion. As he was tumbling, he had felt like he was cushioned, even being held. By who or what he couldn't have said. It would be easier to dismiss if Marcus hadn't said anything.

Marcus stood and took the Frisbee. "I can't do that glow thing. Wish I'd had a camera. What you can't record you can't prove. Shame."

Alex's thoughts stuttered with images. Late night in his apartment. The flash in his bathroom mirror. Other times, too, like the stairwell at the office.

He shivered, then the warmth of the sun settled on his shoulders.

It was only later than he remembered that he and Marcus were standing next to the grove of trees, and they had been in full shade at the time.

THE GROVE of trees had barely shifted into full fall foliage when the last weekend of September shattered into winter. On Sunday, frost danced at the edges of Alex's bedroom windows. Once the building's heating system kicked in on the first of October, that would clear, but for a few days, Jack Frost would dance on the windowpanes of many of Minneapolis' downtown rentals.

On Monday, Alex showed up at Kane & Sutter in a brown cashmere overcoat with a long wool scarf around his neck. He walked, as was his habit, and thought he was prepared for the change in seasons. By the time he was halfway there, he worked his gloves from his pocket and pulled his scarf tighter.

Eliot caught him at the door, even opened it for him and motioned him inside with the sweep of an arm.

"Good morning, Eliot." Alex offered his boss his practiced smile as he slipped off a glove and attempted to work his hair back into place.

"All oiled up?" Eliot smiled, but his eyes glinted with intent.

"Sure." Alex frowned for a moment, not catching Eliot's meaning, before he recalled needing to be "ready to fire on all cylinders."

"Good man. Lane just called. Sophie Verden arrived at the airport this morning, and they're on the way." Lane Shaw manned the company's limo and ferried clients wherever they needed to go.

"Today." Alex's thoughts reallocated the morning's schedule. The change in the season must have frozen his brain. "Okay, thanks for the update. I'm totally prepared."

"I knew you would be. Let me warn you ... no time. The car's here. Winter wrappings off, my man. You've got someone to meet. First impressions and all that." Eliot clapped him on the shoulder and moved toward Stacie Laughton at the reception desk, probably to ensure that she was "oiled up" and ready to "fire on all cylinders" also.

Precisely on time, Lane opened the door with a leather-gloved hand, his mirrored sunglasses giving him a rakish appearance. The woman who stepped past him was elegant but not overdressed, with a smile as precise as ever seen on a fashion magazine cover.

Although the clock on the wall clicked over as Sophie Verden passed the threshold, and everyone else had found their place at their desks, she somehow made everyone else seem late.

Alex still held his cashmere and wool. He shook his hair back and prepared a smile. When Eliot intercepted the beautiful Sophie with a smile of his own and an outstretched palm, Alex freed up one hand and took two steps in their direction.

Eliot introduced them. "Sophie, this is one of our rising stars, Alex Morton."

She slipped off gloves and held out her hand. Her handshake was cold—pleasantly so—but her eyes were warm. "So, Alex. I've heard good things. From a few people, in fact."

"Really?" he asked. "I didn't realize my reputation traveled."

"Some presences do," she said softly before her expression brightened as she looked around the glossy and sunlit interior of the building.

He told himself she meant *career presences*. He told himself a lot of things, actually.

All afternoon, Sophie's perfume followed him. Floral, faintly smoky. It stirred something half-remembered, the way smelling church incense might stir someone who hadn't prayed in years.

Through the glass walls of the building, the day developed a February tone, taking on the frosted glitter of ice and leaving the sky the color of tin. Alex found himself increasingly jittery but told himself it was only the season making him restless. Seasonal affective disorder, caffeine latency, too much screen light—there was always a diagnosis to keep miracles at bay.

Through lunch, he expected to be called to a conference with Miss Verden, but instead he drifted from meeting to meeting on rails of politeness. When people laughed, he synchronized half a second late, as though editing his normal human behavior in post-production.

He missed childhood's simple ratios: work equals reward for effort which ends in praise. Adulthood was compound interest on uncertainty, especially with the perfume from his one meeting with Miss Verden tracing his steps throughout the morning.

During lunch, Renee teased him. "She's here today? Do you have your proposal ready?"

"I'm not marrying her." Alex felt caught out.

"Oh, so who's got what on his mind? Business proposal, Alex. Get your thoughts back on business. I could however come up with something based on that wedding march everyone plays in church weddings."

"You could forget you said that, too." To distract

her, he brought up his father. He kept meaning to visit him—drive the four hours to Madison, eat somewhere quiet—but every weekend had folded into work or inertia.

"You could just do it." She had her phone searching out the best restaurants in Madison. She turned the screen to him. "See? The reviews say quiet and low key. Exactly what you're looking for."

"You know the rest. The thought of facing that neat apartment, the smell of disciplined solitude. It makes me both guilty and tired."

It did, too. Sometimes he imagined knocking anyway, saying, I've done everything right; why does my life still feel borrowed? But then what? His father would probably nod and suggest a tax advantage savings plan.

By late afternoon, he had given up on his meeting with the elegant Miss Verden, but his mind was full of her laughter and the echo of that word—*presence*.

When he left the office after dark, the Minneapolis skyline had melted into glacial colors. Surprisingly, late September snow flurries cartwheeled between the fingers of the skyscrapers silhouetted against the sky.

A faint shimmer danced above his shadow on the sidewalk, as if the streetlights couldn't quite decide whether to reveal everything there was to see.

8

Strange Echoes

TWO DAYS later, Renee texted him in all caps:

REN: U WERE AT HONEYCOMB BAR THE OTHER NIGHT??

Alex frowned. He had been drowning in endless spreadsheets the last few evenings. Besides, free evenings normally meant poker and pseudo-philosophy at Marcus' apartment, not an evening out at the Honeycomb.

"You ever notice," Marcus once said, shuffling the cards, "how similar a poker game is to a service at church?" He began to lay down the cards. Ray Finnagan and Chip Strahan, poker buddies and sometimes fellow Frisbee throwers at the park, each had a drink.

Alex recalled his friend's claims to believe anything alcoholic counted as communion wine if consumed with sincerity.

"How's that?" Ray pulled his cards to him as Marcus dealt them out. He had sharp eyes and was focused on Marcus' hands. He didn't look up and would know every card on the table.

"Ignore him," Alex countered. "He's distracting you from winning. He thinks he's lost enough for the month."

"Me?" Marcus paused with the cards in his hands. "Nah, but think about it. We meet once a week, act like we know what we're doing when this is all mumbo jumbo, and we put money on the table for some other pudzo to walk away with."

"Who are you calling a pudzo? Just because some of us understand the game. You gonna deal or not?" Ray rapped the table with his knuckles.

"I get it." Chip pulled a second can from the fridge and popped the top. He took a long swig. "Most adults are just kids pretending they know how everything works."

"Sure. That's what people're doing at church. Pretending—"

"And helping them pay the rent." Marcus was back to dealing the cards. He was done with the church distraction and ready to start the game.

"Rent knows what we are, that's for certain," Alex said. "Predators with PayPal."

Marcus stopped shuffling and laughed. "That's good, Alex. Dark humor—it's the first symptom of enlightenment. There might be hope for you yet."

On their last poker day, Renee had crashed their get-together with her obligatory guitar, and when Marcus started tossing skeptical spiritual jokes around the room, threw popcorn at both of them, calling out, "An obvious symptom of enlightenment is splitting your hair into a metaphor. Don't."

They had laughed and then played until darkness softened everyone's edges. Alex liked those nights, and it *was* like a church service of sorts: their private ceremony against the encroaching cynicism that went with learning that the adult world was exactly the same as the one they'd occupied at ten, twelve, or fourteen. The same players arrived at the playground, only the stakes were bigger. In the adult world, everyone didn't get a fresh start after an overnight refresher. There wasn't always someone to pick up the pieces, tape the wounds, and say, "Hey, no matter what happens, I've got your back." That's what Renee, Marcus, and to a lesser degree, Ray and Chip were all about.

Still, a voice inside him countered his claims of a "cadre against the world" in their poker night friendships. It narrated alongside the laughter and smiles: *They love who you are here. Tomorrow, you have to be the PowerPoint version, the one wearing a tailored smile and sharing self-assured witticisms*.

Tonight, he watched the snow whirl outside the window. It floated like it had all the time in the world to get to the ground, as if nothing was of so much importance that hurrying could even be considered. Despite the spreadsheets eating his computer screen, the hypnotic swirls of white lightened his mood and left him feeling relaxed, like when he had been a boy at his parent's home, never considering that the snow that was so beautiful was also bringing high utility bills and hours of shoveling walks and driveways. When he was grown enough to see some of it, his mother had shrugged it off with, "The world is full of helpers you'll never see." She would ruffle his hair and, at the time, he'd thought she meant him. He wondered if he still qualified.

His phone jarred him back into the room. *YOU THERE?*

He typed back: *Didn't even leave the couch last*

night. The poker game was cancelled. Why?

She replied instantly. *Bartender swears u chatted w/me, bought me a drink, disappeared. Wearing same jacket too. Clone much?*

He grinned. *You wish. Next time invite me and I might be there. In the flesh.*

She returned: *I might just crash your poker game again. You people give me good song material.*

Alex threw back: *I'm signing off.*

He stared at the messages for a full minute, then locked his phone and breathed out a laugh that was anything but amused.

"Sure," he muttered. "Because my doppelgänger has social skills."

He placed his phone beside his laptop and stood, picturing a lemon seltzer from the fridge. He was in the kitchen when he remembered that he'd planned to pick up more at the shop yesterday and was distracted by a pickpocket who had seemed ready to finger him before his eyes opened wide and he turned tail and ran. The clerk had commented, "Man, you got a powerful friend to protect you from that dude."

Did the man suffer from Marcus' Lutheran upbringing, too? Alex joked, "That's my guardian angel. He's got my back," thinking, Renee would love hearing him say that.

The light shifted, and he noticed a coaster on the counter that shouldn't be there. He instantly recognized the design, an angry bee with an exposed stinger and surrounded by the repeated hexagons of a honeycomb.

Honeycomb Bar. Underneath, a paper receipt from the shop. Alex had wadded his and tossed it in the trash. This one was flat and pristine.

He picked it up, glanced at the list of purchases, and smiled. He guessed he hadn't forgotten after all. Lemon seltzer, it said so right there.

He opened the fridge, found a four-pack, and broke one off. Back at his laptop, he turned his phone on and texted: *I must have gone somewhere last night. I have lemon seltzer, and get this, the cashier must have dropped in a Honeycomb coaster. How random is that?*

She sent back: *Random? Only your clone knows for sure.*

He fell back into work as he enjoyed the seltzer he didn't remember buying, and before long, he didn't think of it at all. It was here, wasn't it, which meant only one thing: that pickpocket had scrambled his thoughts, but he was back on his game.

Still, that night, he dreamed again of the man on the lake—himself, or not-himself, standing serene on the ice that never broke.

9

Fireflies in the Boardroom

ELIOT ASSIGNED him a presentation—the Coomer files come back to haunt him—although Alex didn't mind as it was something he knew intimately from hours poking and prodding every aspect of the business. As his father always said, "Preparation is the start of perfection, and clients always expect perfection."

That wasn't the source of the butterflies in his stomach. Sophie Verden was.

He had met her two additional times, but never in isolation. Lunch in the company canteen and at a sectional staff meeting, each time catching her eye and once shaking hands, and always that perfume that followed him for the rest of the day.

Foodz was off limits as that was his and Renee's spot, but he'd walked by it one evening and pictured Sophie sitting in Renee's chair. It was as if a haze filled the air, obscuring the café from his view, and a voice whispered, *Don't even think about it*. He'd shaken his vision of Sophie from his thoughts, the haze cleared, and he was certain that a hand grasped his shoulder in solidarity. He'd even turned to see who it was, but of course no one was there.

Now, though, the presentation. Eliot hadn't said it as such, but it was all for Sophie. The Coomer files were old hat, important yes, but not unfamiliar to most of the Kane & Sutter employees. Eliot was setting him up to impress, as they wouldn't be familiar to someone in the mid-west development fund field.

This had to go off without a hitch.

Alex opened the door to the boardroom, surprised that the lights were on. He frowned, especially as the company's environmental policy said all lights must be off when leaving a room, and he was fifteen minutes early to set up for his presentation.

One person was already in her seat: Sophie Verden.

"Hello there, Sophie. You are more than on time. How has your experience with the Minneapolis office been so far?" He felt his heart skip a beat, and he reminded himself of the presentation in his briefcase. He was here to prepare, not have his emotions compromised in the moment of his success. He caught the reflection of the two of them in the glass wall on the far side of the boardroom: him with his tie and briefcase, very much the appearance of a successful man on his way to a partnership by age thirty; Sophie at the table, immaculately dressed, with the hint of a smile on her lips. She had been looking directly at him, yet in the reflection, she was looking away, with her attention on something else. He looked back at her and found her attention fully on him. Odd what a reflection will do to the real world, like his bathroom mirror. What it reflected didn't always match what he knew to be reality.

Sophie spoke: "Should I prepared to be wowed,

Mr. Morton? I like being wowed."

He almost stumbled as he made his way to the podium. He caught her perfume, and her words? They were more an invitation than a challenge.

He mumbled a response, unsure of what he said, only that she laughed, and he flipped open his briefcase and pulled out a stack of presentation folders, one for each attendee. When he left a thumbprint on the clear plastic cover of the top one, he realized his palms were moist, and he pressed them against his pants to dry them. With the remote, he initialized the projector so that it could warm up and was relieved when Rick and Shaunkia came through the door together.

"There you are, old man. You want I should get you a coffee? You look flushed." Rick placed his phone and laptop on the table but didn't pull out the chair.

Shaunika paused, took in Sophie alone at the table, and glanced at Alex. She whispered, "Shush, Rick. Can't you see we should have knocked?"

"Knocked?" Rick's eyes went wide. "It's the boardroom, and the meeting's not happening yet. Who knocks?"

"You are as dense as every other man in this building." She called to Alex, "We hope we didn't interrupt. You keep on with what you're doing. I want to meet Sophie."

She settled in next to her, and Alex felt the tension ease. He was interested when a third woman, unfamiliar to him, entered the room, claimed the seat on the opposite side of Sophie, and began to lay out items before her. She spoke to Sophie before heading to the coffee bar for refreshments. An assistant? That was something he hadn't known about.

As he leaned in to place a presentation folder before Sophie, he whispered, "Is she with you?"

Sophie touched his arm—an electric move—and said, "My assistant. She was delayed. Shela Cartier. You'll meet later."

The promised meeting—not quite what he expected—happened during the presentation. The lights were down, and Alex stood to the side with the remote pointing at the projector in the ceiling. They were on the third page, and he was telling them of the plan he had implemented for market growth for Coomer's cosmetic division, when a flickering light from the direction of Sophie's assistant distracted him. He stumbled on an easy word, and everyone turned his direction. He started to point out the light, small as a candle flame, hovering just behind the client's assistant, but no one else seemed to see it.

Alex blinked hard. The flame didn't move but pulsed brighter when Eliot made a self-absorbed comment about Alex's gift of helping Coomer "crush the competition."

For a second, he could swear he heard a sigh. The room was mostly dark, and he turned to see who it was. The space behind him was empty. So, not human.

He realized he'd hadn't heard the sigh, not through his ears. He had felt it, like that warm feeling on his neck he sometimes got.

Sophie caught his eye across the table and smiled knowingly, as if she knew what he saw. That, somehow, was worse than the flame itself.

He smiled briefly and laughed off his verbal

stumble with: "Slip-ups show I'm human. But I know you're interested in the Coomer story and how Kane & Sutter is taking them to the next level. If you'll turn to page four ..." and he clicked the remote to move the PowerPoint document to the next panel.

As the lights returned and people began gathering their things, Alex enjoyed the expected hands on his shoulders and the obligatory accolades of "Great presentation, Alex," and "You're the man, Alex, always batting a thousand."

When he killed the lights and exited the boardroom, Sophie cornered him in the hallway. Her assistant was down a bit chatting with Rick. She purred, "Are you feeling it too?"

"Feeling what?" He pictured Renee and her "vibes." That weird thing in there? No one ever saw his weird things other than him, not that anyone had ever said.

"The air changed in there when you entered the room. It was like it remembers you. During the presentation, you seemed thrown off by my assistant. What was that about?"

"What do you mean?" He knew exactly what she meant, but how could she know? No one else had seemed to notice it.

"You have something about you. A glow, perhaps." She laughed. "I know, an aura of perfection. That was an outstanding presentation, and you mastered that slipup. It was just what you needed to bring your presentation home."

"I'll pretend it was intentional. I think I just need sleep."

"Maybe," she said. She leaned closer. "Or maybe

sleep's when you remember who you are."

Her words echoed all the way home. Inside his apartment, the blinds were open, and through his reflection, the streetlights illuminated the early evening streetscape. He found an actual glow around his reflection and chuckled. The glass was misty and catching the light from outside. He closed the blinds to shut it all away, but when he dropped his shirt onto his bed and stepped into his bathroom, in the mirror he caught a brief flare of light at his back.

He looked closer, but it was gone. He could have sworn it was in the shape of wings folding shut.

He hit the shower lever and set it to hot. A fogged mirror reflects nothing at all, and he'd had enough of lights for the day, especially ones in the shape of wings.

10

Borrowed Realities

BY FRIDAY, reality and dreams had started trading secrets. At least that's how it felt.

Sophie Verden's words crept in when he least expected: "Maybe sleep's when you remember who you are."

Who he was? He tried to shrug it off, but there was the dream-man's familiarity, the nighttime connection with a person and a situation he'd never experienced in real life. Then he'd hear a whisper, "So, I'm not real?"

He'd turn a street corner and see the shimmer in the glass again. A faint outline of light, never much, just for a moment before it vanished. When he stopped to study his reflection, it was gone, then as he looked away, his reflection would hold its gaze just a moment too long. If he looked back, of course it returned his attention, staring into his eyes as though it was reading the disquiet inside.

One day, he whispered to the man in the glass, "Who are you? I mean, to me, who are you?"

The familiar warmth brushed his neck and he heard—rather felt—a warmth of recognition that was all-enveloping, as if he were wrapped in someone's protective arms. His hands were in his pockets, and he pulled them out and rubbed his sleeves.

"I've got your back," he heard someone whisper into his ear, and he turned. No one else was in the reflection, just him. A woman was across the street, preoccupied with a large shopping bag, and not paying him any attention. He was alone. "Oh, man. Now I'm hearing things."

Recent snow still filled in the empty spaces on the sidewalks and in the alleys, and it mounded along the curbs where plows had deposited it. The cold, lack of lunch, something had him off. Renee was unavailable—at a music symposium, he thought—and he'd worked through lunch. He needed to get out of the cold. He pulled out his phone for an Uber when a cab turned the corner with the sign on top lighted. He slipped his phone into his pocket and raised an arm to hail a ride.

"Thank you." He dropped inside and closed the door. Warmth, oh so nice. "That was convenient. I was about to call an Uber. Here's the address." He slipped a card from his coat pocket and held it over the seat.

"I don't need it. I remember the place." The cab driver looked at him a second time and frowned. "Didn't know you cut your hair."

"I likely need to. Is that what you mean?" Alex ran his fingers through his windblown mop to settle it. He wore his cashmere with a wool scarf around his neck, which covered part of his hair. He pulled the scarf free and shook his head.

The thing was, Alex hadn't touched the length. And he rarely took a cab. How would this man know if he did or didn't cut his hair? One more unsettling thing for the day.

Joey's Kaffe Shop appeared on the left, and Alex tapped the cabbie on the shoulder. "Joey's," he said. "New destination. Thanks."

"I thought you might." The cabbie grinned. "I dropped you here last night."

"That's a good one. Doppelgängers everywhere." Alex paid, wrapped his scarf around his neck, and opened the door.

"Yessir. Maybe I'll see you again tomorrow."

"In my new haircut." Alex gave him a thumbs up, closed the door, and headed through a break in the curbside snow. "Wowser," he said to himself. "That was weird."

He refused to look at his reflection as he opened the door to Joey's. He didn't want to see what he halfway expected to be there.

A RACK ON THE wall accepted his scarf and coat, and Alex soaked in the aroma of Nordic coffee. Despite Joey's name, he was Swedish, with a scraggly blond beard and kinky hair in a topknot. Alex placed his briefcase on a free table and headed to the counter to order.

"The same as yesterday?" Joey lifted his head to acknowledge Alex. He was leaning down with both elbows on the back edge of the counter and talking with a customer.

"What did I have yesterday?" The cabbie flashed through his mind. What had he done that he didn't remember? Better, where had he gone?

"You were in twice, ordered the same each time." Joey gave up on the customer and headed Alex's direction.

"Then yes." Must be a glitch in the world, and he might as well go where it took him, see what he got.

"Head on to your table. I'll bring it over."

A thumbs up, and Alex fell into his seat. He glanced at Joey, watching him preparing the drink, and thinking that it seemed like a complicated concoction for the barista to remember *without Alex telling him what he wanted.*

Before Alex could get his laptop up and running, an amazing drink appeared at his side. It was ... and he hesitated before looking up at Joey questioningly.

Joey shrugged. "A venti, quad, half-caff, non-fat, no foam, extra hot, peppermint, white chocolate mocha with light whip, two pumps sugar-free vanilla, one pump classic, a dash of cinnamon, with a splash of soy milk. Yeah, I questioned it the first time yesterday, but you insisted both visits, so I've got it now." He laughed. "Enjoy, my gubben."

Alex pulled it closer and inhaled the aroma. How did Joey know? Yes, the man from yesterday, but you'd think Alex would remember being here twice the day before. But this coffee, he'd been creating this concoction forever, one ingredient at a time. He'd never dared to order it but had wanted to.

Now someone who looked like him had beat him to the punch. Exactly to the punch. How was that possible? The city seemed to be *duplicating him.*

Or maybe it was returning the borrowed fragments he misplaced while asleep. His dreams had been all over the place lately.

Rather than open a spreadsheet from work, he double-clicked his journaling document. He didn't have his paper notebook with him, but he uploaded his handwritten journal regularly, so he added the date, took a sip of the coffee—ah, just as he'd imagined—and placed his hands over the keyboard.

He journaled because Renee told him it helped. He scrolled back a few entries and read the contradictory observations, the ones Renee said to never reread. *Just write them, Alex. You don't plan journaling, you just do it.*

- Dream: walked across the lake again. The man said my name like it was a prayer.
- Reality: colleague quit suddenly; project fell apart, but nobody blamed me. Lucky timing?
- Coincidences are stacking.

He added:

- Got a haircut yesterday. The cabbie said so ... and knew I wanted to stop by Joey's.
- Joey said I ordered my dream coffee twice yesterday, and I never told anyone what it is.

He stopped writing when he caught, in his peripheral vision, a faint silhouette by the window. Same height as him. Same build. In his brown cashmere and wool scarf. Thick blond hair. Watching.

When he turned fully, the silhouette was gone—but his reflection in the glass lingered just a heartbeat longer than it should have, smiling faintly.

Alex found his coat and scarf still by the door, and he breathed easier. It would be a cold trek to his apartment without them.

He added one more journal entry.

- Saw myself standing by the door. Can't avoid myself coming or going.

He chuckled as he closed his laptop, but the shiver down his spine said this was getting weirder by the hour.

11

Tell Him to Tip Better

SATURDAY EVENING transformed Foodz into a comedy club.

Alex walked inside and shed his coat to find Renee setting up for open-mic night. He called, "Do you have the sign-up sheets out?"

Open-mic night was about the comedy, but it was also a financial plan for the café. Alex and the owner, Lottie Warburton, had discussed the falloff in customers over the weekend, and open-mic night had transformed her weekends. So, yeah, it was Alex's idea, but Lottie had implemented it.

And it was a perfect fit for Renee, as she could share her poems and the occasional song when the comedian pool ran dry. So, she helped Lottie with the set-up when she needed her and filled in as barista to give the café a break.

"The stars are aligning. The clipboard is behind the counter. The stand is in the walk-in."

"The walk-in freezer?" He laughed. "You mean outside?"

"I do not mean outside. That's your subconscious trying to get out of work. Hustle to it before people start to show."

She wasn't completely on the money there. Two tables at the back had diners giving them occasional glances. They might stay for the show, but the café was open straight through, and food would be served during the comedy routines. Not everyone wanted to eat during the performances and some chose to arrive early to get food out of the way.

By the time Alex retrieved the sign-up stand, two potential candidates were inside the door and unwrapping scarves and removing thick gloves. One was a young woman with green hair, and the other was tall and thin, and he grew thinner as he peeled away his outer layers.

Marcus joined them halfway through the second set. The lights in the café were dimmed, and the back wall was transformed into a stage with spotlights. Backlit letters spelled out Open Mic Night. Renee sat with Alex wearing a Foodz apron. She was between orders.

Marcus placed his phone on the table and grinned. "Our golden boy alive? He's not been abducted by spreadsheets?"

"I check in daily," Renee said, "mostly to confirm he's eating. I couldn't get him to order tonight. See what you can do before his aura fades completely."

"I eat," Alex protested. True, he nursed a cup of coffee, and it was still steaming.

"Coffee is not a food group." Renee stood and slipped her apron over her head. She laid it over her chair and retrieved her guitar case from Alex's feet.

"You going up?" Marcus pointed to the stage and turned his grin on Alex. "She prays for these slow nights, I bet."

"Who told you tonight was slow? This was my first chance to sit down, and now, I'm back on my feet." She seemed pleased as she lifted her guitar and began to tune it. She bumped Alex's shoulder with the head of the guitar as she adjusted a tuning key. "You still seeing the mystery twin in dreams?"

He hesitated. "Sometimes." He didn't mention Kaffe's or his windows at home, and especially not the glow that resembled folding wings.

"You pudzo, maybe he's your subconscious wingman," Marcus said. "Biggest flex ever—having a guardian angel who looks like you."

"I'd be happy if he made the bed each morning, the one on my side of the mirror."

Renee laughed and added, "It's your apartment. You pay the rent and buy all the food. Tell him to tip better. If he'd going to live in your dreams at night, he needs to share the expenses. Dream rent isn't cheap."

Marcus laughed. "I follow a podcast by Sheldon Francks, and he says angels are basically noncorporeal, intellectual beings that bridge the gap between the divine and humanity. So, maybe your angel is doing that, acting as a bridge."

"A construction angel, is that what you're saying?" Renee had her phone face-up on the table with a set of lyrics showing. She was picking out an appropriate tune, as her chance to share was coming up.

"I did not, but if he has a six-pack and muscles like the guys on that crew on I-94, I'm switching religions."

"Your religion needs to be the gym, and then you'd have your muscles. Okay, this guy's finishing up. Applaud for my song when I'm through if you want a free coffee from the bar."

She abandoned them with a bright smile and her guitar in hand.

"Sheldon Francks? I don't know him." Alex pulled his coffee closer and wrapped his hands around the cup. The talk of angels had him chilled, either that or customers entering the café and letting in the cold from outside.

"I'll send you a link. Francks focuses on their role in protecting, guiding, and praising, as well as their nature as separate substances in scholastic philosophy."

"Scholastic philosophy?" Alex made a face.

"Classic Aristotle mixed with Christian theology. He says angels aren't real, not like corporeal. They're all spiritual energy to guide us by means of the angelic realm." Marcus pushed Alex's shoulder. "Don't tell me that doesn't fit your dream-Alex."

Alex chuckled, though his laugh was slow in coming. Marcus' description carried an element of truth he couldn't pin down.

Under the stage lights, Renee's song that night carried a phrase that made his skin prickle: *"We walk the lake between what's real and right, our mirrored hands refusing night."*

The crowd clapped politely, while Alex and Marcus stood and hooted and cheered.

"A little overkill?" When she returned, she gave them the side-eye as she placed her instrument in its case.

"You said applaud, so we did." Marcus gave Alex a fist bump. "When do we get our coffee?"

"You two. You are going to be the subject of my next performance up there. You might stay away. You won't appreciate how much I roast you." With the case closed and at Alex's feet, she slipped her apron back over her head and exited for the coffee machine.

Marcus kept his eyes on her as she built the coffees.

"What, are you afraid she'll do it wrong?" Alex teased.

"That she'll put something in it I don't like. I couldn't tell if that was sarcasm or intent. What do you think?"

Alex looked down at his coffee. "I'm looking forward to hearing more from Francks."

"But Renee, that's real. Hey, what's she doing now?" Marcus stood and abandoned Alex as he headed across the room.

Angel. Alex let the term swirl in his head like the steam from his coffee, about as vacuous and likely as quick to disappear, something he couldn't hold in his hand if he tried.

Steam from his cup curled upward, shaping for one brief second what could have been the outline of wings. He blew on it, and the wings disappeared into the shadows and darkness.

A touch on each shoulder. Fingers, hands ... a light brush of warmth. He turned, no one there ... except for a shift in the reflection in the glass, one that evaporated as quickly as the steam from his coffee.

"Okay, Sheldon Francks, where are you when I need you?"

Then Marcus returned with two cups of coffee, and the next standup took the stage.

Part Two

Ripples

1

Smoke and Glass

EVERY OFFICE tower has its ghost stories—usually about layoffs, not luminescence.

Kane & Sutter was no different.

And winter kept them in full swing ... especially when the wind howled and snow battered the glass. Somehow the days closed in, voices echoed differently, and no one wanted to walk the stairwells after dark.

When paystubs appeared in mail cubicles, eyes were on the lookout for pink, as in termination notices. Voices whispered, "It's happened before. Did you hear about Liam?"

Every empty desk became a conversation about whether it was vacation time, a frozen pipe, or them not returning ever.

Then one day, the Canadian vortex was especially angry, and it gripped the city's towers and shook them repeatedly. Even through the atrium's thick glass, the voice of the wind moaned with longing ... for what, no one dared talk about.

By the first week of March, the cleaning crews at Kane & Sutter were whispering that something odd was happening on the twenty-second floor. It filtered through the building by shared emails, two uploaded videos, cleaning carts abandoned during the night, and shaking passkeys when supply doors were unlocked.

Alex heard snippets, but he pretended not to notice. Stacie Laughton at Reception laughed and shared with Shaunika about the lobby lights. When Alex entered through the front doors, they seemed to dim. She wouldn't notice, she told Shaunika behind one hand, except that she usually arrived first—except for the cleaners, who were finishing up to head home for the day. During morning break, Shaunika shared the story with Alex as a funny one-off, that Stacie thought the lights dimmed when he walked by. Of course, Shaunika expected it was Alex's electrifying personality that was sucking the power from the fixtures. Now that she knew his secret, she was determined to learn how he did it. She wanted a full partnership, too, if that was where Alex was headed ... and she was certain it was.

On Wednesday, he bumped into Rick Calloway while visiting the coffee bar. The man struggled with two boxes of specialty paper needed pronto in the copy room. Of course, Alex insisted on carrying one, and on the way, he waved at Shaunika to let her know where he was headed.

He cracked a joke about Shaunika's story of the lobby lights.

"I've seen it." Rick looked away, and Alex was certain he shivered.

"Seriously? When?"

"You likely don't want to know. Hey, how are you and Sophie getting along? I heard Eliot might be assigning her to you."

Rick seemed to want him to drop the discussion.

Later that afternoon, while retrieving a stack of prospectus folders from the copy room, he walked in, and each printer he walked by began shooting out blank pages. He was relieved no one else saw it, and he tried to gather up all the paper before anyone came in.

To make matters weirder, twice that day, his elevator paused between floors as if deciding whether to trust him. The second time, Sophie's assistant, Shela Cartier, was inside with him. His "Oh, no, not again" was already out of his mouth before he could suck the words back.

While at his desk, he pretended none of it had happened. People who noticed too much in corporate life rarely got promoted. It was hard though, especially as he couldn't unsee the way the reflection of his hallway silhouette hesitated each time he turned the corner.

The end of the week couldn't come soon enough.

SATURDAY, he tried sleeping late. However, it seemed his subconscious had other plans.

He found himself standing inside an office corridor that felt infinite, with fluorescent lights stretching into the horizon. It was clearly Kane & Sutter's, from the company colors to the logo design beside each door.

He clearly remembered the previous night. The poker game was scheduled for Friday, and it had run late. Afterwards, he stood in the shower an extraordinarily long time, hoping to wash the week from him, he guessed. He'd run the spray so hot that he began to perspire once the water was off, and he had to drench himself with cold before toweling off.

Even falling asleep, he remembered his shower as clear as day. He was relaxed from the heat, and once between the sheets, he'd taken two deep breaths, and the night had folded in on itself.

What he didn't remember was waking this morning, brushing his teeth, or getting dressed. Besides, it had to be Saturday. The game last night ... Ray Finnagan had taken the first hand, but Marcus had cleaned up on the second. If they played last night, this would be Saturday, not the day he was scheduled to be in the office.

And where was everyone else?

He headed down the hallway and never seemed to get closer to the end. The names on the doors caught his attention. Each door bore a version of his own name: ALEX MORTON (STRATEGIST), ALEX MORTON (SON), ALEX MORTON (WHO LIES), ALEX MORTON (WHO HOPES).

From one doorway poured soft blue light. He stepped through and emerged onto Lake of the Isles in deep winter. The ice glowed under his feet like backlit glass.

Why was he not surprised to see a second figure already there—identical face, simpler clothes, eyes calm? And with eyes and nose and mouth that were familiar to him from seeing them for over twenty years in every mirror he'd passed.

And the figure glowed ... not much. It could be the light from under the ice, but the glow was as certain as that door he'd walked through.

"You're late," the familiar face said.

"For what?"

"For remembering."

Alex looked away. "If this is about my father, I'm not sure I want to."

"You love your father. I know that for a fact."

"Right." Alex's laugh was sour. "The problem goes the other way round."

"Then let's move to the real reason for this meeting."

"Meeting? I'm at work, but I don't think I am. I went to bed last night, and I suspect that's where I still am. So, here's my question for you. Are you real?"

"Real enough to keep promises you forgot you made."

Then came the cracking sound, and the ice webbed beneath him, fractal and beautiful. He reached for his twin's hand but woke grasping his blanket, with the sound of his heart hammering loudly in the quiet of his room.

Before the dream slipped away from him, he pulled his phone from the bedside table and opened his journaling app. He set it to voice mode and began to recite the dream into his phone notes.

He slowed when he repeated what he said to his twin. "The problem goes the other way around." He'd never said that to anyone else, and to say it aloud made it seem like it might be real.

He held the phone, with the screen lighting his arms and chest with a sickly glow, before deleting the note minutes later, embarrassed by the sincerity following him into the real world from his dream.

It was years since he'd thought those words. How had his dream twin found them and dragged them back into the light once more?

He spent an hour re-living that hunting trip from so long ago. He'd wanted his dad, not the animals they'd hunted.

He'd not gotten what he wanted, but he suspected his dad had. "Preparation breeds perfection," something Alex had grown all too good at achieving.

2

The Uninvited Twin

RENEE AND MARCUS were arguing over empanadas when Alex arrived at their usual Saturday spot, with his tan cashmere coat unbuttoned against an early thaw.

Renee waved him over. “Please inform this philosopher that not every unexplained event is ‘epistemic fatigue.’”

Marcus smirked. “I use big words to avoid smaller thoughts.”

Alex dropped into the chair between them. He looked tired enough to make them both pause.

“Losing sleep over my big win last night?” Marcus kicked the leg of Alex’s chair.

“What? How did I not hear about this game last night?” Renee slipped the platter in her direction. “I guess I’ll need to eat all these to feel better. Can you see my wounded aura? Feeding it will surely be the cure.”

“Yeah, that’s fine. Just coffee for me.” Alex relaxed his head backwards, studying the ceiling for a bit before closing his eyes and taking a deep breath.

Renee leaned across the table. “Okay, confession: your vibe is weird.”

"My vibe?" Alex didn't open his eyes.

"Hey, Renee," Marcus said, interrupting. "This man shows up, and I'm now cattle fodder? Sorry, Alex. I know Schopenhauer likes to go on about the insignificance of humanity, but sheesh! I think of you as a friend. Can't we spend a little more time on epistemic fatigue? I was just getting warmed up. Tell her, Alex. She takes over like this all the time."

"My vibe?" Alex repeated the question but still didn't open his eyes.

"Yes, your vibe. You've got that haunted CEO energy. You're smiling at things that haven't happened yet."

"I didn't think I was smiling. I thought I had my eyes closed." He lifted his head and put his best practiced smile on his lips. "Better?"

"Not really. Now spill, or I'm ordering more empanadas, and I'll force you to eat half of them."

"If I must." He tried to explain the dream, making it trivial. "Probably stress. My brain's doing interpretive art projects."

"Maybe your brain's bored of spreadsheets." She eyed him with the same tone she used for off-key singers at open-mic night: gentle curiosity mixed with a subtle dare for something more high stakes. "Write it down next time," she said. "Dreams are the body's audition tapes."

He smirked. "Mine's getting canceled in rehearsals." He pictured the words on his phone and the cringe they'd given him. He didn't mention that he *had* written it all down—and as quickly erased it.

"Keep the footage anyway."

She said it lightly, but he pocketed the advice like

a talisman. "In my pocket." He patted his shirt pocket before finding his phone in his coat's interior pocket.

"Okay," Renee said carefully. "There's got to be more. You dream all the time. Lay it on us. How many weirdness units?"

"Define 'weirdness.'"

"Anything you wouldn't say out loud to your boss."

Alex sighed. It was one of the reasons he was glad to be away from the office this weekend—and why the dream had thrown him off so strongly. It had taken him back there, the very place he was trying to avoid until Monday.

He said, "Someone in accounting swore I gave her final approval on a report. My signature's there. My shirt, even—she described it perfectly."

"That's good, right?" Marcus had stolen back the empanadas and was nibbling on one. "I mean, as long as no one was cooking the books. Get it, cooking the books?" He held up the half-eaten empanada and grinned.

"You had to have been there." Alex knew the rest of the story, one he had no explanation for.

"So, what's the problem?" Marcus made the tasty treat disappear, and he pulled a napkin from a stack to wipe his hands and lips.

"Problem? I spent that hour in a meeting ten floors up."

"That's a riot. I can't make the elevators go at normal speed, and you've got them on speed dial. Or have you joined the Enterprise crew? Beam me up to the thirty-second floor, Scotty."

"Seriously, Marcus. Are you able to can the yapping for a minute? I think Alex is seriously weirded out by this. Tell us more, spreadsheet-meister." Renee set her phone face down, crossed her legs, and leaned in with one elbow on the table and her chin in her hand. She soaked in Alex's face.

"Eliot checked the sign-in. By all accounts and records, I was really ten floors up."

Renee blinked. "So, congratulations on achieving bilocation, Saint Alex. But seriously, doesn't the building have security monitoring?"

"In the elevators. Eliot doesn't think we need to pull the footage. He says that me making that meeting and getting that approval on the record at the same time is great for my chances at partner by thirty."

"Does that mean he's good for it? My good friend, a full partner. Can you give me a raise when you get your corner office?"

"I might toss you out of the window of Alex's corner office." Renee picked up her phone, clicked the screen, and said, "Remind me to toss Marcus from the window. The date is the day Alex gets his corner office."

Alex allowed himself to smile. Almost. "I wish this were funny."

Marcus chewed thoughtfully on a fresh empanada. "If there's two of you, which one pays rent?"

"They'll split it." Renee patted Alex's hand, giving it a final rub before she noticed the plate of food. "You creep, you're eating my share, too."

"Thank you, guys, for being so concerned about my week. I'm glad you consider it only slightly less important than a plate of empanadas."

"It is important," Marcus said. "It's just also creepy."

For a moment, the silence stretched to awkwardness. Finally, laughter came thin and forced. Outside, a wedge of rotting snow tumbled from the building parapet and rattled the café sign, loosening the tension.

Still, Alex felt it like an omen trying to dance to the rhythm of a song it had yet to learn.

3

Winter Confession

MIDWEEK BROUGHT the first real anomaly.

The day started normally, with a brisk walk to work accompanied by his morning view of the Nicollet Bridge. The early sun glittered on the surface through the bare branches of the trees. In summer, trees would obscure the bridge and only driving it would sing its praises. Now, though, if you knew when and where to look, there it was in its wintry, slushy glory. The sun would warm the roadway later, but for now, it was as frosted as the flakes in a bowl of morning cereal. Slush along the sidewalks had crisped up overnight, and car tires crunched as they passed.

Inside the Kane & Sutter tower, nothing amiss. Stacie greeted him, Rick stood at his desk with his cup of coffee attached to his hand, and the clock overhead blared the time, daring anyone to not be in their place when it clicked down the last second.

Even Eliot was out and about. He called, “Morning, kid. Tomorrow, Sophie for certain. I’ve got plans for you two.”

Then Eliot was off to juggle words with another employee, verbal sparring that was either their step up the ladder or the precursor to a possible demotion out the door.

At his desk, he greeted Shaunika, who already had a steaming cup of joe at her elbow. He kicked off his outdoor shoes and pulled his office brogues from his bottom desk drawer and exchanged them. One had a scuff on the toe, and he rustled in the top drawer for a mini tube of polish and brought the shine back to office minimum.

All normal, no copy machines spitting paper at him, and no overhead lights dimming as he walked by. Then, the sun was out, and through the glass, it outshone the weaker interior lighting.

Still, a regular day following a regular morning, with not even a shadow of wings in his bathroom mirror.

He looked up to see Amy Witherspoon heading his way with a stack of folders in her arms.

"Amy." He smiled and greeted her. If she had folders, she'd likely just come from the copy room. "Copiers running smoothly? I heard they were acting up the other day."

"Hi, Alex. Nothing amiss I'm aware of. I have this for you." She flipped down the stack and worked one loose. "I hear you're teaming up with the new lady. She's very pretty."

"Sophie?" Alex laughed. "So Eliot says. It's not happened yet."

"Hmm." She handed him the folder. "This might say differently."

The tab on the top said Sophie Verden and had a sticky note attached in Eliot's writing that said Alex Morton, Stat.

"That is you." She smiled and tapped the sticky

note.

As she walked away, he thought, *Okay, not* not *normal*. For Eliot, this was actually pretty normal. Still, he hadn't been given access to Miss Verden other than a few words in the hallway. He'd spoken to her assistant more than to her.

Before he could open the folder to see what Eliot had lined up for him, his desk phone buzzed.

"Alex here. How can I help you?"

"Brian here. About that rescheduling message you dropped on my desk a few minutes ago. The timing was perfect. Eliot had me on a flight to Boise, and I was headed out the door. I would have wound up on the wrong side of the country. Atlanta is a long way from Boise."

Brian Stanford worked on the floor below, either an elevator ride or stairway trip away, and with the elevators acting up, well, that told the tale of that. They knew each other well enough to chat about the Twins but only that. They had attended a game together the summer before.

"Hey, Brian. Sorry, I just got to my desk. I'm glad it worked out, but it couldn't have been me."

"C'mon, Alex. You can't shrug this off. We talked. The Twins, 12-2? You were carrying that blue folder. You said, 'Don't let the numbers mislead you.' Word for word."

"That's something I would say, but if it was me, describe what I'm wearing." He wanted to find this amusing, but with the week he was having, it was a reach.

And Brian did, even to the shoes Alex had worn into work, the slush-encrusted ones. He'd mentioned to Alex that Eliot would expect him to change, and did he need to borrow a pair, as their feet seemed about the same size, and Brian had an extra he wouldn't need for several days.

"Okay, whatever, Brian. How can I help you with the reschedule?"

"I need you to send me the Humphrey files, just for the past six months. I can't locate Eliot, and my new flight is in three hours."

"Give me fifteen minutes."

The files were an easy task, but the conversation was too much like yesterday, when a trainee thanked Alex because he'd given her directions to the lounge area, only he'd been on a conference call during that span of time, with his headset logged into the system and timestamped against his duty log.

He texted Renee for lunch but received no reply. Marcus was available, but he only had half the hour, as he wanted to catch the "New World Theology" podcast at noon. Could Alex pick up something to go and join him at his desk?

Alex wanted to bounce the blue folder and the rescheduling snafu off Marcus, see what he thought, but the podcast covered Open Theism, and as he set the food on Marcus' desk, he caught the tail end of the podcast, with the host restating that human free will could change the future God intended.

"Did you catch that?" Marcus was all animated. "He thinks the outcome for mankind is not preordained."

"Like heaven and hell?" Alex enjoyed podcasts too, but this was a bit off the rails for his taste.

"Be serious, Alex. Don't forget, I was Lutheran.

Heaven and hell are a given to Lutherans. It's the path mankind follows to get there."

"Ah, very interesting stuff."

"I thought so ..." and the rest of their half lunch hour was shot with Open Theism.

Later, one thing the podcast host said kept swirling around him. "Human free will can change God's plan." Alex didn't consider himself particularly religious and hadn't attended much as a youth, mostly the services everyone else catches: Easter, Christmas, and sometimes with friends. How much could free will meddle with God's plan? Didn't Him being God mean mankind didn't have the power to matter in the grand scheme of things?

That night, he walked home past the old stone church near Nicollet Mall. The doors were locked but light poured through the stained glass, with the colors flickering on the leftover, rotting snow like pale blue breath on ice.

He paused, with his hands jammed deep in his pockets, and whispered to no one, "If you're real, if you're listening, can you just tell me what you *want*?"

No response, just the sound of distant cars, and—faintly—the sounds of rustling fabric catching in the wind.

Like wings.

The similarity brushed his thoughts like a moth around a lightbulb. He turned, his heart hammering.

Nothing.

Then fresh snow began to fall, slow and heavy, and in the hush, he could swear he saw footprints forming beside his own, keeping pace as he tried to look away.

He caught his reflection repeating the phrase in

one store window, "Human free will can change God's plan." And Alex wasn't talking when his reflection was. He shivered at the window ghost repeating itself in the glass' reflective surface.

He stepped into his apartment with relief and whispered, "If you exist, it's about time for you to pay your half of the rent."

The joke didn't quite land. The hallway light flickered twice and stabilized.

How many chills could a man's back take before the world quit misbehaving?

He didn't know, but he was heading for the shower. No more chills allowed, not tonight, anyway.

4

Sophie's Smile

THE NEXT MORNING, Sophie Verden found him chatting with Marcus near the elevators.

She wore an icy blue business suit, highly tailored, with a white velvet collar and a black shirt. Pearls shimmered against the black, contrasting with the suit's white piping along the seams.

The day was early, he and Marcus had a few moments, and they were delving once more into free will. After the previous evening, it wasn't Alex's discussion of choice after more dreams of the lake and the ice, with the dream-Alex holding out a hand, giving him the choice of joining him or not.

"I am real," dream-Alex had whispered. "You are who must decide whether to believe or wake up in the real world. Free will is a thing."

Real world? The real world was morning in front of the mirror holding a razor; eating a bowl of instant oats because he'd snoozed his phone once too often; and forgetting his scarf on the way to work. That was the real world.

Who'd choose that? And yet, when Sophie walked up, he was glad for free will, even if Eliot still hadn't signed her account over to him.

"Rough night?" she asked.

"I look that bad?" He shrugged and tried to laugh it off. "I guess you'd better define rough."

"Come now." She smiled and turned her attention to Marcus. "Office talk says you two are tight. Is that the correct word?"

"Could be." Marcus looked at Alex and grinned. "I call it a cosmic connection. The cosmos speaks, I interpret, and my friend here absorbs the truth from the stars."

"What truth have you received lately?" She shifted her eyes to Alex and fought a smile.

Alex answered, "Free will, per the New World Theology podcast. We're changing God's plan for the world as we speak."

"Oh." She chuckled. "That's a big one. So, you two are into podcasts? Should I try this, what did you call it, One World something?"

"New World Theology." Marcus had a new audience. "I grew up Lutheran, and although I left the Church, I've kept an interest in my spiritual side."

"Meaning he doesn't have one." Alex looked at his watch. "We're headed up. Are you needing a ride?"

"Sure," she said. "Are you offering me your car?"

"It's hardly ours," Marcus said. "And yes, if you want to ride with this pudzo here."

"Yes, I would like that, that is if the pudzo doesn't mind." She winked at Alex playfully.

Alex growled, but when the doors opened, he half bowed and waved her in with, "Ladies first."

"Yessir, my good man." She laughed.

"Why the question about a rough night? Do I really look that rumpled? My suit's just back from the cleaners, and I'm fresh from the skivvies out. I even combed my hair this morning."

"He hardly ever does that." Marcus tried to cut off a chuckle but was distracted when the car stopped at an unexpected floor. "What? I didn't push anything."

"That's for me, my destination. I'm looking forward to being on your team, Alex, but I'm off here for the day." She slipped out as the door began to open.

"Wait." Alex held the door. "You haven't said about my looks."

"Your looks are just fine." She paused and crossed her arms, causing small diamonds in her bracelets to shimmer under the overhead lights. Her lips teased him with a grin.

"Then? You can't expect me to endure the entire morning with this on my mind."

"Okay, then. Sure. What I saw was this: You look like you've been walking through dreams instead of sleeping."

"Walking through dreams." Alex felt himself sag backwards, as though the props from under a sailboat were stripped away, and he was sliding backwards onto cold, hard ice. "How ... would you know?"

She touched her lips with one finger and blew him a breath of a kiss. "Because that's how everyone looks before they remember."

She turned and headed towards the maelstrom of cubicles and supply room doors.

Before they remember what? Alex almost asked, but before he could call her back, Eliot's hand appeared on the elevator door.

"Alex, my star pupil!" He turned to Sophie with his glossy self-assurance and overly indulgent smile and called, "Not so fast, Miss Verden." When she turned, he waved her back, getting the attention of everyone near enough to hear him. "I know you two have met. I've been working on tying up my account assignments, and it's finally done."

Eliot's hand on Alex's shoulder pulled him from the elevator and left Marcus to hold the door. The elder statesman put his arm across Alex's shoulder, gave him a quick manly tug, and patted the side of his face. "I want you leading the Verden account next month."

Sophie smiled, slow and triumphant.

"I, um," Alex was rarely at a loss for words, but with the beautiful Miss Verden standing there, and the thought of the time they'd spend together, well, his brain was mush at that point.

"Go ahead," Eliot encouraged with the firm pressure of his hand on his shoulder. "What do you have to say?"

"I won't let you down," Alex said. He'd looked forward to this for weeks, and now that it was offered to him, it felt like the life was sucked out of him.

Eliot leaned in. "Never say that, Morton. It's not about letting me down. It's about *never falling*."

Alex couldn't tell whether he meant career ambition or gravity itself. Either way, hitting the bottom would take its toll.

As Eliot commandeered Miss Verden to escort her to her destination, and the elevator doors closed the two men inside, Marcus let out a whistle.

"I know." Alex tried to blink sudden fog from his eyes. "You can't deny her beauty."

"It's not that." Marcus was wide-eyed. "You should have seen what happened when Eliot put his arm around you."

"I was there." Alex took a deep breath, preparing for the twenty-second floor.

"Nah, you had to be where I was. A glow surrounded you. Man, free will or not, someone up there likes you."

"It was just Eliot." Alex made a point to grin as he said it.

"Yeah, just Eliot." Marcus had his eyes on the floor, and the elevator dinged to announce Alex's destination.

"Then, lunch? Or do you have a favorite podcast scheduled?"

Marcus looked up and grinned. "Hey, pudzo, you know me."

"That's what I mean. Maybe Renee's free—"

The door sealed off before Marcus could reply, and Alex didn't mind. Getting the last word in with Marcus lifted his spirits just enough to wave at Amy Witherspoon as he hit his desk and the time clock on the wall announced it was time for the workday to begin.

5

Raising the Temperature

ON TUESDAY he started taking the early train again, just to watch people.

Walking to work kept him in his head too much, so nah. He needed people around, even if he didn't know them and they didn't know him. Just faces, the chatter and hubbub, and the smell of train and oil and brake dust ... it comforted him. He wanted ... no ... *needed* the small democracy of commuters aboard the train.

He wore headphones but no music; he preferred the rhythm of steel and rail. The headphones said he was occupied, off limits, and needed his distance. Miss Verden's comment, his dreams, and Marcus' description of the glow he'd seen swirled in his head like an ice floe trembling and ready to break the dam.

For a time he leaned his head back, closed his eyes, and let the memories of the birchwood flow like a waterfall from the past into the present: his father, the fishing trips they'd taken, and the words of wisdom his father had shared with him.

Words of wisdom. Alex felt his eyes grow damp. He enjoyed his city life, the hustle and the bustle, the warmth of Eliot's approval at a project well done. And yet, at times, he dreaded seeing his boss walking toward him. The smile, so bright, seemed manufactured for charm, and the thing was, Alex had noticed his own smile, just as bright, and how it began to feel strained after a day at the office.

Renee, he thought, what song would you make of these feelings? Would it be sad, funny, or charmingly quirky? Tick tock, the song of the clock / Hear it sing from its wooden cage / Its voice rings out bright and clean / The chime is the knife of the mage.

He chuckled. Mage rhymed with cage, but what did a magician have to do with a clock? Nothing, which was why Renee was the song meister, and Alex stuck to his spreadsheets.

He sat up to check the train's progress, and that's when he noticed a tall man in an immaculate coat, his face blurred like fogged glass. He wore a neck gaiter of gray cloth pulled up over his mouth and nose, pandemic style. It was a while since Alex had taken the train, but he was certain the man was one he'd seen before, a person he'd begun to think of as the Commuter. Always the same carriage, same seat, same 7:42 departure. He never spoke with anyone and always wore the same neck scarf over his face.

The scarf didn't explain the blurred upper half of his face. Alex blinked several times and gave up. He chalked the blurriness up to bad eyesight and habit. Still, the man's stiffness made the air tighter, like being in a soundproof recording session just before the music starts. Even Alex's headphones didn't explain that.

At one stop, an old woman boarded. She was in an old-fashioned knit cap with a fur border, and she carried a brown paper package wrapped in string. Her plaid coat could have been from 1940. Her feet shuffled down the aisle in U.K.-style wellies, and she took the seat across from him.

"You're glowing, dear," she murmured softly.

He took in the lines in her face, her reddened cheeks, and the slight otherworldliness that had entered the train with her. The Commuter was still focused on nothing, as if she hadn't just boarded.

Alex laughed awkwardly. "Good moisturizer."

Still, he glanced at his hands, unable to control the instinctive movement. He rubbed them, feeling their dryness, knowing his reply was a bridge over the awkward comment, and there was no moisturizer involved. He smiled at her, hoping to ease the situation.

She pursed her lips as if considering his answer but crossed herself before placing her brown-paper package in the seat beside her. She pulled a small bundle of knitting from a pocket and gave it her full attention.

When Alex looked back at his reflection in the window, he thought he saw someone crouching behind him. He pulled his headphones off and twisted around—of course, no one was there. As he settled back into his seat, he closed his eyes to process ... there had been something, he was sure of it, like wings inside the glass. He dared to look towards the window again, and all he saw was the normal Alex face that stared back from his mirror each morning.

Once he got to the office, his schedule distracted him from the events on the train. Despite the prestige of being assigned to the Verden account, he still had a full plate at his table. Projects tended to stretch into weeks and months, and then some were on-going, with regular maintenance and input sessions. Eliot hadn't taken any of those away, just added another for Alex to manage.

Then coming out of the café at lunch, Jerry Culbertson from the Records Department waved him down and asked to walk with him back to the office.

"Hey, man," Jerry started, while giving Alex a quick fist bump on the shoulder. "How's your day been?"

"About the same as the last time you punched me." He laughed to show he didn't mean anything by it. It was a thing Jerry did, always punching even if he'd just spoken to you five minutes earlier.

"Yeah, right. Hey, man, can I talk to you about something?"

"Ha, ha. You already are, so shoot. I think it was Pat Benatar that sang hit-me-with-your-best-shot. Go ahead. I'm ready."

"No offense, Alex. You're a good guy, and Eliot worships you, I think. But people have been commenting on odd things about you. Don't get me wrong, this isn't from me, just repeating what I've heard."

"That's the warmup, right?" Alex wasn't sure he wanted to hear the next part.

"Yeah, it's one of the interns. We all know they're a little light upstairs." Jerry laughed and circled his temple with his pointer finger. "Anyways, the intern said it looked like light was bending near your chair."

Alex had to laugh. "And you're telling me this why? Seriously, light bending near my chair? It's called sunlight."

"That's not the only thing. Shelly—" Shelly Clarkson was with the daytime cleaning staff. "—always crosses herself when she empties your recycling bin."

"Okay? She's worried about cross contamination. So what?"

"Only when she empties yours. You get my drift?" Jerry smiled to diffuse the incidences. "Just saying, didn't know if you knew."

A memory swirled in Alex's head. That morning, during a meeting with an elderly client in Alex's portfolio, Eliot had tried to strong-arm the client with charm. Alex had seen the incident from his client's viewpoint and stepped up for her, even offering to rework an updated proposal to her satisfaction. Surprisingly, Eliot had backed off when Alex interrupted. Now, something the client had whispered to her assistant came back to him.

"Do you feal that heat?"

And she'd been looking at him when she said it. Alex was so focused on dancing around Eliot's possible irritation that he'd not had time to do more than listen and move on. Then after the client left, Eliot surprised him with, "You got a lot of power in you, kid. You and whoever's smiling on you, keep up the good work."

Alex realized what had bothered him about Miss Verden at the elevator. Whenever she or Eliot entered the room, warmth flared at his back—not the comfort kind, but the warning kind.

He realized that upon entering that meeting, he'd caught a flash of something: a man, his *own face*, standing behind him in the door's reflection, holding something the light turned to gold. His breath fogged the glass, but the figure's didn't. Then the conference room door opened, and the image dissolved.

"Ah, the office. We're still good, Alex? I mean, no intentions, no hard feelings, right? I'm on your side." Jerry wrapped a hand around Alex's upper arm, squeezed it, then waved as he moved away.

"Right, Jerry. We're good." He returned the wave.

Maybe Marcus could fill in the cracks forming in the world around him. His Lutheran upbringing ... he was certain Lutherans believed in angels. So, a good ex-Lutheran should know, if anyone would.

If he could convince his friend that it wasn't all a joke just to play him.

6

The Therapist

HE AWOKE EARLY the next morning, no alarm, just instantly alert. His phone rested on his bedside table, dark and pending with future calls, wake-up alarms, and reminders of life as an up-and-coming corporate associate. He studied the ceiling as the night's dreams filtered through his thoughts.

He was nine. They had yet to move to their new house, and a storm broke over Madison that summer. It came rolling low across Lake Monona, dragging a ceiling of bruised clouds behind it. Thunder rattled the porch screens and sent his father to the basement to check the fuse box, while his mother stayed by the window, half-smiling at the lightning.

"You'll miss it someday," she told him.

"Miss what?" He enjoyed her hand loosely resting on his shoulder.

"This." Outside, lightning painted the clouds, fairy writing on the sky. Then, seconds later, the house rumbled, shivering the glass in the windows.

"What will I miss about it?" It was just a storm, and while they were exciting, there were always more in Canada, slowly making their way into Wisconsin.

"Storms are the sky remembering it can speak."

Alex didn't fully understand but loved the sound of her voice. She was the sort of woman who talked to seedlings as if they were confidants. His father called it sentimentality.

Alex only later came to the realization that his mother's way of speaking revealed her faith without the sermons they heard when they attended services at the church.

As the light failed, and even the clouds became invisible, the storm battled the darkness for possession of the sky, with wind, distant rumbling, and eventually a torrent of wet on the rooftop and windows. For a time, he climbed out of bed and positioned himself between the glass and the curtains, and through the beaded water creating shimmering streaks down the window, felt he was part of the sky.

When morning came, two trees had fallen in the field behind their rented duplex. The yard invited him out to explore with its smells of wet earth and ozone. In the birchwood at the edge of the property, he found a thrush stranded beneath a fallen branch, its wings trembling but intact. Overhead, the tree limbs shivered, shedding the storm's aftermath, and showering him with leftover night. He crouched, the tears of the trees running from his hair, and whispered, "Shh, buddy—it's okay," the same way his mother soothed him whenever the adult world turned loud.

He worked the small body free. It shivered, blinked at him, then hopped once and flung itself back into the air. A handful of silver feathers caught the rays of morning sunlight and floated upward longer than gravity should have allowed—sparks instead of fluff, the moisture on the tiny wings glinting till the small bird vanished.

In the dream, he remembered something else from all those years ago, another shimmer, other wings, the glint of light from among the tree trunks that made up the birchwood. It was there, and yet it wasn't, a shape almost human yet translucent, watching him with patient affection. He blinked, and it was gone.

Later that night he tried to tell his parents. "There was someone in the woods."

His father chuckled without looking up from the paper. "Neighbors, maybe. Nobody lives out there."

His mother simply asked, "Did you feel afraid?"

"No."

"Then maybe it wasn't meant to scare you."

Two weeks later, the curated calm of his sheltered childhood cracked. His father stood at the back door where Alex and his mother had looked out over the storm and said, "No matter how much, it's never enough."

The argument—and that's what it became—started about money, then drifted to aspirations, and ended—like many things in adult life—with silence. From his bedroom he heard only the muffled slice of a suitcase zipper. Each wordless sound entered him like a new rule.

Goodness doesn't always win people's approval. Sometime the "room" takes everything. You can try to game life, but it will always steal the lot.

Sometimes, the best you can do is just keep breathing until the noise passes.

For years he measured every conflict by that night—the scale between noise and silence.

Now, the silence of his bedroom was deafening. Why he remembered that storm and his father leaving he didn't know. He needed sound, and he reached for his phone and tapped his music on. He sank back into his pillow and tried to focus on the feel of his sheets against his arms and his legs.

They were real; this room was real; the storm had passed long ago, and the birchwood was likely an apartment complex now. Eventually, the echo of the dream faded, the darkness in the room folded in on him, and even the music lost its hold on his ears.

ON MARCUS' INSISTENCE, Alex booked an appointment with Dr. Julian Milt, a corporate wellness consultant with the calm diction of a podcast narrator. Dr. Milt had worked with Rick after his separation the previous summer and seemed to achieve wonders. Rick praised him, anyway, and he had gotten back together with Rebecca, so some concrete success there.

Dr. Milt was in the Kane & Sutter Tower, with offices also on the twenty-second floor, which was convenient, but he did work for the company, so that was that. His part of the building was not the open, expansive part exposed to the sky. Alex followed a corridor away from the light towards the north side of the structure.

"Marjorie," Alex said, as he entered the office foyer. Marjorie Breakwater was Mr. Milt's assistant long before Alex came onboard at Kane & Sutter.

"Mr. Morton!" Marjorie was chirrupy and positive, exactly the sort of person people enjoyed seeing when they were scheduled for visits with the wellness consultant. "It is so good to see you this morning. First, let me congratulate you on your step up the ladder with the Verden account. You will get your name on the board before thirty. Everyone in the office is certain of it. Let me ring Julien to let him know you're here."

Alex took a seat, and within minutes, the doctor's door opened, almost closed, then fully opened to reveal the therapist, smooth, calm, and very much in control of the moment. He held a clipboard in his hand with a pen attached.

"Alex, come in. Thank you, Marjorie," he called, as he waved Alex inside.

"Doctor ... or?" Alex left it as a question.

"People always ask, but I say my father's name is Dr. Milt. I'm Julien, so yes, first names."

"So, your father's a doctor, too?" Alex had a flash of his father's suitcase snapping closed in the middle of the night.

"Was." He smiled brightly. "Life happens. But you, Alex, you asking about my father. Are you here about yours?"

"Why ... why do you ask?" It was eerie how perceptive the man seemed. How did he know?

Dr. Milt chuckled. "Most twenty-somethings are. It's the nature of the corporate world. After all, why are you at Kane & Sutter? To prove to someone you can do this, be the best, top out the leaderboards? Otherwise, you'd be in Austria teaching snowboarding."

"Or Hawaii on a surfboard." Alex could sense what Dr. Milt was doing—making a connection—and it was working, even as Alex wasn't certain he liked it.

"Is that where you want to start?" Dr. Milt

motioned to the couch, and he took an armchair that angled out from his desk. The windows were covered in dark wood blinds, with a tall plant anchoring one corner, a very relaxing space that felt like a cocoon of safety.

"I'm not sure where to start," Alex admitted. It was their first session, and while he had dreamed of his father, it was yesterday that prompted him to be here.

"Not surfing, then." The doctor smiled. His eyes glinted, although later Alex would remember it more as a shifting of the light, even a ripple of reality. "Say whatever's inside. This is confidential. You are, shall we say, my patient, and I can offer you full patient confidentiality."

His eyes did that ripple thing again.

Alex decided to take the risk. "It's ... reality that's starting to echo."

Now that it was out, he realized how bizarre that must sound. Reality echoing? Yet, in bed that morning, the memory of the storm and his father leaving had seemed just that, an echo of the past invading his present.

Dr. Milt smiled gently. "Echoes only occur around boundaries. Perhaps your mind is telling you one exists that you're pretending not to see."

"Between what boundaries?" His father had given him boundaries. His mother, faith. He guessed he had something to prove to his father, and he'd let his mother's faith slip through his fingers.

Hadn't he? If not, why did he feel his life was so manufactured and that he had to work so hard at it?

Dr. Milt drew him back into the room. "That depends. Work and self. Self and image. Dreams and whatever you fear dreams might expose."

That hit Alex in the birchwood and nearly left him breathless. He studied the man's calm exterior, the smooth expression that didn't condemn or judge. Except for the eyes, but then, the good doctor smiled, nodded, and glanced at his hands as if to say, You can trust me totally. Alex slipped on the banana peel and began to describe the mirror moments, the lights, and the impossible incidents Jerry had described to him.

When he finished, Dr. Milt folded his hands. "Tell me, what do you believe about angels?"

The question startled a laugh from Alex. If they were discussing angels, shouldn't he be visiting a medium or a priest? "I believe coffee exists. Angels, not so much."

"Interesting." Dr. Milt jotted a few things on a pad of paper and looked up with his polished smile. "Because belief is the last sense to fade."

Something about the way his pupils shimmered—like liquid pouring inward—made Alex look away. The last sense to fade ... whatever that meant.

"Do you journal?"

Alex looked back into the man's face, grateful that his eyes were just eyes once again. "Yes, but only because a friend insists."

"So do I. I need you to provide me with data for my intake notes. Take this notebook and journal any experiences you have, including your dreams. I want you to leave it with me the next time I see you. That takes care of us for this time. I'm so glad you shared with me."

The doctor stood, and with little fanfare, Marjorie ushered him out the door.

7

Searching for Purpose

HIGH SCHOOL was easy for Alex. The academic parts, anyway.

Connection with people and situations wasn't. He excelled in debate, economics, schedules—anything with outcomes, but to sit around at a burger joint and just shoot the breeze, or to be at the lake with friends and cook hot dogs with nothing else on the agenda, that was harder.

He received invitations, and people seemed to like him. However, he didn't have a well-oiled plan for stepping into unfamiliar situations, to shift gears when people showed up that he didn't know, or even how to step away from the event when it was winding down. Sometimes he stood around, waiting for … something … someone to say, "I see you're out of here, Alex. Later, dude." He felt unsure who to hug, who to shake hands with, how to interrupt a conversation to say he was hitting the road.

Often, it was easier to just not go.

But he did build connections with people, and he hoarded the feelings of warmth when giving away notes before exams, sitting quietly by panicking class-mates until they calmed, even once fixing the rusting latch on the janitor's cart without being asked. He couldn't always say what made him do those things, but each act made him feel threaded back to something more important than just working to earn top grades. It was like he was making a difference in the grand scheme of things, at least in the person's life he interacted with.

At seventeen he started running at night. He liked the solitude, the rhythm of sneakers against dark pavement. On those routes, he could sometimes run effortlessly for hours, as if the wind were lifting each leg, giving him support, taking away the strain. When he paused for a drink from his bottle, he'd turn behind him to catch the breeze, and there was nothing there. The air around his face was completely still. Yet, when he began to run again, there it was once more, the push, the lift, the help with each step. He chalked it up to imagination—his body's own encouragement. He was training, and isn't that what training is supposed to do, make the activity a normal part of his skill level, effortless even when it seemed difficult to others?

He knew he must be giving it more effort than he thought, when in the corner of his eye, small particles of light would drift like lazy fireflies keeping pace with every step. Eyes did that, didn't they? His coach said the extra strain on the body put pressure on the retina, and therefore, the particles of light, what his coach called "seeing stars."

After graduation, he took the summer to rethink his plans. His father's words had him looking at the corporate world, and that path required more than just running at night with stars in his eyes, no matter how effortless it seemed. So, from the first day of college, he determined to reinvent himself. He researched and memorized a repertoire of jokes, standing for hours in front of his mirror while he polished his delivery. He felt like he had an audience in the glass, that his reflection was laughing with him at the funny spots, and helping him time his routines until they rang with clarity.

Then there was his GPA. He'd done well in high school, but college was a fresh start, one that didn't just go away at the end of each year. His studies ate into his free time, for which he was grateful, and pursuing fraternity bids masked the isolation he tried to push aside. He was sometimes surprised but always appreciative when his newly honed social performances kept the invitations coming.

Professors admired his composure. Whatever the class or the assignment, Alex took it in stride and never missed out on getting assignments completed on time. During his four years, he was paired with outstanding roommates. Even when they butted heads and he expected a clash, it never happened. Alex would head home for the weekend, only to return on Sunday to find the situation eased and his roommate eager to see him again. His junior year during a late-night conversation, his roommate told him he envied his luck.

Luck? Sure, Alex had no trouble getting the professors he wanted, and the classes he chose were never full, even though others complained about being shunted to second choices. Then, student aid grants showed up just in time, even when Alex was certain he couldn't continue another semester without working a full-time job. The night after his "lucky" conversation, he noticed how he fell asleep with his fingers crossed under the pillow—not superstition exactly, but something that felt like negotiation. After his roommate's comment, professors, classes, and grants swirled in his head, and he found himself whispering, "Let tomorrow feel purposeful, not just busy." Lucky, he almost said, but he refused to call it that.

One evening, his phone rang, and it was his mother.

"You're happy, sweetheart?"

"Of course." His day had been a ragged whirlwind of activities. Several times he thought he couldn't get it all done, then as if someone were helping him, tasks got magically completed when he wasn't looking.

"You still noticing things?"

"What things?" The finished report that he didn't remember turning in? The lab he forgot about but received full credit for? The clean shirt in his dorm room locker when he woke up late? Those sorts of things? What was there to notice? That happened to everyone. It must, if it happened to him.

"The small ones that happen when you're not trying too hard."

He promised he was. In truth, he didn't have time to notice those things, not the way she wanted him to; he had to accept them and let them slide off his plate. The corporate ladder required college connections, bonds formed in his fraternity, and inquiries into the paths that would open a position after graduation. He was already building his corporate future in his imagination, and it was requiring most of his attention.

Yet deep beneath the gleaming polish of corporate

preparation remained what he called the "better itch," or a reflex toward helping others. He knew his time should be about himself. Wasn't that what college was about, preparing himself for a lifetime career? Still, that "itch" survived nights of studying and sleep-fogged semesters where he barely found time to slip off his shoes. It made him offer over-indulgent classmates a ride home, donate more than he could afford to progressive causes, and smile at stranded tourists in February and offer them directions to their destination. When he weighed the cost of goodness next to his plans for corporate success, sometimes that goodness felt like weakness, and sometimes it buoyed him like a jolt of pure oxygen.

After college graduation, with a job offer in hand, ambition finally landed him in Minneapolis. Giving his mother a hug, he told himself he would find his purpose there. He had to follow a paycheck first, because who could live without that?

He had found the paycheck and was on an upward trajectory, but the hoped-for purpose? That was more difficult. However, the lie had worked long enough to carry him to twenty-four—and sometimes he still hoped for purpose.

On the January morning he first glimpsed his reflection behaving separately, that childhood shimmer in the birchwood surfaced fresh in his memory, as if the same unseen companion had simply waited for him to look again. He still remembered the sound of the thrush taking flight—the thin rush of air when something fragile proves it isn't. He recalled thinking: If the world really is full of helpers you can't see, maybe one of them saw me too.

That night, he recorded every detail he could remember.

- Dream: same lake, same companion.
- The ice: now clear, with faces frozen beneath ... versions of myself, each reaching upward.
- The figure beside him saying: “Every time you keep silent when truth is asked, another part of you drowns.”
- Result: I looked up, I was alone, and the sky began to crack open.

He had woken up gasping, with his apartment smelling faintly of ozone and burning wood, and he sat up and began to cough.

A beam of light glimmered across the floor, brighter than the streetlight through the blinds could account for. When he threw back the bedding to inspect it, the light vanished, leaving only silence and the faint vibration of his phone.

He pulled out Dr. Milt’s notebook and opened to the first page and wrote: Another Dream. He added the date and began to write it down.

8

Stopping Time

DURING LUNCH a few days later, Alex found Priya Kapoor waiting in the building's atrium, carrying both textbooks and skepticism under one arm. A law student a year younger than him, she was brilliant and fiercely logical, the perfect person to bombard him with the voice of reason when he felt he was going off the rails.

"Renee texted me. Said you're having metaphysical migraines."

"Glad my friends respect confidentiality." He chuckled, enjoying the banter. He didn't mind, as she understood his struggle as an immigrant daughter balancing the American dream with her family's inherited traditions.

She studied him carefully. "You look ... different. You know I tell you that you work too hard—"

"And have repressed anxiety. What is it from this week, that my father left when I was a kid?"

"Likely, but no. Your aura ..." She held up an open palm and circled it in front of his face. "No, not repressed anxiety ... well, yes, you have that, but that's not what I'm seeing. It will come to me."

"Can you be more specific? I need to know if my

clients can see it too." He made light of it, but the question was real, especially after his recent dreams.

She pursed her lips as she studied his face, then sighed and relaxed into herself. "You seem harder to focus on, somehow. Like a candle behind glass."

He forced a grin. "Guess I've achieved enlightenment."

"Or you need a CAT scan."

He wasn't sure she was joking. "Renee's at a symposium, and Marcus only gives me half a lunch."

"Podcasts, again?" She grinned.

"You know, modern, metaphysical theology, that sort of stuff, but yes. So, have you had lunch? I'd like company, if you've got the time."

"Let me check." She pulled out her phone and scrolled with her thumb, nodding, checking a second time, then slipping it away. "I cancelled my lunch date for you. So, yes, I've got the time."

"I *am* special." Alex grinned. Her willingness to accommodate him on the fly was part of her allure as a friend.

"That's why I'm here. Renee and I talk, you know." She nodded as if to say, "Of course I can make time for you. Friends, duh."

As they headed outside to the café across the street, a gust of wind slammed against the revolving door, reversing it before it halted with a shudder. It came to within inches of Alex, and he put up an arm to protect Priya.

"Oh, whoa!" Her eyes went wide.

"Yeah, that was close!" He took a deep breath, certain his eyes were as wide as hers.

"No, no. It wasn't the door." She peered around

him, searching.

"It's just me, you, and the door." The door was still frozen, and he lifted his arm to push it to get it started.

"No." She touched his forearm to stop him. "For an instant, I saw the faint outline of someone behind you. He had his palm raised, shielding you when that door almost hit you."

Something in the enclosed space rustled, like crumpled paper or the brush of bird's wings. Air brushed Alex's face, and he felt a hand on his shoulder. Warmth on his neck felt like a hug and a whisper of encouragement.

Priya shivered. "Did you—feel that?"

He nodded slowly. "Yeah."

Yet, there was only sunlight filling the glassed enclosure, bouncing harmlessly off the reflective surfaces.

Talk during lunch was intentionally light, as they both took time to absorb what had happened. He asked about her classes, and she shared bumping into Marcus in the elevator one morning. When he inquired about why she was at Kane & Sutter, one of her classes had referenced an old legal case involving the firm, and she was doing research.

"Nothing to do with my team, I'm certain." He laughed. When she didn't, he frowned. "You know Eliot. I've told you about him, my boss, but even more, my mentor. He thinks I've got a great future in the corporate world. I'm certain he'd stay clear of anything like that."

"It's an old case. And I'm just doing research. So, how's Renee enjoying Boise?"

Alex got it. She had shifted the conversation to

safer ground, and they enjoyed their food when it arrived.

THE NEXT DAY, with Renee still away, lunch with Priya was again a thing. Light snow swirled as they headed back to the familiarity of the same café.

"Yesterday, I've got to know." She had her arms on the table and was fully focused on him. "Something stopped that door, and I know what I saw. Or perhaps I should say someone stopped that door."

He relaxed into her inquisition and confided in her, and she listened like a litigator. She didn't take notes, not on her phone, but he could see her eyes clicking off each detail, categorizing them, and lining them up against one another.

"So," she began, sitting up as though she had assessed a case and determined the outcome. "Duplicates, dreams, lights, and ghosts. Possible diagnoses include stress disorder, insomnia, or divine audition tapes. Which do you prefer?"

"None sound flattering. What are divine audition tapes?"

"None rarely are flattering. Divine means God and angels and stuff. I think you need a vacation."

"And if God and my angel follow me on that vacation?" He chuckled to show he didn't think it was a real possibility.

"Then at least you'll hallucinate in warmer weather."

"Ha, ha. Then it'd be the heat. No way I need heatstroke."

She smiled, kind but unpersuaded, and pulled out a sheaf of papers from a folder. She laid them on the table and spread them out, each one showing a different locale that would offer beaches, relaxation, and sunshine. He perused them, pointing at the tanned, smiling people, not certain he could take the time to do that. He shared that Eliot was pushing him to embrace his ambition "for the sake of his rising star." He didn't share that, at times, he felt his boss also considered moral shortcuts perfectly acceptable.

As they crossed the street back to the office tower, a gust of wind sweeping snow through the downtown juggernaut of buildings halted in mid-motion, freezing the snow in midair, and revealing a car coming directly at them. They stepped backwards, and the car missed them by inches, with the whole thing taking less than a second.

Priya breathed out slowly. "You feel that?" she whispered. "Every flake was suspended like glitter on invisible threads."

He nodded. He was more aware of the car's taillights now disappearing around the corner. Then, as if the sky breathed out extra moments of time it held in its grip, the world resumed, with Uber drivers honking as if offended at the momentary immobility of the day.

Neither mentioned it again, but that evening, she texted him.

PRIYA: Physics of stopping time. Googled it. Unresolved.

ALEX: Who would have thought?

Her text consumed him until he fell into bed and sleep took him.

9

Breaking Point

THE NEXT WEEKEND, Marcus threw an impromptu small-group dinner, half intervention, half distraction.

Marcus attended as the host, but Priya and Renee were present also. Alex was the guest of honor, although no one shared that with him. They met in the building's common area, which had a serving kitchen tucked in under a lowered ceiling. The grand space, a seating area with a 360-degree fireplace, offered four-person tables, heavy, padded seating, and wingbacks nearer the fire. The flames were gas, but gas was as good as gold when Old Man Winter tried to steal their warmth.

The four attendees sat at one of the tables, with the remains of taco salad littering their plates. In the kitchen, food packaging and cooking utensils painted the story of events there. The conversation stayed light until Alex mentioned his latest dream: the self-duplicate now speaking in his *voice*, warning of "a betrayal by fire."

"Oh, this is too much." Marcus, ever skeptical but mixed with equal parts curiosity, pushed his plate back to make room for his arms and leaned into the table. It groaned ever so slightly with the pressure.

"We were just starting to understand your ice-self. Remember the versions of you under the ice?"

"What?" Renee had been humming a new tune and tapping away at her phone, her "habit" of creating songs on the fly no matter where she was. "So, your ice subconscious now has a flaming bodyguard? Look into my eyes, Alex. I have something to say to both of them. Tip better. Dream rent isn't cheap."

He wasn't sure he should share his latest dream, one where his ice double had spoken with his mother's voice.

"Being kind to everyone around you isn't the same as finding safety."

He wanted to ask what that meant, but she—he—was already fading, replaced by the city skyline reflected perfectly in the frozen water.

After that dream, he awakened with an ache that wasn't physical: it was nostalgia for something unnamed. It outlined a hole in him, one that was partially filled by the friends with him tonight, but as empty as ever when he stepped back into the world of his apartment, solitary walks through the city streets, and slaving away to fulfill Eliot's increasingly dubious goals. He sometimes tried to fill it with coffee, but coffee just sharpened the edges of the question: "What is your purpose in life? Have you found your focus yet?"

Marcus rolled his eyes at Renee's observation. "Dreams don't predict; they process. You, Priya, give me your thoughts. Should we all chip in and send our friend for a little rest and relaxation? If transportation's a problem, what say we inquire about any angels needing overtime."

"Stop it, Marcus." Priya put her hand on his forearm to forestall any further teasing. "During our lunch the other day, I thought I saw something too, and it stopped a door from blowing into Alex. Right after that, it was as if time stopped so we could step out of the way of an oncoming car."

"I give. I didn't hear about that." Marcus held up his hands as an offering of submission. "Dreams are there to work out problems in our daily lives. They serve as resolution meters, where the stranger our dreams, the more we need to work out."

Renee frowned and tapped the table right in front of Alex. "Except your dreams keep syncing with the latest headlines, dude."

"I haven't dreamed about Russia, Gaza, or climate change." Alex noticed that the conversation had turned fully to him. He wasn't sure he wanted to rehash his dreams that much.

"Here's your daily headline: that client who almost tanked your project—didn't you dream about that the night before?"

Priya stared into her glass. She had talked about the revolving door, but Alex was relieved she hadn't told them what she'd seen stopping it. As far as the snow freezing its position in the sky ... well, wasn't there a waterfall in Hawaii that tumbled uphill due to heavy winds? If a waterfall could stop in midair and flow backwards, he was confident that snow could do the same.

"You're all overthinking this," Marcus insisted. "Alex's stress hormones are auditioning for *The Exorcist.*"

"Heads-turning-backwards *Exorcist*?" Renee

shivered. "I watched part of that one time, and I swore off it forever."

"What is this *Exorcist*?" Priya was a slow eater, and she was still spearing bits of salad and eating them off her fork.

"Wow, but you don't know about *The Exorcist*?" Marcus' eyes twinkled. "This little girl gets infested with demons, and her face turns all funny—"

"Stop." Alex pushed his chair back and stood. "My dreams are weird enough. I don't need those kind."

"You guys want to move to the fire?" Renee pointed with her head. They were indoors, but the room stayed chilly in winter. "No one else is here, and I can clean this up later."

They pulled up chairs to prop their feet on the circular hearth. The flames didn't crackle, but the light shifted in patterns of yellow and red, and the warmth was real.

"She's not wrong about the predictions," Alex said quietly. "Last night the dream said something else was coming. Something about a choice."

Renee gave him a soft look. "Usually that means you already made one—you just haven't admitted it."

He laughed it off, the sound brittle. "Don't worry, I'm not starting a cult."

Marcus raised his glass. "Cheers to that. If you do, at least make the robes comfortable."

They drank. Outside, the storm that had been brewing all day finally gave in and threw out a long shaft of lightning, with fingers of the beast breaking off into a series of snapping tendrils and decorating the sky for over a minute. As the lightning pulsed and forked over the Mississippi, the building rumbled with a low-pitched tremor.

Just as the lightning reached the end of its tether, a final flash, white enough to silhouette the shadow of opened wings across the windowpane for one impossible second, worked its way across the heavens before folding in on itself and fading to black.

10

The Mask of Success

THE SUNDAY after Marcus' intervention, the weather cleared, with any leftover clouds hugging the Canadian border far to the north. In the direction of Lake Superior, Duluth was likely shivering under a new load of thunder snow, but the local parks were sled ready, and a few people even wore shirt sleeves as they tossed footballs back and forth.

Alex happened to bump into Brian Stanford who had a new girl on his arm.

"Brian!" He called and jogged his way. "I've been thinking, it's early for baseball, but a radio show I listen to is offering presale tickets at a good discount. If you want to get together this year?"

That was when he noticed Brian's girl.

"Alex, meet Cherie. Cherie, meet Alex, my work brother." Brian wore a red woolen cap with a blue tassel—the Twins' colors—and his jacket said TWINS across the back in giant block letters, with Minnesota just underneath in a smaller cursive.

"Brian, you didn't tell me you worked with someone who's a Twins' fan." She looked up at him with a pretend pout. She shifted her pout to Alex. "So, is this a boys' thing, or can girls join in?"

He was on the verge of assuring her she was welcome, when he felt that familiar warmth at the back of his neck, and a whisper that was as much in his head as in his ear said, *They won't be together then.*

Alex backtracked with, "Once I get some available dates, I'll let Brian know. He can get that information to you."

They walked on by, with Cherie holding Brian's arm wrapped in hers and looking at him with adoring eyes. However, just as they walked out of sight, she turned and gave him a look that said something it shouldn't.

The next morning, Brian entered the elevator after him, just the two of them, and he ducked his head.

"Tough morning?"

"Something like that." He glanced up sheepishly. "Sorry about Cherie."

"How's that? She seemed nice enough." That last look ... he wasn't saying anything about that.

"I thought we were out for an afternoon in the park. She only wanted a final free meal before she cut me off." He sighed heavily. "I'm glad you didn't give her the ticket dates. She would have probably accepted and then expected to go with you. Are we still on for one of those?"

"You bet. I never say no to a Twins' game." He laughed.

"Even with Cherie?" The elevator had stopped at Brian's floor, and he held the door for a moment.

"I'd have to think about that. Okay, I did, and it's a big no."

"Smart man." Brian laughed, released the door, and disappeared just as it closed behind him.

At his desk, he greeted Shaunika and noted his

inbox as he draped his coat over the back of his chair. The week was just starting, and it seemed fuller than ever.

"Shaunika, has someone already been around delivering folders?" He lifted the top one, expecting it to be the Verden account, only to read: Baumgartner Florals. He'd never heard of Baumgartner Florals, so it must be a new account.

"Eliot put those on your desk. Personally. I guess that means they are especially important."

"Right. They all are, according to Eliot." He ran a finger down the spines of the folders, counting. If Eliot expected him to focus any real time on each of these, that meant he was doubling his responsibilities. He had four meetings with Sophie last week—she refused to allow him to continue calling her Miss Verden—meaning he saw her nearly every day. She was always nearby now, or so it seemed, an orbit both flattering and exhausting.

Following one meeting where Eliot was pitching a new idea, Alex could see weak legal wording in the proposal, and he'd asked Eliot for an extra day to rework several sections.

"For?" Eliot frowned, and the room felt colder. Shela Cartier, Sophie's assistant, reached for her sweater.

"Legal did go through this?" Alex had a copy of the proposal—as did everyone in the room—and he hit several areas with a highlighter.

"Of course." One of the legal team glanced at Eliot with a frown, and Eliot said, "Or they will, as soon as this meeting is over."

Oddly, as soon as Eliot switched from falsehood to

truth, multiple electronic devices in the room glitched. Several phones began to ring, despite claims that they had been silenced, and the fire alarm blinked twice before going dark again.

Sophie's phone was face down on the table, and it vibrated once. She turned it over, tapped it, and smiled. She reached out to get Alex's attention and murmured, "You're brilliant when you stop doubting yourself, Alex."

He almost missed the faint hiss when she said his name, as if the air itself recoiled when she let it slip through her lips.

She touched his sleeve. "You could go far, Alex." There was that hiss again. "But only if you learn which voices to ignore."

The meeting concluded with the legal team collecting all the proposals and assuring everyone that new copies would be forthcoming.

Following an afternoon drowning in clearing his inbox, Alex was haunted by the way Sophie had said his name. As beautiful as she was, and as much as she appeared to give him exactly what he dreamed of, including admiration and potential companionship, he felt emotionally compromised when he was with her.

Before leaving, with his inbox stash mostly cleared, his finger hovered over his power button as he prepared to log off his laptop. He hesitated and realized she hadn't meant his critics. It wasn't his critics he had to ignore. She'd insinuated something deeper—*voices unseen?*

He pictured the whisper when meeting Brian at the park. *They won't be together then.* He'd thought it was intuition, something he'd unconsciously recognized in their interactions. Now he wasn't certain of anything.

He touched the power button, and the screen flashed before shutting down: DON'T.

Just that word, white letters on a jet-black screen. And a reflection—of someone standing behind him.

When he spun, the office was empty.

As the week progressed, things began to fall in place for him, like a second proposal where legal checked the wording and sent him a note of thanks for catching the weak sections. Small coincidences multiplied. He missed an elevator, only to hear that someone's thermos had exploded, and everyone's shoes were ruined. Twice, when he was alone, the elevator speaker whispered, "Good morning, Alex," before he pressed his floor. Email drafts auto corrected to phrases he never typed, as if an A.I. bot had access to his computer, even though the company had a rigid firewall and real-time activity monitoring to keep unverified A.I.s out.

Once, it changed to "You're not alone" as he watched, before returning to his original words. Every time he tried to rationalize why the glitch happened, the rationalization melted into doubt and suspicion.

He shifted all his journaling to longhand and put nothing about his dreams on his phone or his computer.

If I'm unraveling, he thought, I want it to at least be in my own words.

The entries in his new journal became dialogue between two versions of himself—one cynical, one patient.

The handwriting of his patient self was neater.

11

Collision Course

HIS APARTMENT became his safe place, except for his bathroom mirror. There he ran the shower to fog the mirror as often as he actually showered.

A podcast during breakfast talked about loving the human that was gifted to you on the day you were born. The host said, "Imagine that your one job in this life is to take care of and protect your human. You will have other jobs, sure, because that's life, but the only job that really matters is caring for your human. The rest are inconsequential. Parents love their children because they are theirs. You must love your human because he is yours. You can't trade him in at 21 or 26 ... this human is the only one you get, and your job is to give him the best chance for happiness that you can."

Alex found the podcaster's premise interesting in a metaphorical sort of way—as in angels assigned a person to cover as their guardian and protector—especially with what had been happening lately. Then the podcaster put a twist on the story.

"Your human is you. A parent is cautious about who their children spend time with, the quality of their sleep, and their food choices. They don't put them in danger, because they are theirs, and they love them too much to put them at risk."

The kicker came next.

"Even when they don't like their children, they still love them and care for them. You don't have to like yourself to love yourself. Take care of the human you were given the day you were born."

Images of child-Alex flooded his thoughts. His parents had cared for child-Alex, and then his mother after his father abandoned the family. Now it was Alex's turn. He thought he was doing everything right, but sometimes, when he was with Eliot, he began to reevaluate if that's what he wanted future-Alex to be when he reached his age.

Was being mentored by Eliot the best way to assure his human's best interests and future? If he wanted to rise in the corporate world, it had seemed so when he stepped onto Kane & Sutter's stepladder.

The podcaster's story had him thinking. He spooned up a final bite of oatmeal, and his phone vibrated, telling him it was time if he intended to catch the early train. Self-reflection and the reevaluation of his life choices would have to wait.

Arriving at work, his desktop calendar reminded him he was scheduled with Dr. Milt the last thing in the day. A text mid-morning was a welcome distraction.

REN: How's that dream journal coming along?

ALEX: Into my second notebook.

REN: Notebook? What is this, the twentieth century? Foodz for an update! Today!

At the café, he was grateful for Renee's fully focused attention as he shared some of what had been happening. She pinned him down on the longhand, and he sheepishly revealed his computer's auto correct autocorrecting things he didn't think it should auto correct. He held back about the "You are not alone," but he shared turning off his laptop, the word DON'T, and the ghostly image in the screens.

"So, just computers." She relaxed and smiled. "Remember when we met back in college?"

"Ha, ha! How could I forget? I thought you were the coordinator for our team, and you had no clue either."

"We were all just volunteers, and they forgot to assign us a coordinator. We had to figure out how to move that urban aid project forward on our own."

"We did it, though." He picked up and swirled his coffee. "Your vision, Renee. I told you that then, and it's still true. We all earned our congrats, but it was your vision."

"Yeah, like I'm the Statue of Liberty. Even she gets tired of holding her arm in the air."

"Your point?" She always had one. Her dream journal was a success. He trusted what she "dreamed," and he smiled at the play of words.

"And what's that smile for?" She returned it, even as she asked about it.

"You, dreaming up a dream journal to keep track of my dreams."

"Ah, because you're so dreamy." It was a poke, and she smirked. "So, any other opportunities for song material other than an elevator that talks to you? That's facial recognition, by the way. Not weird, not by a long shot."

"And Eliot telling the truth and all the electronics glitching?"

"Eliot! I'd glitch too, if I suspected him of honesty.

You don't see what I see, and maybe that's best. It's why I write songs no one wants to hear. People can't bear the honesty."

"You do a great coffee."

"Hence my job as a barista. The singing barista, that's my new moniker. I'll send out a promo: Coffee and Truth, by the Singing Barista. I'm sure that'd hit like a ton of truth bricks."

DURING HIS MEETING with Dr. Milt, the therapist began with a single question that changed everything:

"When the reflection speaks, do you answer?"

Alex froze. No one, not Marcus, Renee, or Priya had ever asked that question. Marcus usually cracked a joke that if Alex's angel had a six-pack, he wanted a pass to his workout facilities. Renee kept him in line with sarcasm, saying, "Yeah, my mirror speaks to me, too, telling me I should get more sleep." Priya would send him to Bermuda for a week in the sun.

Dr. Milt held his fingers entwined, with his pointers forming a small temple just under his chin. His calm precision said that he had seen this before, and that delusions could be conquered by reason. His tone stayed calm and measured.

"You should. Reflection is communication. You deny it too long, and it finds alternate messengers."

"Are you saying my hallucinations have—spokes-people?"

"I'm saying truth often wears more faces than one."

As the session continued, Alex felt less and less hope that Milt could help him, that his reflection-detection meter would soon overwhelm his senses, and that he might well be referred to Mental Health Fairview before he could make his mark in the firm. He avoided the doctor's eyes, and when Milt spoke, he closed his and sensed the movement of warmth around him, as though his arms were being caressed by something not quite solid.

When he left Dr. Milt's, Marjorie's desk was vacant, and he let himself out. The office with its myriad of cubicles echoed with emptiness. Outside, ash dusted the sidewalk. He frowned, certain he would have seen newsflashes if a fire had occurred anywhere near downtown. A few feet away, the ash thinned and quit. He looked up, tracked the outside of the building, and located his floor and the likely location of Dr. Milt's office. He found himself enveloped in cedar smoke and the sharp, metallic aroma of iron.

The scent lingered in his jacket all evening: cedar smoke and iron, with the iron taking on a slightly musky, mushroom-like odor, which he recognized as the result of skin oils on iron and the chemical reaction that ensued. Whose skin oils? He hadn't handled bare iron, so how could that be?

That night he dreamed of a man who looked like himself, one with wings and a flaming sword. It didn't seem frightening, rather comforting, as though someone was looking out for him and wouldn't allow him to come to harm.

The dream faded as he moved into his morning, but the warmth didn't. It was his best sunrise in a very long time.

THE POKER NIGHT was cancelled for the week. Ray's daughter had a birthday, and his ex-wife seemed to know just when to schedule it to cause him the most inconvenience possible.

On Friday, Marcus arrived with Vietnamese take-out and bad philosophy. “Maybe your double is what you’d be if caffeine evolved consciousness.”

Renee followed him in, and when she found her place at the kitchen counter, she tapped her chop-sticks against her drink. “Tell your double to tip better, too. You need better stemware.”

Alex smiled, grateful they could joke. The humor grounded him, even when it mocked him. *Laughter is proof the dark doesn’t own the room*, he thought.

As this was poker night, and its replacement was impromptu, there was no agenda. They chatted a bit, avoiding the obvious, like angels, glass doors that magically avoided Alex’s face, and elevators that liked to talk to him personally.

Renee did have her guitar attached to her like white on rice. She pulled it out, strummed a few cords, when Alex requested, “A cappella, if you don’t mind.”

She stilled the strings with her hand and began a simple tune, no guitar: “We walk the lake of life between what’s real and right ...”

The sounds from outside the apartment faded, and even the fridge muffled to nothing. Marcus stopped chewing, the furnace worked in a vacuum of sound, and only Renee’s voice was there.

Alex felt space fold inward, bringing momentary peace thick enough to taste.

When the final note faded, the lamp beside him brightened for one single heartbeat—then dimmed again.

Renee frowned. “Old wiring.”

"Probably," he said, pretending to believe it. Inside, another voice whispered, *Or rewiring what used to be into something brand new.*

12

The Lake Returns

IN THE FOLLOWING weeks, Alex's inner narration became constant—and began to resemble his journal, commentator and confessor.

He began to question every part of who he was, why he'd chosen the corporate footprint, and how he related to those around him.

After a harrying day at work, when Eliot pressured him to just "sign the client's signature" on an updated form, he'd felt the cold emanate from the man and questioned if he was doing the right thing by refusing to do something he felt was wrong. Would the client have agreed to what was in the paperwork if he were here? Likely, Alex thought, but the point was, the client wasn't here, and that made it forgery. It wasn't honest, and if he did it once, it would make it easier the next time. Before long, it would be about convenience rather than necessity, and he could imagine stumbling into a vast cauldron of consequences.

That night, in his journal, he angrily asked himself, *Why do you chase perfection?*

For the first time, Eliot had lashed out at him, storming out over the signature, telling him it was no big deal, and he'd better buck up if he wanted to remain in the company's good graces. The room had darkened with the words, and Alex's laptop rebooted during the tirade, telling him Eliot wasn't kidding. The truth had come out, and it wasn't in Alex's favor, not as far as the company was concerned.

Why did he chase perfection? He lifted his pen and considered ... because he was honest? Because Marcus respected him? Or was it Renee, who he knew had a romantic thing for him, even if she never pursued it ... or Priya, chasing two worlds, the old one her family had left behind and this one, the American dream that her parents didn't understand?

The truth found its way to the paper: *Because his father called perfection a virtue.* Love, parenting, his mother, none of those played into his father's rules. Perfection, perfection, perfection. And despite his abandonment of the family, Alex still strove to live up to his image of what a man should be.

A day later, he was heading into Joey's, and a young woman with two small children crowded the counter. She was talking them through the cocoa options on the board, and they couldn't decide what they wanted. Everything caught their attention, and the children constantly changed their minds. Joey caught his eye and shrugged, and Alex mouthed, "Black."

When the family stumbled into the booth next to his, the mother noticed his black coffee and seemed embarrassed that she had stolen his chance to order. Black was, of course, available, but it wasn't on the menu. In Joey's, it was a last-minute quickie for people on the run, and here Alex was nursing a black. That couldn't be intentional, and she was so sorry.

He shrugged off the offense, observed that children were a handful, and he could have one of Joey's specials anytime.

Just then, Joey delivered Alex's venti, quad, half-caff, non-fat, no foam, extra hot, peppermint, white chocolate mocha with light whip, together with two pumps of sugar-free vanilla, one pump classic, a dash of cinnamon, and with a splash of soymilk coffee just like before.

The mother paled. "And you were drinking black? I'm so sorry. Let me pay—"

He hadn't let her, but once he was home, in his notebook, he scribbled, *Why do you forgive strangers?*

He didn't know the woman, and to let her pay for his coffee would have made her feel better, he was sure. Her kids were blissfully oblivious to the entire thing, so that wasn't it. He knew one thing, after she'd turned her attention from him, he'd felt the warmth of having down something right; and even more unusual, the bell over the door dinged twice, even though no one had walked through.

Had he expected Joey's second coffee? Would he have been upset if the barista hadn't offered it and considered the black good enough? It was, after all, what he had requested.

After several minutes of thought, unable to come up with a fair reason, he felt a nudge on his hand and in his heart. He wrote: *Because your mother taught you helpers hide in plain sight.* He frowned at the sentence, crossed out "your" and wrote in "my." He chuckled. He never called her "your mother." Where had that come from?

It seemed he was haunted by guilt. If he did what

Eliot wanted, his morals were wrenched aside. If he confronted the man, he felt himself slipping on the corporate ladder and disappointing his father. When things happened for the good, things that lately he didn't remember doing although his co-workers assured him he had, he felt guilty he didn't remember. It was like he wasn't in control, that life was skittering along just ahead of him, and he was riding on someone else's coattails.

Why can't you forgive yourself? He wrote the words carefully and underlined them three times. The third time, it all smudged, or at least his view of it did. He pressed a hand to his face, and it came away damp. He'd finally opened the ache that never seemed to heal. His dad leaving... somehow, Alex had convinced himself it was his fault. Leaving his mother in Madison? Each time she called, the guilt of her loneliness consumed him. Trusts he'd broken, even when the people returned forgiveness; unintentional slights; laughing at awkward times; jokes that hadn't gone over well ... it was too much. Why didn't his life come with the perfection that his father demanded?

Because you prefer cleaning others' wounds.

He didn't record the comment and wondered if everyone held board meetings with their conscience, or if his was simply louder.

He knew the solution was the same as it had always been: When you're unsure of things, do something. Step out, step up, just be the responsible one that shows up and starts. Everyone else will step up to follow your example.

That was what he did over the next several days, determined to push the guilt away and leave success in its place. He focused more during staff meetings, backed Eliot before clients, and spent extra hours each evening at his desk. He even tried to answer Dr. Milt's questions as honestly as he could.

Still, through the hum of responsibility, he found himself repeating a quiet mantra: Leave places kinder.

It became instinctual. He helped interns without recognition, sent anonymous donations, and carried groceries for neighbors twice his age. At Joey's, he complimented the coffee, left a larger tip than normal at Foodz, and picked up his groceries from the shop rather than calling in delivery—and still left a tip for the next delivery guy that came in. Motives blurred between altruism and superstition—maybe grace, if such things existed, needed exercise.

His next dream was vivid beyond compare.

He stood on the same lake, with ice under his feet, and in the distance, snow-covered hills were alive with white-tipped trees reaching towards the sky. His companion still boasted his hair, eyes, and jawline, and he wore the simple clothing that hid the power that Alex knew must be there.

His other self—whether angel or ghost—was no longer silent during the dream. The man crackled with power, the sound of a recently frozen river ripping ice from the shore as it barreled past the watchers alongside.

"You've wandered between faith and fear long enough," dream-Alex said. The words were deafening with the roar, and yet, each one was perfectly clear. "The choice is coming. And you already carry the weapon."

"What choice is coming?" Alex couldn't hear

himself over the roar, and yet, he saw the man's recognition of his question and knew he could hear it as clearly as Alex had his.

"Look down."

In Alex's right hand, light flared in the shape of a flame. Then it lengthened, not into a sword, no longer just fire, but becoming both.

"What if I don't want any of this?" he shouted.

"Then others will decide for you."

The man's clothing began to buffet in the wind, and wide wings opened at his back. Light glistened behind him, sparkling off each feather, until the light grew around him and he subsided into the brilliance.

Alex looked around, now alone, and he was frightened. Who would decide for him? He looked at the flame/sword and hefted it into the air. The flame whipped in the wind, as if the molecules in the air could extinguish it if they battered it enough. The wind roared, and the ice buckled under the onslaught, and yet the flame burned brighter. Beneath the surface, faces—Eliot's, Sophie's, even Dr. Milt's—stared upward, mouths moving in silent accusation. Then the ice broke, and he felt himself falling through.

He woke trembling, with the familiar smell of fire and iron in the room. He hit the bedside switch, and the light came up. His bedding steamed, and when he searched through the fabric, a scorch mark revealed where his hand had been.

He looked at his hand, ran his fingers across his palm, and found nothing. He put his hand to his nose, and there it was: fire and iron, certain and sure.

He pulled his journal from a drawer, opened it on his lap, and began to record.

13

The Morning After

AFTER WRITING down the dream, he reread what he wrote critically.

- Lake: still frozen.
- Me: the other one, still there.
- Unusual this time: fiery sword.
- Thoughts: Who's coming for me?

That was the essence, but it was like understanding a spread sheet by only reading the column headings. If you knew the entire set of information, then it made sense. But the details would begin to slip, and you'd lose the essence of what had happened.

He tried again.

- Dream: vivid beyond compare.
- Same lake: ice under my feet.
- In the distance: snow-covered hills.
- My companion: still me but in simple clothing.
- Different about my companion: crackled with power.
- Another difference: no longer silent.
- He SPOKE: said I have a choice and a weapon (what choice; didn't get to keep the weapon ... what's with that?)

- Decision: I must make one ... or it will be made for me.
- Under the ice: Eliot, Sophie, and Dr. Milt (means?)
- Afterwards: iron and fire odor in the apartment; hand not burned.

The first list made more sense. The second carried more emotion, especially since he'd just been there. He pushed his hair from his face and studied the blinds. Lights flashed, and he threw back the bedding and walked to the window. Outside, the parking lot revealed a fire truck. No siren, but the lights were flashing, meaning they had been called, but there was no obvious fire. He shrugged and climbed back into bed.

Sleep didn't come. He checked his phone every fifteen minutes, certain it had been an hour each time. Finally, it vibrated, and he realized he had managed a few hours sleep. In the bathroom mirror, red eyes peered back at him. No glow of wings, flashes, or blinking lightbulbs, and for that he was grateful.

A morning shower was in the works. He usually didn't have time, but this morning, he would take it. He baked under the hot water and was glad the mirror was a cloudy sheet. Nothing to see, or at least nothing he wanted to see.

Breakfast consisted of the simplest things in his kitchen: water to boil for oatmeal and a sliced bagel in the toaster oven. He set out a block of cream cheese for the bagel.

Renee called first. "You okay?"

"Define okay." He checked his bagel, and when the water started to steam, he poured it over his oats.

"Marcus said the smoke detector in your building went off last night. Half the block swears they saw sparks at your window."

"I saw the fire truck." The toaster oven dinged, and he slipped the browned bagel onto a plate. "There was no fire. I'm about to have breakfast."

"Then what *was* it?"

He settled in at the bar, giving himself time to think. After a long pause, he said, "The inside of me, trying to remember what it's made of."

"I don't know how to answer that."

"I put it in my dream journal, so you can read about it later."

"I don't like later. Text it to me."

"Seriously? How?"

"I forgot, paper. Later sounds good." After a moment of silence, she said, "I think your doppel-gänger's dream rent just went up."

He laughed, really laughed, and almost spit out part of his bagel—partly because it was funny, but mostly to keep her from realizing how hard he was shaking.

"ALEX, GOOD morning!" Sophie Verden was sitting at his desk when he arrived at work, very relaxed—like a woman who had claimed her spot. She wore a red, low-cut dress, with her hair tightly styled and her features done up in alluring makeup.

"Oh, yes, good morning, Sophie." He looked at Shaunika's desk for help, only to find her chair empty.

"Your workmate is with Eliot this morning. He called her in for a performance review."

"That's not for another month—" He caught

himself. Why would Sophie have information about who Eliot was calling in for reviews?

"How inconsiderate of me. I'm in your chair. Let me move out of your way."

She was looking directly at him as she spoke, but her reflection in the glass separating the cubicles clearly showed her looking toward the elevator. He turned to see what she was watching, and he caught a shimmer of red and steel, of smoke and iron, and it disappeared as ash settled to the floor.

Sophie's eyes grew wide, and she hissed, "Not now. I'm not finished with Alex."

He heard the hiss and felt warmth brush his neck. The smell of iron and flames surrounded him, and when Sophie tried to go around, the smell grew stronger and the fire alarm began to sound.

"That has to wait." She moved her hand in the air, and the alarm silenced itself. "Alex—" hissing again "—later today. Can we schedule a consultation at eleven?"

"I'll mark it on my calendar."

As she moved away, the odor of iron and flames faded, but it never left him for the rest of the morning.

THAT EVENING, while trying to put off meeting the dream-Alex again, he drafted an email to his father.

Subject: Long Time.

I'm fine, I think, Dad. Work's good, though weird things keep happening.

I can hear your response. Weird doesn't make a partner by thirty. However, Mom would laugh. She always said angels work overtime when adults forget their bedtime prayers.

Don't worry, things aren't THAT weird. I'm not off the rails, and I really enjoy being at Kane & Sutter. I'm still working to make you proud.

I know you don't like to hear about things like this, so I guess writing this is just to pretend I can tell you how I feel. I hope you're well.

Love, Alex.

He ended it there but didn't send it. Just reading the words felt like opening an attic door, one where old memories gathered dust, and being inside was a scramble in the darkness.

Who wants to scramble through old memories, anyway?

When he shut down the laptop, its dark screen returned his reflection—as if waiting to answer his question.

He whispered, "Not tonight."

The reflection smiled faintly, approving.

14

A Man Doubled

THAT EVENING, as city lights glittered across the thawing sidewalks, Alex found himself in the complex's fitness center, a large glassed-in area totally isolated from the remains of winter just outside. Through a glass partition, the indoor pool fractured overhead lights into the workout room, shattering the coming of night into glittering fragments.

He pressed a towel to his face as sweat beaded on his skin. His loose tank and lightweight shorts were drenched. A circuit of the machines with twenty minutes on the elliptical had him eyeing the spa for a bit and then into the pool for a cooldown.

He kept his eyes from the glass, specifically from his reflection in the slick surface. That double image, one from the front side and the other from inside the thick panes—if he could avoid that, he could avoid his father, the hint that something was going on around him that he could barely sense, and even his newfound caution at being around the beautiful Sophie Verden.

He worked his shirt over his head and dropped his shorts to reveal trunks underneath. Under a showerhead, he rinsed before entering the spa and sinking as far down as he could get and still remain connected with air and life. He welcomed the smell of chlorine—better than smoke and iron—as he dipped his head completely under and let the action of the jets vibrate his skin. He came up gasping and stood, checking the pool for who else might be in the water. He let the remains of the chlorine drip from him as he stepped out and headed that way. What was the purpose in a towel, as he would be even wetter in the pool? One other person occupied the far end of the pool and was swimming laps. It was the wrong direction, but then, the water didn't know direction, only resistance.

He fell forward into the water, which was heated but chilly after the temperature of the spa, with his arms outstretched. The surface peeled away as the water consumed him, washing down his skin and bringing him back to reality. When he returned to air, he began a slow backstroke across the surface. Overhead, the ceiling revealed the building's pre-formed concrete ribs, with round, half-dome pendants nestled inside, creating a series of eyes that critiqued the activities in the pool with an illuminating glare.

Pausing in mid-stroke, he let his feet drop. He located the ladder along the edge, ready to make his exit. He couldn't touch, but the motion of his hands kept him afloat just fine. Without thinking, he glanced toward the glass facing the outdoor Minnesota cold, and he caught the room's reflection. He was low and could just see the coping around the pool along the bottom of the window, with the back wall revealing gym equipment deeper in. Someone was getting out of the pool, a man wearing trunks much like his. The man turned and smiled, and it was him.

His mirror image had moved *ahead* of him, doing what Alex was intending, and that took weirdness to the next level.

The reflection-Alex worked his fingers through his hair and shook the water off his hands. Rivulets of wet worked long fingers down his torso and legs. He gave Alex a thumbs up. *Soon*, he mouthed.

Behind the reflection's shoulders flared a faint outline of wings unfurling.

And for the first time, Alex didn't laugh. He whispered, "I see you."

He swam to the side of the pool and exited just where the reflection-Alex had stood. Water from his hair was in his eyes, and he worked his fingers through his hair and turned to where he was when he'd seen the man. Of course, the pool was empty except for the swimmer doing laps at the far end. He shook the water from his hands and caught himself whispering, "Soon," before he realized he was the person he'd seen.

If it wasn't him, at least they had been doing the same thing. He shivered, unsure whether it was from the cold or the experience.

He grabbed a towel and began to work it over his hair. That was one question he wasn't prepared to answer.

ONCE DRESSED, he was unwilling to head back to the apartment. Renee was working tonight, so he determined he would support her job by dropping in for a coffee. He stepped directly outside, and the chill in the air prickled his skin.

"Whoa," he let out. Yet, to go back now for his coat was anticlimactic, and he braved the temperatures for Renee's sake.

He stepped through the door at Foodz to dimmed lights and the Open Mic backdrop in place. "Yeah, I'm out of touch. Maybe later."

"Not later."

He turned to see Renee in her Foodz apron with a tray and steaming coffee in one hand.

"You must be a chilly boy. Hold there while I deliver these." She smiled and moved into the darkened space.

By the time she returned, Lottie was announcing *Gary Olheitzer, the brightest young comic in the Midwest.* Except, he looked to be forty, hardly young.

"Some nights are better than others." Renee slid her tray onto the counter. "You, though, braving the cold. Bare arms. I don't even do that."

"I was in the pool, well, the spa first, so I'm warm inside where it counts." He shrugged off his gaffe with the outdoor weather. "You have a few moments?"

"See that?" She pointed at Gary, who was ripping through jokes like they were a dime a dozen. "I have until he'd done. Now, what do you need?"

"I saw him again." He pulled his shoulders in, not exactly embarrassed but uncomfortable stating it so baldly.

"Can Priya verify that?" She teased and tapped him on the shoulder.

"Priya was not in the pool with me." He caught her frown. "The place is surrounded by windows. I was thinking about getting out, and the reflection of me did just that before I could."

"Time travel, right? Don't think too hard on this. You were thinking about it, so your mind saw what you wanted to do. Call it a vision if you want, but I call it preplanning. Oops, Gary's done. I have to go. Are you hanging around?"

"I'm headed to my place. Thanks for keeping me grounded."

"Anytime for an angel like you." She laughed, gathered her tray, and moved into the crowd to collect used cups.

Angel, he thought, as he moved back into the chill. He remembered the wings. Those hadn't been on him when he got out. He looked back into Foodz and studied his reflection in the glass. Yes, there was the double image he expected to see.

Pedestrians streamed around him, oblivious to his internal dialogue. But one passerby—a woman with a briefcase and tired eyes—paused, staring at the same window. "Do you feel that?" she asked softly, rubbing her arms as though warmed by sudden sunlight.

He nodded.

"Strange," she whispered. "A glow, almost like someone wants you protected by a shield of light."

He had seen it, and with it confirmed, he could no longer imagine it away.

Part Three

The Broken Mirror

1

Power Failure

MINNEAPOLIS PULLED another spring prank: sleet in April.

With a few days of sun under the city's belt, everyone was convinced that warm weather was here to stay, but Minnesota was the same as every place in the nation: Wait a few minutes, and the weather will change.

The day had started mildly for no other apparent reason than to lure people outside. Alex's phone suggested a possible weather concern for later in the day, but the sun was streaming in, and he couldn't resist shirt sleeves under his jacket. It would feel good on his arms to spend some time outside at lunch, maybe at the park with Marcus, if he could divert the man from his theological podcasts. He was telling Alex that "anything angel" was what he was after. There had to be something in there that explained what he was experiencing.

Alex even bypassed the train station. Why spend more time indoors when he could be out in glorious nature? March had been harsh, but maples in the park were already budding, and many of the earliest trees were swelling with a blanket of downy green.

The silver maples and many of the red buds already popped with blooms. Their leaves would come later, but the signs of spring were there.

He began his walk in full sun, while braving blocks of shadow from the surrounding buildings. By downtown, light clouds blanketed the sky, and the wind turned as he approached the Kane & Sutter building. Sharp flecks of water-ice began hitting his neck as he ducked through the revolving doors.

"Good morning, Stacie. I bet no one expected this." Dark spots turned his coat into a leopard-skin cape, the true sign of his life in the concrete jungle. He smiled at the memory of a movie he'd seen growing up of a kid who lived wild in the Amazon with his mother and went to visit his father in New York City.

He was still in the jungle.

Alex's boyhood had felt like a jungle, he had moved to the jungle, and how he had the cape to prove it.

"I see that smile. You timed it perfectly, almost. Check your shoes. There's the mat."

Yes, his had left water prints. He returned to the mat at the entrance and swiped several times before crossing the marble lobby. Other people were scurrying in, and the area was becoming more compacted by the minute, with shoes dripping and the latest group shaking out umbrellas.

Yet he had a clear shot, no matter which direction he walked. Other people were dodging umbrellas, apologizing for accidental fender benders, and stepping aside. That was good manners, but he tried not to notice how people automatically sidestepped him at the last second, as if some invisible fence gave him a few extra inches of space, perhaps even pushed them away. They didn't seem to notice, but he did. Not one umbrella or briefcase touched him, even when he was at the crowded elevator entrance with a dozen other people.

When everyone sardined inside, shoulder to shoulder, only his had clearance with no contact. When the elevator doors closed, the mirrored panels caught his reflection twice, faintly out of sync, like it had so many times over the past few weeks.

He reached past several people—who conveniently leaned just far enough out of his way that he touched none of them—and pressed his thumb against the cold metal for his floor. "Don't start again," he muttered quietly.

A faint breath fogged the glass, spelling something for half a second—letters so small he almost missed them: STAY TRUE.

He blinked, and they melted away. He tried to catch the eye of anyone who might have also seen it, but everyone seemed to be in their navels and oblivious to anything other than getting to their desks on time.

THE FIRST TIME the lights blew out at Kane & Sutter, winter had been in full bore, with an Alberta Clipper tearing at the city and vibrating windows. The firm had locked the revolving doors, and everyone was shunted to the regular doors on either side. It was snow battering the building, and while no one could prove it, everyone blamed the storm.

It became almost an occasion, searching for candles (yes, there were a few) and engaging flashlight apps on their phones. Computers still illuminated workstations, but their batteries were temporary, and automated backup programs began to overwhelm the oldest of the machines.

Once the batteries went down, there would be no reserves left.

But ten minutes later, the building's backup power systems switched in. The floors shuddered—differently than the wind—and the lights flickered, with the accompanying beeps, whistles, and whirring that said electronics were coming back to life.

Everyone got a quarter-hour break on the clock, with no penalty, and something to share for several weeks afterwards.

Today, the bite of ice during the morning rush fizzled out to colder temperatures and a light overcast. Candles emerged with the first bites of ice, but with no storm and the sun trying to break through, it didn't look like anything. The morning went on as normal, with meetings, emails, and coffee breaks as usual.

It wasn't normal, however. Electrical pressure began building inside the cubicles, with paper crackling and pens giving off sparks when the lids were loosened.

The monitors couldn't be ignored, either. They began to hum, at first just under most people's hearing, then louder. One or two people flipped theirs off and on again, and the IT department suggested people power down and reboot their computers. No matter what they tried, the problem continued.

Alex not only heard the hum, but he also felt it inside, pulsing at the same pitch as the blood in his veins.

He was heading back from a meeting with Eliot

and Sophie when the electrical pressure became overwhelming. He paused and stood at the center of his floor. Around him was a chaotic cacophony of hubbub, phones ringing, computers beeping, and a whine somewhere in the ceiling. He felt the temperature shift.

A fluorescent tube ramped up in brilliance and began a slow climb in volume. It buzzed, ratcheted to a sharp vibration, then *popped* and rained glass chips over him and for several feet around him. He shook the glass from his hair, brushed at his clothing, and tried to laugh it off when the entire floor went dark.

No storm, no wind, no reason for the power to be out. The office became half-dark, half-bright, with the shadows cast by the large windows becoming brush strokes of deepest black, like a photograph caught between exposures.

A phone rang. The buzz of conversation died, and it grabbed everyone's attention.

"Lacey speaking. Are the lights working on your floor?" She covered the mouthpiece and called out, "It's Vince from IT."

No power surge was detected, and yes, the IT department had power, as did every other floor in the building.

The elevator dinged, and Eliot Kane stepped out, smooth as ever. He stopped beside Alex and took in the glass on the floor. "Happened again, didn't it?"

"What do you mean—again?" Alex asked.

Eliot smiled faintly. "Buildings with history remember their prodigies."

And then he turned and called to the rest of the staff, "It's all good. We don't know why the backups aren't kicking in, except that this is the only floor without power. Be patient, as we're working on it."

Interestingly, he left a scent behind: ozone turning suddenly bitter, like something burning its way through the air freshener dispensers in the vents.

Alex felt the unseen presence rise behind him and knew—*knew*—he wasn't alone in that room.

2

The Shatter Café

HE TEXTED Renee:

ALEX: Taking the afternoon off. You free?

After the glass incident, he found himself in the men's room picking through his hair for errant shards. In front of the mirror, he inspected his hairline, searched from different angles, and when light glimmered, worked yet another shard of glass free.

They were lightweight and became dust at the slightest touch, but they were glass, and he didn't want fluorescent light dandruff flaking from him all day. Finally, he leaned over the paper bin and worked his hair violently and was satisfied to see glimmers of glass residue turning free of his scalp.

He also removed his jacket and shook out the seams and under the collar before setting it aside. He found glass in his shirt pocket and sighed. It was likely in more places than he could count, and that's when he pulled out his phone to text.

After several minutes of reflection in the mirror, he slipped on his coat and stared at his image with his hands tightened on the sides of the sink. Where was his other self? In this mirror, or was he only in his bathroom mirror? Yet, he'd seen him at the coffee shop, in the windows around the pool, and in his living room windows. He touched the glass and studied the distance between his skin and the reflective material on the opposite side.

"Do you live in there, or should I look for you somewhere else? In my dreams, maybe? If you are part of my dreams, why do I see you when I'm awake?"

He thought, *Am I awake ... or is this just another of my dreams?*

The fire and iron, and the scorched marks on his sheet ... he hadn't dreamed that.

His phone vibrated.

REN: For you? Always! Foodz?

ALEX: Not Foodz, please. He wanted somewhere unfamiliar that wouldn't trigger him.

REN: Suggestions? Or can I choose?

ALEX: Where have I never been?

REN: Follow my lead, fair warrior.

She met him on the street, with her guitar case on a strap over her shoulder. "Is your subconscious bodyguard joining us?"

"My dream-Alex?" He chuckled but wasn't in the mood to be amused. "Hopefully not."

"Ominous. Should I hum a few oos to settle the ether?" She closed her eyes, lifted her hands with her thumb and pointer forming a circle and hummed, "A-U-M," which sounded very much like ah-oo-mm. "There, is that better?"

"Funnier, anyway. How far to the mystery eatery?"

"Behind St. Anthony Main, so manageable. You'll like it."

Along the way, he did his best to avoid windows, but it was the city. They held up the storefronts and were the backdrop to every corner and curb. Occasionally, his eyes met himself, and he searched for a glow or for the vaporous image of wings.

Renee noticed. “Are you finding yourself?”

“What?” He frowned. “Strike that. I know what you mean, and it’s not me I’m looking for.”

“Your guardian angel, then? Any sightings? I know a good priest who wants to do an exorcism on someone who’s alive and kicking. I’m sure you’d do.”

“I’m sure I wouldn’t.” It got him to thinking: Was his “angel” something that needed exorcised? Had he done him any harm ... he remembered the feeling of someone at his back after the lighting incident ... he rephrased it, someone who *had his back*. His eyes moistened, and he wasn’t sure he wanted to push that aside too easily.

The sign beside the door of Renee’s eatery announced the business as The Shatter Café, and inside, it overflowed with mismatched furniture occupied by nervous students. A list of hand-written options filled a chalkboard, with colored chalk and an eraser in a tray at the bottom. The counter to order and where the food was delivered were the same, with two fresh-faced workers taking orders. Three people were in line.

“Can I write in my own?” Alex hefted one of the sticks of chalk.

“No, you cannot. But, if you could, what would it be?” As she asked the question, she shrugged her guitar off her shoulder and stood it on the floor.

“An order of wisdom. To know what this is all about. Focus maybe on what my purpose in life should be.”

"That's three. There's enough choices on the board already, don't you think? Do you want to overload those two behind the counter? If so, your bodyguard might have to step in to cover the shortfall in brains."

"As always, my conscious speaks up. I'm returning the chalk to the tray."

When they reached the counter, she ordered fish fingers, while he went for a turkey on rye, and the worker handed them a tag on a metal stake with a wire base.

"We'll bring it to your table. If you will," and she checked a seating chart, "take number three. It's that way. Have a good lunch." She pointed towards a table in a window bay.

When they were settled, Renee took one look at him and said, "Okay, either you've seen a ghost or became one."

He told her everything: the blackout, Eliot's cryptic words, the feeling that someone else had *answered* him without a sound.

"Do you want my metaphoric or mystical advice?" she asked.

"Both."

"Metaphoric: quit your job, write a memoir. Mystical: maybe stop pretending this is normal."

"I'm not hallucinating."

"I didn't say you were. Sometimes the universe rents a billboard before it hits a wall."

Her flippancy made him laugh again, a fragile refuge. Then her gaze drifted to the window behind him, and she fell silent.

"What?" he asked.

Renee's voice was small. "There's ... light around you. Like gold dust."

When he spun, it was gone—but the reflection on the window kept glowing for three heartbeats longer.

THE FIRST HALF of their lunch was quiet, with the focus on the food and specifically not on what they'd seen in the window. By the time they'd cleared the plates, she leaned forward and whispered, "What about that therapist you've been seeing?"

"Dr. Milt?" He felt the frown on his face.

"He knows, doesn't he? I mean, if you're taking the afternoon off, what can it hurt? Do you want me to call to see if he can work you in?"

"No, I'll do it."

That's why he found himself outside the door with its nametag boasting: Dr. Julian Milt. He grasped the doorknob and pushed it open.

"Mr. Morton!" Marjorie, bright and chipper as ever, touched a switch on her desk. "Julian, your appointment is here."

The box clicked and said, "Thank you, Marjorie."

"You may go on in." She smiled and pointed but didn't stand to show him the way or open the door. She must have figured that he had been here often enough and no longer needed her assistance.

He entered the neutral-toned office with its shuttered windows and calming ambience and took a seat.

"Tell me what brings you here."

"Company policy," Alex said. "A concerned friend, maybe."

Milt's smile was of the curated type, and this time

it exuded empathy. "You've been here before, and you did call me for this special session. Let's pretend you want to be here. What would you say?"

"Apathy in expensive shoes." He sidestepped the truth that his visions were distracting him from his job. He glanced at his shoes. They were expensive, and that was the truth.

The therapist's pen hovered. "And underneath the sarcasm?"

"Fear of being average," Alex admitted before he could stop himself. "And increasingly weird dreams."

"About?"

He hesitated. "Someone who looks like me."

"This has happened before. Does he help or harm you?"

"I'm not sure yet."

"Let's talk about that. Have you begun to answer the questions he's stirred in you? After all, his questions are really your questions."

The doctor was skilled, too skilled; their conversation looped back to guilt, until Alex felt hollow, with his subconscious peeled from his inner self like last year's paint.

When the session was over, and he stepped back into the world of buildings, city streets, and the crush of people, one question lingered: *Why do you need everything tidy, Alex?*

The answer was there, just as it had always been: *Because when things got untidy, people left.*

3

Marcus Makes It Real

BY THE TIME he was through with Dr. Milt, Alex hit the streets without Renee. She did have to work sometimes, and tonight was one of them.

He didn't recall if she was working at Foodz this evening, but if she were, she had a job to fulfill. On occasion, she might make time for him, but even Lottie had a limit to her patience, and he wouldn't do that to his friend.

He thought of Ray and Chip, except Ray had to run on a schedule with his daughter and ex-wife. What sort of friend would stir up that level of silt when there were other options? Chip, maybe. Alex checked his watch and pulled out his phone.

ALEX: Leaving work. What's up?

He didn't expect a quick response, as his friend was likely doing the same, and if he remembered correctly, Chip commuted via an electric bike. Not an ideal venue for whipping out a phone for an unexpected text.

He pushed open the door to Joey's and nodded to the scraggly, blond Swede. Surprisingly, every table was empty, and he fell into the corner booth and slipped to the back. Customers were rarely this sparse, so he didn't expect the loss of a booth for one person would decimate the evening's till too drastically.

You're welcome, a warm breath seemed to whisper in his ear.

He glanced around, didn't see anyone, and gave credit to the vinyl on the bench. Escaping air made very real sounds sometimes. He whipped out his phone and stared at his text messages, hoping for one from Chip.

"Man, you have timing, my gubben." Joey appeared at the end of the table and wiped at imaginary coffee stains.

"Maybe not. My text is being ignored." He turned his phone to show the unanswered text.

"Maybe yes. My chairs were full fifteen minutes ago. The fancy coffee? No one in the way this evening."

"If my text gets a response—" He shrugged and didn't finish the sentence.

"I get it. You must go. A hot chocolate, then? I prepared a new batch. As you can see, there is no one to enjoy it. On the house." He had finished the table, and he stood folding and refolding the towel.

"Will you sit with me and talk? I'd appreciate it."

"Only when I have no customers."

"Deal. Hot chocolate sounds good."

"Be right back, my gubben." Joey tossed the towel over his shoulder, leaving the front hanging slightly lower than the back.

My gubben. Alex didn't know that he considered himself an "old man," but he wasn't Swedish, and sometimes the meaning didn't jump the barrier.

Joey returned with two cups, and he slid in across

from Alex. He placed each cup on a cardboard coaster and centered them before them.

"Don't often have the pleasure." Joey picked up his cup and inhaled the steam.

"How's that?"

"To sit and enjoy my handiwork. This smells delicious."

"I never enjoy my handiwork. The clients benefit from it, but it never lands in my paycheck."

"This is not in my paycheck either, but I am still enjoying it." Joey sipped from the cup, and his eyes opened wide. "Drink up, my old man. You will be pleased."

"What, I'm not your gubben any longer?" The chocolate drew his attention, and he brushed the steam his direction.

"We are friends for the moment, so I can say this. I am not really born in Sweden. Right here, yes, Minneapolis, although I don't often share that. Saying my gubben? My mother is from the old country, and she calls her uncles that. It's the one thing I picked up." He leaned in for a second sip, and when he glanced at Alex, his eyes narrowed. "Do that again."

"I didn't do anything." Alex chuckled to get through the moment. He was about to give up on Chip.

"The steam. Brush it towards you."

He did, and Joey had him hold the cup higher and do it again.

"There, around you. The steam is leaving you a message. Too bad things like this never show on film. I would like to take a picture."

"Of what?"

"Your wings of steam, of course—"

Before Alex could roll his eyes, his phone vibrated.

CHIP: Hey, man. Emergency dental appointment. Was just there last week for a cleaning. Don't know how I broke a tooth.

ALEX: Sucks. Man, take it easy and avoid the popcorn.

CHIP: Easy for you to say. Your jaw's not screaming at you.

Joey said, "That's your call to go?"

"Sorry, Joey, but yeah."

"A small drink, then. You can't let the chocolate go untasted." He pressed his cup to his lips and took a long slurp.

"Yeah, man, sure." He was surprised at how *chocolatey* it was. He now understood the children's argument over their drinks. "Yah, worth every dime."

"Especially as you did not pay any dimes for it. Go, I enjoyed visiting."

Before Alex could stand and slip his phone into his pocket, the door burst wide, and a group of twenty or more crowded in, laughing and talking about a man doing pantomime and the crowd that had caused a total standstill for pedestrians who wanted nothing more than good coffee.

In his apartment, he went from window to window, closing blinds and creating a barrier between himself and the glass. No reflections allowed. He was certain that Joey's comment was no more than cheerful banter; after all, the man was known for charming his customers. But that exact description, after what others had described seeing?

The door banged, and when he opened it, Marcus barged into the apartment armed with liquid refreshment and bluntness.

"You're seeing lights. Fine. Pretend it's radiation poisoning if it helps. But maybe keep a log?"

"Deer in the headlights, that's me. I just got in from the office, and Joey at the Kaffe Shop said something weird to me. Don't expect me to follow you."

"Just what I'm saying. Another thing for your log. Let me see your phone. I can download an app—"

"I don't need an app. I have a paper log. It just doesn't obey physics."

"Great. Let me see it. I can publish it. Let's call it *Haunted by Myself: A Consultant's Memoir.*"

"I like you, Marcus, but seriously? Nobody's reading anything I write. If anything, give it to Renee for inspiration. She can make something of it if anyone can."

Undaunted, Marcus pulled out two cans, handed one to Alex, and headed toward the couch. Alex joined him, pulled the tab, and after one sip, set the can on the arm of the couch and twisted it like a corkscrew, this way, back, and this way again.

Marcus leaned his head back, staring into empty space, and asked, "You actually *feel* it, don't you?"

"Yes. And I'm not sure 'it' likes sharing a lease."

Marcus studied him, then said more softly, "If your angel's got a six-pack, I'm still switching religions."

That brought out another reluctant laugh—proof that humor could rebuild sanity one joke at a time.

That night he dreamed himself as a boy, standing in the hall while his father packed boxes.

"It's not your fault," the man had said, eyes on the floor. "Adults get complicated."

"I can fix things," young Alex replied. He was

certain that if his father was leaving, he hadn't learned the lessons from the fishing trips well enough.

His father knelt and took his shoulders in a way he never had in real life, looked Alex in the face for a long time, and whispered, "Then don't grow up."

He woke to the sound of dripping water and sat up, instantly alert. His first thought was that Marcus had rinsed the cans before dropping them in recycle, and he checked to find the sink dry. The ceilings were fine, and besides, it wasn't raining outside. He'd showered before hitting the sheets, and that was his next place to check.

He hit the bathroom switch and froze. He had grown used to heating the shower to fog the mirrors, but that left everything dripping. The only water was on the mirror, where water droplets were emerging from the glass and running upward instead of down.

He wiped the surface with a towel, wanting the entire night to return to normal. The glass cleared except for his reflection, which stayed fogged—a face watching him from the far side of nowhere, and within the misty outline, he glowed, faintly luminous.

He turned off the bathroom light and laughed, a single absurd bark. "All right. You have my attention."

In the dark, the glow was brighter, enough to make every surface in the room visible. When he returned to bed, the glow followed him. Only when he closed his eyes did it go completely away.

4

Sophie Unmasked

TWO DAYS LATER Eliot appeared at his desk and pulled a small envelope from his jacket pocket. Alex shivered as though the temperature had dropped. Overhead, the warmth flooding from the ceiling shifted into a higher mode, with the volume of airflow catching on the corner of a file folder in his inbox.

"Good morning, kid. Something for you." Eliot flipped the envelope around like a card shark at a casino table to reveal Alex's name in a feminine script. The light caught on the glittering silver ink and flashed with a metallic sheen. When he spoke, Alex's laptop screen compressed into a straight, horizontal line, then blinked off. Then the logo reappeared and changed to say "Rebooting."

He got the connection. Eliot. This was an easy truth, as the other computers on the floor were unaffected. In the conference room, a bigger truth had shut down all the electronics. He shivered, unsure if it was the cold or Eliot.

"Thank you, Eliot." He accepted the envelope. The computer was coming back online and required his input to connect to the tower's systems, but that could wait. "Should I?" He mimed the flap opening.

"Absolutely. You want to read this, kid. This is your step up in the firm. Be smart, and you've got it made here." He tapped his temple and grinned. "You do want this, don't you?"

"It's what I've worked for since high school." He opened his desk drawer for his letter opener. The blade reflected his first success at Kane & Sutter: Alex Morton, Top Closer, with the date. He ran it under the flap and set it aside. The front of the embossed card inside glittered with the same silver ink, S. V., printed in a stylized looping script.

"Open it. Read it." Eliot rolled his finger for him to get to it.

Inside, a full paragraph in the same silver ink and feminine script was signed with Sophie's name.

"What do you think, kid? That's at the finest restaurant in the city. I can already see your name in lights. Let's knock this one out and get your name at the top of the leaderboard. What do you say?" Eliot winked. "The Capital Grille. On the company's tab, too."

Indeed. Sophie was inviting him to a client dinner.

"This might outclass my wardrobe."

"Already covered, kid. We have an account at both King Brothers and Jaxen Gray. I've got Lane waiting with the car outside. Are you ready for the biggest change that's ever happened in your life?"

He didn't think being ready had anything to do with it. This sounded like a summons.

In the car, Lane with his mirrored aviators seemed to be in cahoots with whatever Eliot had cooking. After two hours, and with the new suit hanging in the car, they looped by Heimie's Haberdashery to ensure Alex had the perfect shoes to complement his new threads.

Back in the car, Alex hit the control to roll down the interior window. The intercom seemed too impersonal. “I appreciate you taking me around, Lane. Think we’ll make it back by quitting time?”

“Thank you for asking. My quitting time is your quitting time. The car is yours for the evening.”

Eliot was serious, and a chill worked its way down his back. Sophie had been in Minneapolis for some time, doing what—besides the various meetings with the team at Kane & Sutter—he didn’t know, but he’d been drawn into it.

He still didn’t have a handle on her business needs, and that was something he prided himself on. It was as if her company had appeared out of the ether, fully fledged, with a past and financial connections that were there on paper but hard to track when he tried to trace them.

Her money was real. He’d seen the amounts that moved from account to account, and he’d already received bonuses for benchmarks. You couldn’t discount the money ... if you didn’t research the sources too deeply.

Sophie was at the restaurant already and waiting at a secluded table. Linen tablecloths, dark walls, shimmering glass. Minnesota culture at its finest. And Sophie was the finest looking woman in the room, dressed in silver lamé, and refracting the lighting like a weapon.

Paul, attired in a white top and dark trousers, walked him towards the table. Sophie raised her hand and smiled. “Alex, I knew Eliot would get you here.

How was your day of shopping?"

She knew? When he'd thought "cahoots," he hadn't guessed how much. It left him rattled.

Or maybe this was her circle, and she understood the difference between his financial situation and hers. And that when he stepped up, his finances would follow, but for now, it took Eliot's tab with the company for him to measure up.

"Hello, Sophie. You are stunning, as always." He pasted his company smile on his face, and he knew it worked when she returned it. Paul pulled out his chair, and he seated himself.

"Thank you, Paul," she said with a small wave of her hand. "Food anytime."

"Do I need to order?" No one had given him a company card. This meal could easily top a grand. He could cover it, but it was something to consider.

"I've already taken care of it." She touched his hand and quickly moved hers away. "And so that you don't have to worry, client dinner, client request, client credit card."

"Thank you." He relaxed a breath he didn't know he was holding. "So, we're discussing business tonight?"

"Perhaps. Look, here's our meal. Let's leave the discussion until afterwards." Smoothly said with a sultry smile.

He returned the smile, but the servers were placing plates on the table, and that took precedence to any conversation.

The starter: lobster and crab cakes with what looked like lemon basil aioli. And bread, thick and crusty on the outside. If this was the start, what would come next?

"We're having double lamb rib chops, honey roasted. So don't overindulge." She placed her embroidered napkin in her lap and turned to the sommelier who offered her a choice of wines. "Yes, Jay, that will be fine, and for my friend, also."

His mind buzzed. It was like she was reading his thoughts. One very odd thing was how she kept looking behind him, as if something distracted her.

Midway through the meal she leaned close. "Eliot thinks you're ready for more responsibility. You and I could achieve real power here."

He sipped his wine, refusing to wince at the sharp, alcoholic bite. "Power for what?"

"To rewrite the limits of what others can do. To stand where no one else dares. To be the man on the mountaintop who can jump and never hit bottom because of your success."

Her words slid over him like the heat from a bonfire. Under the tablecloth, her hand brushed his, and every instinct screamed *cold*.

The familiar warmth brushed his neck and whispered, *Manipulation ... take care.*

Across the room, a mirror above the bar cracked from corner to corner without anyone touching it. A server with a tray of plates paused, looked at the crack curiously, and shook her head, puzzled, before moving on.

Sophie's smile never faltered. "You're waking up, Alex. I'm proud."

"Of what?"

"Of what you could become—if you let go of the one following you."

Prickles crackled across his skin, each individual

hair standing up. *The one following you* ... Was that what had distracted her? He thought of the reflection at the pool, with Priya in the revolving doorway, and the feeling of someone having his back when the lightbulb burst and shattered him with glass.

If you let go ... and the face from his mirror through the misted glass; the water running upwards; the flaming sword he could feel in his hand even as his skin prickled.

And her knowing that Eliot had sent him shopping on the company's tab. He felt a vice around his conscience. Waking up to what? What would he have to sacrifice from his life to be what this woman was manipulating him to become?

You're seeing it, the warmth at his neck seemed to whisper. *Trust your conscience. Trust me.*

He pushed back his chair. "Dinner's over."

As he glanced in the cracked mirror, the light just over their table flickered, and in the reflection of their images, hers was ringed with shadow, and his flared with a brief, defiant burst of light.

OUTSIDE THE restaurant he walked. Ride with Lane? Not in a million years.

He didn't know how far he traveled or even the direction, but street after street and corner after corner brought him to the Honeycomb Bar. It was a familiar name, so he pulled the door wide and was inside.

He smiled at who was on their small stage, a familiar face with an equally familiar guitar.

After she completed her set, Renee found him. "Cool threads. Did you rob a bank or get a bonus?"

"Client dinner at The Capital Grille. The threads

belong to the company."

"The Grille. Oh." Her eyes opened wide. "Who paid?"

"The client." He smiled but didn't really want to talk about it. He needed distraction.

"Okay, don't confess. But you're smiling at ghosts again. You need fresh air that isn't haunted. I've got one more set before I close the stage down. Wait on me?"

He agreed, and back on the street, they walked along the river at midnight, with the city streetlamps catching ripples on the water. It was like the light could barely speak and was being choked off at every turn.

"I keep thinking the world's about to lift its disguise," he said.

"Maybe it already did and you blinked."

"Wouldn't you tell someone if it happened to you?"

She thought about it. "Depends on who asks. People want inspiration until it doesn't fit a calendar."

He liked her honesty. He liked that she didn't pretend wonder was free.

When they reached the pedestrian bridge, a gust hit hard. Renee staggered, but an unseen force steadied her.

"Thank you for the hand on my shoulder." She smiled at him.

"It wasn't me," Alex said. And somehow, he wondered if it was. Something had stopped that glass door. Priya had seen it. Or she had seen someone.

A hand?

His breath in the chilled air came out as pale fire.

5

Priya's Proof

THE NEXT MORNING was hard to wake to, hard to endure. Sophie's ... *threat?* For some time, she had made him uneasy, but nothing like at The Grille. He wasn't sure she would harm him, but she wanted him to compromise on his conscience. He was convinced of that, and that was something he'd never do.

Then the gust of wind. He'd have thought nothing of it, even with Renee certain he'd caught her to keep her from falling, but after that mirror over the bar. That was as clear as a testimony in court. And it connected the time in the revolving door to the wind on the bridge.

Had those been an attack? Could it be that he was being helped? *And maybe his friends, too. They were being helped because they helped him.*

Who knew what was possible any longer?

Priya wasn't a believer, but she was a legal mind trained to trust evidence. Renee was a trusted supporter, but she'd offer a quip as soon as a quote. At times, that was exactly what he needed, just as at times he depended on Marcus' comic sense of timing. His six-pack joke was already a fixture in Alex's mind, but it didn't help with the metaphysical mystery of what was taking over his life.

He knew Priya had finals on her agenda, so he played it safe and sent a text.

ALEX: I'm caught up in the crazies. You won't believe the half of it. Do you have time to listen?

The wait for her reply was interminable. A lemon seltzer from the fridge gave him something to do with his hands, and he walked to the window and turned up the blind to try to focus on the views. A mother was walking a toddler in a carriage, and the sun through the trees shifted across her, giving her clothing a camouflage texture. Even with the shadows, there was only one of her, no glow, and no shadowy images to suggest the metaphysical world was tugging at the reality that all humanity knew and accepted.

When his phone vibrated, he jumped. He knew his nerves were shot, but he didn't realize how much. He glanced at the screen.

PRIYA: Mom's insisting on a traditional lunch with all my cousins. So, yes. Thank you! Where?

ALEX: The park?

PRIYA: Perfect!

ALEX: I'm headed out now. Take your time. I'll wait.

Once outside, the air filled his lungs like the first time he'd taken a breath. Rich, sweet, with a hint of hickory chips in someone's backyard cooker. Life was still happening for other people, which meant the world wasn't totally topsy-turvy, just his little part of it.

Priya was nearly half an hour in arriving, and when she saw him, she lifted an arm and called out his name.

"Alex, I made it. Mom insisted I bring fresh pani puri." She held up a paper bag with faint grease spots at the bottom. When she dropped beside him, hip to hip, she leaned into him and continued, “She’s cooking *everything*. You have to eat some of these, or she’ll never let me escape again.”

“Then I guess I have no other choice.” He reached into the bag and pulled out one. It felt heavy. “Stuffed?”

“Always.” She removed one for herself. “They are a mix of sweet and savory. No one knows for sure—” She bit, laughed, and almost didn’t keep it in her mouth.

“Savory?” He grinned.

“You have no idea. I think she seasoned the potato filling with red chili powder. Try yours.”

He bit and discovered a creamy custard and took the whole thing in at once. “Sweet,” he laughed as he licked his fingers.

“Oh, you. I wanted sweet, but I don’t dare sample more. The one was more than enough.” She rolled the top of the sack. “Now for you. My time is yours. Tell me about the crazies.”

“And you’ll explain why they’re not?” This time, his voice shook, and he couldn’t control it.

“Until I experience something supernatural, that’s what my mind does. It’s why my teachers tell me I’ll one day be the best Indian lawyer in Minneapolis.”

He told her everything: Sophie’s threat, the mirror cracking, the pressure in the air. When he finished, she sighed.

“I understand that you *feel* haunted. *Being* haunted is entirely different. *The Amityville Horror* and *The Exorcist*? Everyone has seen those, and yet, not a shred of incontrovertible proof. Nothing with a judge’s stamp that says, yep, fully proved and real. You can trust me on this."

"Is a cracked mirror real enough?"

"You're sure there's no other possible reason? The foundation in the building could have shifted, perhaps a screw came loose. Who knows?"

"The timing, though."

"Coincidences do happen." She looked at him hard. Her eyes seemed to say, *How can you not see this?* Then her shoulders relaxed, and she gave in. "Okay. I'll watch. You do something metaphysical. Glow. That's what I want to see."

He blew out his cheeks. "You won't see anything."

"Then we'll both know it's stress. Overwork does that, and I happen to know they've been loading up on you lately."

"Can we do this somewhere besides in the park?"

"Your apartment or mine?"

"Not mine. I've been weirded out too many times there."

"Then my place it is."

On their walk, two more of the pani puris disappeared, and she remarked that her mother would be pleased to see that they had enjoyed them so much.

Inside, she offered him a glass of wine, as she had an open bottle from the day before. He declined but asked her to go ahead.

As she was pouring her glass, he crossed in front of her apartment window, and something invisible stopped him. It was like running into a glass wall.

"What?" She glanced up and laughed. "Are you stuck?"

"Yes, and I don't know why."

"Oh, I think I do." She set her glass down and moved in his direction, keeping him lined up with the window.

"Are you seeing something?" He could only hope.

"The dust motes behind you are frozen in midair. They're taking on the shape of—" She gasped at a flash of light.

Alex saw it too, but when he turned, it was gone.

"It was just behind you. It's impossible."

"What was?"

"A blaze of light in a human shape, with wings huge enough to fill the room."

He closed his eyes and sighed. If Priya saw it—

Priya gasped. "Alex—your shadow—"

It was moving on its own, as though whatever she'd seen was creating a shadow of its own. The wine-glass on her table steamed as though touched by extreme heat.

He stared at her. "You believe me now?"

"I believe ... I don't have the vocabulary for this. Marcus grew up in church. Have you called him? He might could offer you a better explanation than I can."

Marcus was in a handball game at the Dayton YMCA downtown. He asked if Alex could make it by noon. The facility closed early on the weekend, and they could do lunch together. He suggested The News Room at Nicollet Mall, and it wasn't one Alex had tried, so it seemed an adventuresome fit, especially as he hoped to avoid locations where he had experienced "metaphysical experiences" already.

Marcus showed up in track pants, a hoodie, and sneakers. Alex made a face, and his friend laughed, saying that he picked The News Room for a reason. It was sports themed and he would fit right in.

He listened to Alex explain the mirror, the river, and the therapist's odd questions. There was more, but Alex wanted to gauge his responses before bleeding everything out, especially with what happened at Priya's.

"So, your reflection's unionizing," Marcus said. "Classic millennial burnout symptom."

"Funny. And you eating lunch in public in track pants? What happened to your millennial aspirations?"

"A sign of my self-confidence in what I wear, not burnout." He chuckled and stole one of Alex's fries. "I mean, what's happening could be stress. You know I believe in algorithms, not apparitions, but hey. Friendship outranks worldview. You do know studies show that corporate guys start seeing metaphors when spreadsheets multiply."

"That means absolutely nothing." Alex grinned. "One hole in your theory is that if I'm hallucinating, at least the production values are high. I have a scorched place in my bedding where I held a flaming sword during one midnight session."

Marcus leaned back. "I don't know of any apparitions that would do that. Were you smoking weed in bed?"

"Get serious. I've never smoked weed, and you know it." He pushed back the plate. He'd had all the fries he could take.

"It would explain a lot. You've pegged yourself to some high goals, you pudzo. And you're reaching all of them. You ever wonder if something good could also drive you mad? Like happiness exceeding voltage limits?"

Alex grinned and shook his head, but he also considered the joke longer than it deserved.

6

The Therapist Revealed

WORK BECAME constrained.

Busyness was Alex's solution. Complete a project, hit a milestone ... *achievement.* Avoid self-sabotage, which Renee chided him about when things didn't go as planned.

He recognized part of the problem: abandonment syndrome. When boys' fathers abandon them at an early age, they're always chasing validation in a battle for meaning. He'd deflect that accusation from anyone who said it, Renee excepted, but his determination to make a mark in the company and in Eliot's eyes ... he was trying to feel real in a world that sometimes seemed staged.

His interactions with Sophie now felt that way—staged—although he hadn't decided whether it had been there all along, or if the event at The Grille had opened his eyes. He now tracked who would be in their meetings, and he had "emergencies" when it was just Sophie and Eliot and postponed the meetings. He also worked to hit any Verden milestones ahead of time, send the results to Eliot for approval, and avoid standing under overhead light fixtures when his boss was around.

He couldn't completely avoid Dr. Milt. The sessions were de rigueur for all staff, and they were plugged into the company calendar. Any postponements shifted to the next open session and continued to blink on his individual calendar until it was marked off.

He postponed twice before he gave in to the inevitable.

"Alex, two postponements. You've a busy schedule recently. Thank you for making time for me."

"Good afternoon, Dr. Milt. You know the consulting business. We consult for the clients, and when they call, we jump, er, consult."

"Amusing wit. Won't you have a seat?" The doctor gathered his things from his desk and took his regular chair. He settled back, crossed one leg over the other knee, and smiled. "Now, what shall we discuss today?"

"Life is filled with weirdness. I guess maybe that's a good start?" Alex studied the doctor's expression to gauge the direction today would go. He didn't like to think the man was complicit, but he did work for Kane & Sutter, if not directly, at least in the building.

"Good start. You've been asking yourself some questions. How's that going?" The doctor flipped through his notes and looked up smiling.

He did *not* want to talk about that, and he began to tell about the mirror at The Grille. He left out the context of Sophie's overtones, just that it was a business dinner, but how odd it was to have simply cracked with no outside influence.

"Did Miss Verden have any concerns about the mirror?" Milt jotted down something and looked up.

"I didn't ask her. The dinner was winding down, and I met a friend afterwards."

"And did you talk about the mirror with this friend?"

"Of course. It had just jarred my sense of self ..."

Dr. Milt listened in detached compassion until Alex mentioned Priya seeing the angel's outline. "Tell me about the glow."

"How—how do you know about that?"

"You wrote it down in your spiral. I have it in my intake notes."

"I didn't."

"You must have."

Something about the air curdled. The doctor's pupils rippled once before he looked away. The room dimmed, either clouds shadowing the building or something affecting Alex's vision. In that moment, Alex sank into a level of despair that was unlike anything he'd felt since his father left.

"You fear being ordinary," the doctor said, his voice slower, buzzing with a metallic hum that was slightly offkey. "Yet ordinariness is your only salvation. Give up the notion of meaning."

For half a breath, Dr. Milt's pupils became vertical like the shutter releasing in an old-fashioned camera lens before snapping to round again. Then his voice changed, and the room seemed to shrink.

"You think there's a guardian watching you," he said.

"I don't *think*—I've seen—"

"Perhaps what you see is a projection of your fear. You are working at an important company, and your boss wields power. The mind can do unusual things when it fears loss. If you think you aren't up to the task of performing adequately, well, angels are comforting lies the human mind invents to mask despair."

The lights dimmed again, even though he hadn't touched the switch. Shadows were eating the room. Milt's pupils flared black, iridescent at the edges.

"Why do you fight it?" the doctor whispered. "Wouldn't it be easier to surrender to nothing?"

"You're not the same therapist I've been seeing," Alex managed, looking for a way to diffuse this quickly and easily. Yet, as he said the words, he remembered their first session. The eyes had been there all along.

"On the contrary," Milt said, standing now. "I'm your true instructor. I teach endings."

The air crackled, and the smell of iron filled the office. Alex felt the now-familiar warmth at his neck and a whisper that said, *I've got you*. Then, behind him, heat blossomed, bursting outward, and the shadows in the room splintered and vanished.

A voice—not from Milt, not from Alex—rang through the space: "Not this soul."

Alex was immobilized in stunned silence as intertwining fingers of luminous fire reached from behind him and encircled them both. With a flash that caused Alex to close his eyes, Milt's office stood empty, with scorch marks like a blackened spider's web crawling across the carpet.

When he opened the office door, Marjorie looked up from her desk as if nothing had happened and no one had seen or heard a thing.

"Dr. Milt will be right back, Alex. I'm sorry he's taken so long." She smiled warmly.

Alex pulled the door shut. "We're done."

A door behind her desk opened, revealing the white porcelain fixtures of a restroom. The doctor's smooth, calm smile returned instantly. "Alex!"

"He says you are finished." Marjorie was the epitome of helpful assistance.

"Of course. Same time next week." The doctor nodded, walked across the room, opened his office door, and stepped inside.

Alex couldn't return to his desk. He hit the elevator button and barely held on until it reached ground level. He nodded at Stacie at the reception desk and forced himself outside into unexpectedly harsh weather. The wind howled, and sharp rain pummeled his face. He stepped around the corner of the building and vomited in the rain.

Between flashes of lightning he thought he saw Milt's silhouette watching him from behind the glass walls of the tower with his head bowed and lighted by something eerily aflame.

HE WALKED a long time and had the presence of mind to think: *I can't make a habit of this.* Water ran in torrents down his scalp, his shirt was sodden inside his coat, and in his shoes his feet squished with every step. Passersby turned to him to look, and one taxi, still in old-fashioned yellow, stopped and rolled down a window.

"A ride, sir? I can give you a discount to get you out of the rain."

Alex laughed. "Water doesn't burn. Did you know that? Water doesn't burn!"

"Right, man. I'm off then."

"Thank you for checking on me." He waved the

man on and looked up at the sky. He'd never seen rain this way, the droplets falling directly from the clouds, a whole sky full of needles coming straight at him. They hit his eyes, and he refused to blink. In the moment, he couldn't. His eyes were opened by what happened back in that office, and he could never close them again.

Of course, he eventually had to blink, and in that blink, he understood why people were staring at him, even those who were pretending not to. He was dripping from his shorts to his shoes. Even his fingertips dripped water when he held them out.

He found himself in the park and sat on a bench. Water pooled around his feet. Even in the chill of the rain, he felt the familiar warmth at his back, and it kept him from being as chilled as he would have expected. Protected. Watched over. *Not this soul.* He repeated those words to himself, then aloud, then he laughed and yelled them into the sky. A whisper into his ear said, *Not too loudly. They are listening.*

Then the sun broke through, and the rain dissipated to a spatter and then to nothing at all. He basked in the warmth on his face, and a warm breeze soon had him dry enough to begin the walk to his apartment.

7

Confessions by the River

ENTR'ACTE.

It was a word from his high school days in theater class. It meant a shift from one act to another in a play. It might involve a scene change, different characters, or even the start of a whole new story line, but it almost always meant an extended breather.

An intermission, if you will.

He needed his story line to change, and for the better. And he needed an intermission while it happened, some time off, a chance to reevaluate his life, his choices, and what had been happening.

He began sending himself messages he never opened with subject lines only:

Remember kindness.

Mom said storms speak.

Don't let mirrors talk first.

They filled his inbox like unread commandments. He wanted them to remind him without having to open them, one-line truisms. Some people might call them clichés, platitudes, or adages. He thought of them as proverbs or axioms because he wanted to accept them as established, self-evident, and universally accepted.

He wanted them to be incontrovertible truths. Especially the third one. Mirrors don't talk, not yesterday, not today, not ever.

"Please, God," he prayed one night when it was all too much. "Don't let the mirrors continue to speak to me."

He still wanted what he'd always wanted, at least a part of him, to be at the top of his game, to establish himself as the best, and to make himself into someone his father could hug and tell him that he was proud of all he'd achieved.

He was also awed by the events in the therapist's office.

On Friday, he met Renee and Marcus by the river near the Stone Arch Bridge, where the city lights rippled off the Mississippi's languid and dark water. Music filtered in from Water Works Park where a band was providing the accompaniment for An Evening on the Water, a yearly fund raiser for the Minneapolis Institute of Art.

A riverboat chugged along the shore, part of the Evening's festivities, as attendees enjoyed various activities. People could be heard laughing at a comedian's jokes.

"They're having a good time." Alex looked out over the water, taking in the lives of people who'd never seen fire eat a man who then walked out of a restroom and back into the room in which he'd been totally consumed.

"This is a holy place." Renee closed her eyes and inhaled. "Holy places should be enjoyed."

"Why's it holy?" Marcus snickered. "It's just water."

“Gathering-in-of-all-the-waters is the river’s true name. Or just Father of Waters, if you want the easy translation. It sounds an awful lot like Great Father or even Heavenly Father, if you’re Christian.”

“I thought Tonti recorded it as Michi Sepe.” When Alex and Renee both looked astonished, Marcus said, “I attended school here. I remember some of it.”

“Who’s Tonti?” Alex was willing to go with it for a distraction from why they were here.

“The French explorer in 1682. He was with La Salle as his lieutenant.”

“I’ve heard of La Salle, so that makes it okay.”

“I’m not okay with it.” Renee opened her eyes. “I smell woodsmoke. Anyone see anything burning?”

Alex hoped not. He’d been in Dr. Milt’s office, and that was all the fire he wanted to see for a very long time. Perhaps the odor clung to him and he no longer noticed. The flaming sword ... fire and iron. His hand itched, and he rubbed it against his leg.

Marcus opened his backpack and pulled out refreshments. When Renee started to balk, he held the label under his phone flashlight. It was non-alcoholic, and he tossed her one. Alex held out a hand, got the next one, and unscrewed the lid.

“Are you guys ready to hear what’s in my head?” They were here because this place had no connection to any of the events he’d experienced, there were no reflective surfaces, and no lights to set off a glow if he happened to have one. He’d learned his lesson in Priya’s apartment.

“Will it be you talking or your bodyguard?”

“Renee!” Marcus reprimanded her. “It’s not a bodyguard, it’s an angel. I know a divine halo when I see one, and an angel is definitely divine."

"Wait," Alex said. "Who says I have an angel?"

"Um," Renee temporized. "You?"

"Yeah, pudzo. What else have you been describing all this time?"

"Maybe not this time. Let me tell you what happened at the therapist's this week."

He told them about Milt's transformation, the voice, the fire ... and walking out to discover Dr. Milt coming out of the restroom on the other side of the office.

"His assistant, Marjorie, didn't even know he'd been in there with me."

Marcus swore softly. "So, *therapist-as-demon* wasn't in my HMO paperwork. I almost signed up to attend sessions with him."

Renee reached for his arm. "Maybe it's time to stop seeing new people completely. Or at least have one of us around when you do."

"That's not always possible. If we're joined at the hip, that'll seem pretty strange when I show up at my dentist with one of you holding my hand."

"I said new people. Don't make your life harder than it is."

"Dr. Milt wasn't new. I've been attending sessions with him for months. And remember, I don't choose these meetings or these people. They find me."

"Anything else?" Renee tipped her bottle to empty it and tossed it in a refuse bin.

"Do you really want to hear it?" Alex's drink was half full, and he swirled the bottle absently. The wind gusted, and with the falling temperature, it felt cold and dry. He shivered. He was surrounded by the faint glimmer of fireflies, but he knew it for what it was. Pips of electricity, faint but clear in the darkness, floated from his fingertips each time he lifted his drink to his lips. His clothing likely contained even more, unable to get free.

He would be a static electric powerhouse before morning at this rate.

The party with the band was winding down, and on the far bank, fireflies chased along the power lines with nervous energy, red to his white, the antithesis to a very weird week.

"Of course we do." Marcus slapped him on the shoulder. "Friendship trumps fiery assassinations, even if the man is a demon."

"*Was* a demon." Renee hesitated. "I suppose it's *was*. Do demons die when they burn up, or can they come back?"

"Now who's weirding everyone out? Good going, Renee." Marcus bumped her shoulder with his elbow.

She shivered. "What do we not know, Alex? I'll let you know when my parking meter needs fresh quarters."

He tried to remember it all, from the water running up his bathroom mirror to the ceiling light exploding and the incident at Priya's. When he told of the revolving door, Renee stopped him.

"Like us, right? I thought you were teasing when you said you didn't catch me."

"I didn't, honest. I would have, but it happened too suddenly."

"It *was* sudden. You haven't talked of your dreams for some time. Are you still doing the dream journal?"

"I was handed a flaming sword." He looked out

over the river. The park had gone quiet, but with his stories, the fireflies were back on the powerlines dancing like a choreographed accompaniment to his tales.

"Man, I need me one of those." Marcus grinned.

Renee took it more seriously. "If this keeps escalating, how do we help you?"

"You already do," he said. "You keep reminding me I'm still human."

Marcus grinned and flashed a pretend sword. "For now, anyway."

8

The Lake of Decision

SLEEP CLAIMED him on Sunday just before dawn.

The concept of "still human" had taunted him, keeping him awake. Electric fireflies floated from his skin. An invisible voice pushed equally improbable fire past him. The sword, fire and iron, in his hand *and leaving a scorch mark on his bedding.*

And Marcus' comment, "For now, anyway."

His pillow cradled his head, and still, his thoughts ricocheted from one side of his skull to the other. Was this his chrysalis moment? He was a boy, then a man, and to eventually become the butterfly, he had to break down and rearrange who he was into what he would become?

Kane & Sutter. How had the job come to him? He no longer knew. It was just there, and he stepped into it, charmed into a position he accepted as his due.

He had begun to see it differently.

Eventually, however, the natural *human* need for sleep will override even the wildest torrents of the brain, and exhausted, his bedroom closed in on him, and he stepped into another world.

He stood once more on Lake of the Isles. The ice under his feet shimmered and fractured the light from a full moon. In front of the glowing orb, his angel-Alex double stood backlighted by a moon that looked suspiciously like a nimbus.

His angel-double waited expectantly, ringed by a glow brighter than even the moon, watching Alex steadily.

"I'm still in bed, right?" This place had become familiar, but it was one he only saw in his dreams.

"I waited for you. Your world demands much of you, and yes, this is your chrysalis moment."

The angel-Alex shifted, and he held the flaming sword that didn't burn. Power flowed from it, and real-Alex understood that the flames in Mr. Milt's office had come from this sword. Even as the angel-Alex held it, the fire surged and demanded to be released, not flames containing heat but invoking the divine power of another realm.

"Your sword. I held it once."

"It is for your protection." He moved it from one hand to the other, and the very air seemed to burn as the flames cut a path through the ether.

"I never see it in the real world."

"It is for your enemies' eyes. You are shielded from the power it contains. It flows over and around you, for it is your protection." He nodded, ending the discussion of the sword.

"Tell me about Dr. Milt. I think it was your sword that saved me then."

"You've met them all now," said the reflection. The words were layered with Alex's own voice, as if it were Alex speaking, although the words flowed from the man in front of him.

"What do you mean, them all?"

"Pride, Deception, and Despair."

"Can you explain?" He felt once again the utter hopelessness that overcame him in the doctor's office.

"You already know."

"Despair is Dr. Milt. I ... I wanted to give up, and you saved me."

"Yes. I was there with you."

"But pride and deception—" Alex cut off his question. He did know—or thought he did. "Eliot must be pride. When I'm with him, I can think of little other than how great I can become."

"And the embodiment of deception? What has been revealed to you?"

He pictured the beautiful Sophie and her demand for him to turn his back on his protector.

"Yes, it is she. I am the one who cracked the mirror. You are the one who chose to run."

"So, we're done?"

"One remains."

"Who else can there be?"

"Indifference is chaos unshaped."

There could only be one person that fit that description. He had seen him repeatedly on the early train, and he was always the same. "The Commuter?"

The being nodded. "He rides your every choice."

Alex laughed bitterly. "So, everyone on my train is a metaphor now."

"Everything is a mirror until you choose your side."

"What's the choice, exactly? How can I know until I face it?"

"You already have. Your decision must be to serve the light, or to sell yourself in silence."

The angel stepped closer, until the moon overhead was little more than a halo around his head. He still held the flaming sword, though it did not burn with heat. Waves of internal warmth reached fingers of flame toward Alex, and when the angel's hand touched his chest, it surged through him.

"Soon, the last will test you. Remember: fire protects, not destroys."

When Alex jerked awake, faint traces of frost patterned his bedroom floor in the shape of wings in mid-beat.

CHOICES FOR GOOD. Serve the light. Or he could sell himself in silence, although he couldn't imagine doing that.

Or had he already started down that slippery slope?

At work, Eliot charmed him, appealing to his future in the company, even taking him up one floor to view a vacant corner office and pointing out where Alex's desk might go.

"The Verden account is your key, kid. You get Sophie on your side, and the world's your oyster. You're this company's rising star, and I know you'll make me proud. How does that sound to you?"

His heartstrings ... no, his pride wanted that. The gleaming windows, the river in the distance, the softly murmuring air flowing from the overhead vents. But the angel's words stuck with him: *or to sell yourself in silence.* Was it worth it for a corner office? To give in, be Eliot's minion, eclipse his mother's faith in the divine?

In the moment, he fought the feelings. Only later,

at lunch with Renee, did his head clear and his choice become obvious.

Then two days later, Lacey Sanghorn, a junior analyst, made a mistake during a presentation. Eliot turned on her, his face dark with rage, and she turned pale and fainted. Alex caught her before she hit the floor.

Her first words upon waking: "There was someone with you. He touched you and you shone for a second. It was like sunlight through water."

He pretended he didn't hear. Instead, he said, "You might need food. We've called for medical help."

HR filed it under "stress incident."

Yet that night, she texted him privately.

LACEY: I pulled your number from the company phone tree. Whoever that was with you, thank him.

He typed back three dots.

ALEX: . . .

And then he deleted them.

How could he thank someone he only saw in his dreams?

9

The Commuter

DREAMS BLURRED into visions.

He began to see them without sleeping. They danced before his eyes when the lights were on, even when he tried to push them away. He pulled out Renee's dream journal and laughed sourly as he titled a fresh page as his Vision Journal, Chapter One.

He began to describe what he saw, at first in jilting fragments, then with more assurance. Eliot Kane, his boss, whispering to Sophie under flickering lights; Milt watching from a distance, smiling too widely.

In one dream they all turned toward him in perfect synchrony and recited his father's line: *Focus. Stop thinking about people.*

He woke sweating, and gasping, he whispered into the dark, "No. People are the whole point."

He put his feet on the floor and his face into his hands. Awake, asleep, it no longer made a difference. The visions were everywhere.

Something unseen stirred—a soft, approving rush of air like wingbeats close by.

He raised his head and looked around, but that was a vision that remained in his dreams.

Write it down, the unseen presence seemed to

whisper. He pulled his notebook from his bedside table and opened it. With a click of his pen, he began to record what he remembered. When he was finished, he printed in bold letters: People Are the Whole Point.

Perhaps that was what the dream was about. People. The Laceys and Marcuses and Renees in the world. The Priyas and the Jerrys and the Brians. Even the Joeys and the Lotties, the whole lot of them.

He slipped the book back into the drawer and stood. A morning shower would be nice. He was taking a lot of those lately.

He hoped his water bill understood.

ON MONDAY morning, he couldn't manufacture the motivation to walk to work. The weekend had left him drained, and he timed his routine by the train schedule.

An hour early and two cups of coffee—sorry, Rick, this old man's nearly there—and he felt he could make the connection. Marcus volunteered to be his wing man, and he knocked on Alex's door ten minutes before departure time.

"One, two, all aboard!" Marcus leaned against the wall outside Alex's apartment with his right elbow on the doorframe and his hand on his head. He flicked a corded earbud from his ear and let it drop to his chest to join the second one. His left arm was akimbo on his waist with his overcoat draped across his forearm. His ankles were crossed.

"Who is this casual stranger? Surely not someone who works at Kane & Sutter. Come on in. I'm finishing up my coffee."

"Third cup? If so, I'm reporting it to Rick. You'll never live it down." Marcus grinned, broke his pose, and sauntered in with a briefcase he lifted from the floor in an easy motion. He stood it on the floor just inside the door.

"Second, you snitch. Want one?"

Marcus did, and the last of the brown liquid steamed into a clean cup. As he took a sip, he peered through the fog and dared a question.

"Any bodybuilders during the night? I'm still hoping for my six-pack. It's never happening to this body without divine provenance."

"Divine provenance my foot. You need a few sit-ups." Alex could tell Marcus was working his magic on him. He felt better already, and he thumped a wadded paper napkin at his waistline. It hit and skittered off.

"Ouch." Marcus didn't jerk away, and he grinned.

"Tell it to the napkin. When you're ready, put that cup in the sink and let's go." A timer began to ding, and he silenced it before grabbing his keys and walking towards the door.

With Marcus for company, Alex was distracted, and he let the Minnesota morning wrap him in all that was good about living in Minneapolis. The sun was bright, birds were returning, and the morning breeze was unseasonably warm, with occasional gusts whipping up last fall's leaves.

"Bet you're glad this morning you didn't take that job in L.A." Marcus grinned. "They're expecting ninety today."

"L.A.?"

"Yeah, just out of college. You can't have forgotten this. We were still rooming together, and it was from a big tech company. Apple or Meta or something. Then the call came in from Kane & Sutter, and all the previous offers were instant packing material. We shredded everything just out of spite." His face was bright with the memory.

"I didn't even consider the L.A. job?"

"You *have* been losing sleep. We went there together to interview. A weekend at Laguna Beach? The yellow Jeep? You can't forget me wiping out on that surfboard. Sheesh, you are a pudzo. That was the best weekend of my life."

"So that's how I wound up here." Alex took a deep breath.

"And how I learned that angels have six-packs. I can't wait to get me one of those, even if it means becoming Lutheran again."

"You would not." Alex felt himself becoming mired in the missing memory of L.A. What else was he missing from his past?

That was why the train platform caught him off guard. It was mostly empty when they arrived, just the early crowd of sleepy professionals and coffee steam.

Then Alex saw him: the faceless man he'd half glimpsed a dozen times—tall, with his coat unwrinkled despite the wind, and his briefcase hanging like a pendulum. A blank oval filled the area where his face should be, leaving his features blurred like smudged glass.

Alex's pulse thundered as the man stepped beside him.

"Ready?" The voice came without sound. "It begins."

He looked at the man to see him facing ahead.

Marcus didn't seem to notice anything unusual about his missing face, and Alex wondered if it was missing to his friend.

As the train doors opened, they stepped forward and boarded. Every fluorescent carriage light flickered at the faceless man's presence, as if he drew something from them that they didn't have to give.

People's newspapers bore black ink bleeding upward off the pages, amorphous black feather-like shapes that slowly coalesced into a word: CHOOSE.

Alex clenched the cold rail. "Marcus, are you seeing this?"

"What? An empty seat? Sure, right over there. I'm headed that way. Join me when you get your bearings."

When he walked away and left him behind, Alex knew this was more than just riding the early morning train. The faceless man, the Commuter, was in control.

He muttered, "I choose nothing."

"Then nothing will choose for you." The Commuter had taken Marcus' place, and he whispered the words into Alex's ear. Then, the rest of him took on the same unfocused appearance as his face, and he faded completely away as the train braked into downtown.

When the doors opened, only soot remained on the floor where the man had stood.

10

The Compromise

THAT AFTERNOON Eliot summoned him.

"We have a delicate matter before the Verden account is signed over to us lock, stock, and barrel," he said. "You do understand that securing this account is a masterstroke for us. We're moving into the big leagues, and you're here at the start. As we move up, you move up. You do still want to move up, don't you, kid?"

Behind him, slides glowed on the conference screen, ones Alex had worked on for the Verden account. He could quote the figures on each of the spreadsheets down to the dollar.

"That's all my stuff. It's perfect." He tasted ozone as he set his laptop on the conference table.

"Maybe in our eyes." Eliot sighed dramatically. "This is an urgent client issue. Our eyes aren't the ones that count. You are good, kid, I'll give you that, but Verden's investors need some of those numbers adjusted. For optics. Nothing that changes the bottom line, just how they appear on paper. That's why I've pulled you in. You're the only one who's worked on this, so this is just between us." He slid a thumb drive across the conference table. "Here's what you need. I trust you'll handle it."

When he opened the presentation file, lines of data rearranged themselves across the screen, spelling: DO NOT COMPROMISE.

He blinked, and the numbers returned to normal.

Eliot's voice: "Make it look clean, Morton. We all do our part."

"The numbers aren't there to look pretty, and you know that. If you want me to change any of them, that means you want me to falsify the ledger books."

"A junior associate telling one of the owners what his company can and can't do? Don't moralize." Eliot's tone chilled. "You were always the ambitious type until you started ... doubting."

Sophie appeared out of the shadows. Alex was certain she hadn't been there before. She was at her most beautiful, and her lips shimmered with appeal. "It's just a narrative correction, Alex. The beginning and the ending aren't changing, just the path we are taking to get there. Don't spoil the beautiful destiny we could have together."

As she spoke, the lighting from the projector threw shards of color from her lipstick, and even after his experience at The Capital Grille, her allure pulled him in. Something cold moved beneath her beauty, like oil under ice.

Behind her, the office's glass wall trembled as if pummeled by wind.

Alex felt the invisible warmth gather once more at his back. The air in the room shimmered, brighter than the projector could account for. Somewhere unseen, a sword hissed free of its sheath.

Eliot's eyes narrowed. "You're not alone, are you?"

Alex exhaled a breath he only then knew he was holding. This was the moment of choice from his dream.

"No. I never was."

Light erupted, silent but overwhelming. Shadows became solid objects, and what the light couldn't get through trembled as it tried to get out of the way.

"What are you doing?" Sophie held up an arm to shield her eyes. "Stop it now."

Alex was no longer in control. He felt the power behind him as an oversized subwoofer, and the floor vibrated beneath his feet. In a thrust of wind, light, air, and matter, the projector shattered, and the overhead fluorescent tubes burst one by one as if by evaporation. They were just gone with no glass to shower the floor.

Alex collapsed onto one knee, blinded, and he covered his face with his arms. When his sight returned, Eliot and Sophie were gone, leaving only two faintly scorched silhouettes on the glass wall, surrounded by an imprint of wings unfolding outward.

The projector's screen was dark, as it had no longer had a bulb. Light filtered in from glass panels over the doors. Alex stood, unable to deny what had happened.

He whispered, "Thank you," before opening the door, where it was as though the day had chosen to ignore what had taken place in that room.

ON HIS WAY out of the building, Priya caught him in the lobby. She was in a chair, and when he exited the elevator, she sprang to her feet in excitement.

"Alex, I found something you absolutely do not

know."

"Oh, I know a lot." He fought a desperate laugh, afraid she would see the manic nature of his response.

"Not this. Can I walk with you?"

"Can we talk at Joey's? I need coffee to recharge my system."

"Yes, but this is really important."

"Okay, after my coffee, please."

They walked into an empty establishment, except for Joey behind the counter. He called, "I should know to expect you when it does this. I had a full crowd until five minutes ago. Any table, my treat. As you can see, I have no other customers." He said it with a chuckle and turned to begin preparing a coffee without asking Alex what he wanted. He called over his shoulder, "A black with sugar for the lady?"

"Yes, thank you," Priya returned.

When they had their coffees, she leaned in and spoke quietly. "You remember I told you I was looking into an old case involving your firm?"

"You found something, didn't you?" He set his cup on the table. A month ago, he'd have dismissed anything she had to say, believing any "proof" was manufactured to discredit Eliot. Now, he'd believe anything, even offer eyewitness verification of his own.

"This will prove you're not haunted, just corporate." She placed a leather binder on the table and began to unzip it.

He heard in her words what she didn't say. A corporate buffoon. She knew how to cut to the core of a matter in her brilliant and fiercely logical way, and that was what he appreciated about her.

Kane & Sutter had an old legal bruise: cooking the books for a couple of companies several years back, with Eliot taking the bulk of the blame as one of the heads of the company. It hadn't gone to trial as a settlement was reached, but it had cost the company plenty. Even now the office tower was heavily mortgaged, and one failed account could take down the firm.

Not even Alex could manufacture the surprise she hoped to see on his face. When she frowned and pretended to pout, he laughed.

If she wanted the exciting version, he could tell one even better than that.

LATE THAT evening, before even pulling off his coat, he stepped into the bathroom and looked hard into the mirror. His face shimmered, and one became two.

The second Alex spoke first. "You still think you're broken for wanting good things."

"What are you?" He studied the face that shouldn't be there, saw in it everything that he knew from his childhood up, the nose, the ears, the full lips. Yet, it wasn't him, wasn't exactly the same.

"I'm your reminder. I'm the part of you that never stopped believing that help is out there and it exists for you."

"I feel like I'm talking to myself. Weirdness unleashed."

"Exactly." The second Alex smiled, and light behind the image flared across the mirror. For an instant Alex saw himself, still fully clothed from work, with the person behind him in the rugged clothing of an old-world painting, surrounded by luminous wings. Without knowing why he knew, he understood that those wings were armor—not metal, but luminous with power. A sword of fire in the man's grip radiated peace rather than threat.

It frightened him, anyway.

He whispered, "Why now?"

"Because you finally stopped pretending reason can replace love."

The image flashed white and was gone. When the glass returned to normal, the mirror bore a fine crack down its center, one that wasn't there before.

11

A Lakeside Confession

THE NEXT MORNING arrived long before dawn cracked the sky into the frying pan of sun and shadow.

The coffee machine glared balefully with red eyes as he toyed with an empty cup, not wanting to be alone but unwilling to disrupt anyone else's sleep.

He hadn't been able to fall into the cracks of the night, to allow the events of the day before to evaporate at least for those few hours of oblivion. Instead, the night had spit him out as if he was too tainted to endure.

He looked away from the coffee machine, refused to see the accusation, understood it for what it was. He was the very people who had come to haunt his days and to torment his nights. He remembered now the reason he'd discounted the L.A. offer, the reason he'd blanked that visit with his friend from memory.

Priya's revelation wasn't exactly an unexpected exposé. It was rumors he'd ignored, pushed aside, and refused to face. Now they were in his face. Why? No one who knew him would know he was rising in the corporate world in California. He would always be the Alex who took honors during his college career, then evaporated off the map, sucked up by the machine to never be seen again. They might hear of him occasionally, but he would be shrugged off as no longer of importance. He needed them to see; his father to see; the little boy who had listened to his father packing his bags to see that he had achieved success despite those years of pain.

He had deceived himself into the illusion of success to stoke his pride rather than accepting a position that would allow him to become what he needed to be. He had made the easy choice as he'd run from the despair of not becoming who he wanted to be.

Really, he'd made no choice at all. He'd allowed his future to shape him rather than embracing decisions that could give him purpose.

He couldn't face work and would have to call in sick, but that was an eight o'clock problem. He slipped into his cashmere coat, dropped his phone in his inside pocket, and rolled his scarf for use outside. The nights could still be cold this time of the year, and he needed to be at Lake of the Isles, the real one, not the one in his dreams.

Perhaps the angel-Alex would be there, and they could have the real conversation they had been skirting around the past few months. Unlikely, but what else unlikely had gone on around him? Nothing, that was certain.

He laughed. Who was he kidding? Everything.

He headed southwest. Streetlights glowed in the light fog, occasionally buzzing and once or twice blinking off as he approached. Each time, he wondered if it was his angel, or if a malfunctioning photocell was picking up the ambient light reflecting from porchlights.

One car passed, an SUV emerging from the fog, wearing the fog, and disappearing back into the fog, with the glow of red taillamps marking the final evidence of its presence.

The buildings dripped with the night, and an occasional lighted window revealed other people up and about. The city breathed sleep, blanketed by the sky, accompanied by a melody of rustling branches as they rubbed against one another for warmth.

At the lake, thin ice rimmed the shoreline. Alex pulled his coat tighter around his neck. He knew it was cold, but the ice told the truth of it. He needed to be careful. A dip at these temperatures would be a death in the morning news.

He searched for his shadow man, the vison from his dreams, the creature that had left the crack in his mirror the night before. He looked for wings, a divine nimbus, for the droplets of water in the fog to coalesce into a human form that would call his name.

Nothing. Just the soft movement of water, and even that was hushed into near silence by the heavy covering of darkness.

He crouched at the water's edge. The thin ice, with the black water beyond. Ambitions disappeared into dark water like that. They went under, air came up, and they were never seen again.

That's not you.

He jerked his head up. "Are you there?" The water ... he would never take that step, just that Dr. Milt, Eliot, and Sophie ... if they were the essence of him, how could he ever face another mirror? He had told the Commuter that he refused to choose. How far had he fallen from his mother's words and her vision of grace in the world?

Fully kneeling, with his palms on the cold stone lining the shore, he spoke aloud into a nighttime landscape that had somehow come to embody the choices he must make.

"I want to make things right and experience joy in my life. I want to be the man my friends need me to be even if my pride dies along the way. I want my life to be about the people around me and not about impressing them with my achievements."

Wind brushed the surface of the water, and it carried the cool scent of thawing earth. A faint glimmer settled over the lake like breath catching fire. He stood and brushed off his hands.

"Thank you, but I don't need signs," he said. However, part of him did. An acknowledgement that this wasn't happening just in his head. The lake rippled once, becoming concentric rings of undulating water gliding outward until they disappeared into stillness.

As if touched by the hand of a divine being.

By then, the sun was warming the sky in oranges and reds. He checked his phone and realized he'd bypassed his call-in deadline. He would need to Uber in. Besides, he was curious about the aftermath of the events in the conference room. The imprints of the wings on the walls were real. Surely someone would make something of those, realize he had been in that room, and come to him for answers.

He walked through the revolving door and greeted Stacie. She replied with a smile, and he hesitated. He had seen Eliot and Sophie obliterated by a light so bright he hadn't been able to keep his eyes open.

He asked Stacie, "Has Eliot been in this morning?"

"Eliot?" She frowned as if puzzled by his question. After a pause, her face smoothed and her smile returned. "I think he transferred to another branch. Maybe Spokane? Anyway, he's no longer in Minneapolis. How was your night, Alex? Relaxing, I hope."

"I took a walk to the Isles."

"Before work? You are the adventuresome one. I don't get that direction as often as I'd like. Is it beautiful this time of the year?"

"Very. Thank you, Stacie."

He headed to the elevator and was surprised to discover there was no police tape and no evidence that the fire alarms had gone off. Everything worked perfectly just like it always had.

At his desk, he powered up his laptop and checked the employee message board. One marked as important thanked everyone for their patience with "the brief electrical anomaly" that had reset most of the building's computers the day before.

A one-liner wished Eliot Kane, the co-founder of the company, best wishes on his new position in Spokane.

There was nothing about Sophie.

Shaunika filled in that information. She was pursuing a new overseas venture and taking her account with her.

So, no police reports, no fire alarms, and building maintenance called the conference room debacle "a brief electrical anomaly." Eliot had "transferred" to another branch, and Sophie had "accepted a new opportunity overseas."

Life was moving on as if their existence was being edited out.

Alex sat alone at his desk, watching a dust mote hover in sunlight as it shimmered like a miniature star. His future seemed as remote and unknowable.

His phone vibrated.

MARCUS: Drinks tonight? Or an exorcism? I hear something interesting happened yesterday, and I need to know it all.

ALEX: Both. And there's not much to tell.

Ripples in the water? Would Marcus believe him? Perhaps this time he would.

12

The Crack in the Mirror

THEY MET AT the Honeycomb Bar. Alex joked that he didn't want to run off Joey's customer base too often. They might flock to spots with less disruption.

Marcus didn't catch that, and Alex explained about the coffee shop emptying out twice just before he arrived. He leaned over to look behind Alex and commented, "No wings yet, so likely not a miracle. Someone must have warned them you were on the way."

"My guardian angel?" He used his elbow to poke at his friend. He wasn't even teasing, and that's when he realized he was starting to believe.

"Oh, we're back to that?"

The bar was humming, and they waited fifteen minutes for the doorman to allow them inside. Despite the full count of patrons, the small stage was vacant and unlighted. The dance floor, though, throbbed with music, lights, and bodies.

They threaded their way to the barman and started a tab. The man frowned when Alex requested a lemon seltzer, but it appeared alongside Marcus' more potent concoction, and they collected them and headed into the madhouse.

The music paused, and the DJ called out, "Five minutes until half price at the bar. Start heading that way," and then the music ramped back up as loud as ever.

"I didn't expect this." Alex circled his hand in the air to include the dance floor, the noisome patrons, and the people entering each time someone exited. He nearly had to yell.

"You must have been here on Stand Up Night. It's the DJ's night off." Marcus had to lean in to be heard. "There, those girls are leaving. That's our table."

They reached it just as a waitress appeared to clear it. She let them sit, asked them if they needed refills, and collected the empties and wiped down the table. She left them two coasters just like the one Alex had found in his apartment.

"Do angels visit bars?" He grinned at Marcus.

"In *It's a Wonderful Life,* Clarence did."

"Well said." Alex laughed. He'd forgotten. That made him think: Was his angel trying to earn his wings? He thought not. He was now wearing them each time he saw him.

With the noise level forcing them to yell to be heard while in the bar, Marcus didn't learn much about what had transpired in the conference room, but for Alex, it was a great distraction. He didn't know how long it would last, but any break in his dealings with the spirit world was welcome for as long as he could drag it out.

THEY FOUND a park bench and had their hands in their pockets to fight the rising damp from the river. Alex still felt alert despite the cold, but Marcus had lost some of his focus. It was to be expected after two hours in the Honeycomb.

Even with his buzz, he hadn't forgotten why they were here.

"Okay, Alex, old friend. Let's get this straight." Marcus held out a finger and hit it with a finger on the other hand. "First, you don't remember spending days with your good friend Marcus at Laguna Beach. Second—"

Alex put his hand on his friend's forearm. "I remember now. All of it, so you can move on from that."

"Okay." He seemed to think, and then he tapped another finger as he continued his countdown. "Second, you haven't been back to Dr. Milt. I thought he was helping you out."

"And three?" Alex didn't want to talk about Dr. Milt.

"I didn't see Eliot or Sophie all day. I mean, I know I work on a different floor, but I looked and didn't find them anywhere."

Alex put a hand on Marcus' shoulder to get him to look at him. "Eliot transferred to Spokane, and Sophie left for Europe. I don't think either of them are coming back."

"Oh, maybe that's good. I didn't much like her. She was pretty, but you weren't the same when you were around her. I like you better now that she's gone."

Alex chuckled. "Thank you, I think. Do you think we should get you home?"

"Almost. One more thing." Marcus leaned in with his pointer extended and nearly toppled onto Alex's lap. "Oops, sorry there, old friend."

"One more thing and then you're off to bed. What

is it?"

"I think angels are real. Yep, really real."

"Oh? A change of heart?"

"Me? No. You've always been an angel to me, and I love you for it." He wrapped his arms around him and leaned his head against him. Within moments, he began snoring.

"I love you, too, Marcus. Now let's get you home."

Just like college, Alex thought. *All over again.*

BY KEEPING A raucous duet going, he was able to keep Marcus in motion all the way back to the apartment building. He dug through his friend's coat pocket until he located his keys, and he helped him remove his jacket and shoes and tucked him in before leaving his keys on the bedside table and letting himself out.

Back in his apartment, he shed his clothing down to his pants, socks, and a tee and dared the bathroom. He instinctively glanced at the line down the center of the mirror and remembered the conversation from the night before. He hadn't told his friend about that. He scratched it with a fingernail to prove it was real, and the memories slammed into him.

The mirror-Alex had said he was part of Alex. If they were part of each other, then who was stepping up to guard his back when bad things were happening to him? Alex didn't have those skills ... or wings or a flaming sword. Only the mirror-Alex had those.

Even so, the memory of the scorched bedding kept forcing his thoughts onto a path that he didn't find comfortable or easy.

How did the mirror-Alex, the angel if you will, get from there—in the mirror—to out here where he could affect the real world?

Then the glass made a soft *tick*. He wasn't touching it, there was no impact, just the hairline crack widening, pulling back to form a fisheye image of the bathroom with a dark void in the center. Alex shifted his position and could see himself in the darkness.

He watched his reflection grow larger and then step out of the fissure through the glass. His second self—now unmistakably angel, with glowing, rippling wings and wearing a sheathed sword of liquid light—pushed the opening in the glass wider until all of him could fit. When he stood fully before Alex, the glass slowly returned to its original shape and resealed itself crack free.

"How did you do that?" Alex knew his perspiration must be revealing his fractured sense of reality.

"*I* did nothing. *We* have crossed the line between reflection and reality," the being said.

"Are you ... me?"

"After a fashion. I am you and not you. I began in you and with you, and you have allowed me to become more."

"If you are me and not me, how are we different?" Other than the wings and the flaming sword. Except for that, they appeared pretty much the same.

"You are what you allow to live. I am what you refuse to let die. Together, our survival changes from self-interest to purpose."

Alex whispered, "What now?"

The answer came not in words but in feeling—a surge of grief and gratitude that flooded the small apartment.

Outside, sirens wailed toward some distant fire.

Inside, the warmth brought by the presence of the angel seeped into the walls, floors, and furniture and directly into Alex's heart.

The mirror was closed. The glass had healed itself, now a seamless barrier between the here and now and the impossible. Only by looking *through* the glass was a remnant hairline running straight through the reflective surface on the backside of the glass—the evidence of an angel's passing—still visible as proof that Alex hadn't dreamed the entire evening.

The final remnant of the crack was forever unhealed, forever shining, and evidence that people could change.

Part Four

The Reckoning

1

Half Light

THE MONDAY after Eliot and Sophie vanished, Minneapolis looked washed clean—as if someone had wrung the color from the skyline. With spring teasing the city, mornings arrived earlier, and walking to work on warm days was a pleasure.

It was a wicked tease by a season not fully ready to come awake. Just north of the city, hovering at the far edge of Minnesota, a shadowy band of menace threatened a return to winter.

Snow showers, Canada come to call, offering to share the fun.

For days after Eliot's disappearance, Alex expected a reprimand or at least to be touched by corporate frostbite. Somewhere in the system, there had to be a record of the meeting in which the man was banished by the light. Someone would see a schedule, read a memo, open an email ... see Alex's name and put it all together.

Instead, Kane & Sutter hummed along as though nothing had occurred. No change in schedule, no pushback for losing the Verden account. That was somehow worse—erasure masquerading as harmony. The silence carried a weightless calm that was almost greater than the pressure of compromise his boss had exerted.

Amy Witherspoon sat beside him at the weekly sectional staff meeting.

“Good morning, Alex.” She smiled, brightly cheerful as always.

“Copiers working all right?” He remembered them shooting out blank pages when he walked by. He hadn’t been back since.

“I’m glad you asked. A few moments ago, I dropped a memo on your desk.” She leaned in conspiratorially. “I think Eliot left under suspicious circumstances.”

“Oh?” Around them, the chairs had filled up, and Harry Sutter—in his late sixties and meticulously groomed—stood to the side waiting on the meeting to begin. Alex recognized him but hadn’t been directly involved with him. He’d only reappeared with Eliot’s disappearance.

“He’s flying in. I think that’s on Mr. Sutter’s agenda.”

“You’re saying Eliot’s back?” The announcement was a hammer in his chest.

“Not permanently. It’s all in your memo. I wasn’t prying, but there was no coversheet, so I couldn’t help but see. I thought you must know and the memo was just confirmation.”

He supposed he knew Eliot wasn’t *gone*, as in *vanquished from all existence*. Stacie knew of his transfer, although how it could have come together overnight was a greater concern. Perhaps the man from his mirror also had the ability to control time, rewrite history, or even shift the world onto an alternate existence pathway; and in some other version of this world, Eliot and Sophie had convinced him to alter the spreadsheets. Maybe he was now a full partner in that world: Kane, Sutter, & Morton; although if he was, it likely carried an aftertaste of regret.

Warmth surrounded him, and he felt the familiar voice: *Part of my plan.*

Harry Sutter cut off Alex's internal monologue as he introduced himself to any employees who hadn't had the chance to meet him and let them know that he was temporarily stepping in at the Minneapolis location. He also covered some changes he was introducing until Eliot's replacement came online, but that essential office procedures would continue as normal.

He seemed hesitant but announced that Eliot would be flying in to deal with some unresolved business matters, and that it was temporary. He wasn't to be disturbed with office affairs, but if anyone wanted to give him a final goodbye, do so but don't take too much of the man's time.

He detoured by the conference room on his way back to his desk. He didn't expect to see the doors removed and workmen refurbishing the interior walls. The old lighting was gone and stacked in the corridor, and a new style of ceiling was being installed, with tiny LED downlights rather than the bulky fluorescents.

At his desk, he stared at a blank spreadsheet on his laptop screen, waiting for inspiration. He called it that, but in reality, he was waiting for the consequences to hit him sideways. Eliot's return—however brief and for whatever purpose—jarred him. The intensity of his last interaction with the man was suffocatingly, heart-poundingly back again.

Instead, he heard a whisper—something rising from the base of his skull: *Integrity rarely sends memos.*

He rubbed his temples. "Whatever that means."

But the voice felt warm, familiar, and he thought he got it. His "angel" had removed the threat, but real-Alex hadn't yet conquered it. He couldn't move forward by having his obstacles *removed*. He had to *conquer* them by his own determination and force of will.

He had to step up and prove that he was different, or as his other self had suggested, that his integrity was fully intact, alive and well.

It wasn't a bad feeling, more like being watched over by love instead of judgment. Still, he would like some feedback from the real world, and he pulled out his phone for a group text.

ALEX: Anyone available for lunch?

The replies began to vibrate almost immediately.

MARCUS: ?? You have to ask? Where?

PRIYA: My class lets out at 11:30. I'm free after that.

The final text took a little longer, but eventually it vibrated through, also.

RENEE: I expect this to be good song material. I'm hoping for a recording contract soon.

He sent a final text:

ALEX: The usual, Foodz, quarter of.

He tried working, but he'd read Amy's memo, which didn't tell much, and had to turn it upside down to keep it from stealing his attention. Underneath it, the next folder contained updated documents from

Baumgartner Florals, and he titled the spreadsheet and began to enter column titles. However, every spreadsheet cell shimmered with faint gold edges until the numbers blurred. He finally surrendered, shut down his computer, and told Shaunika he was taking an early lunch. He'd adjust his timesheet later, but he had to be somewhere besides here.

The last thing he saw on the monitor before it powered off was his own dull reflection. It smiled a moment *after* he did.

"WHAT DID I say? Corporate shenanigans, not angel manifestations." Priya pulled out her phone and opened a file. "Here, the same thing happened last time. Eliot was transferred to Minneapolis when he almost tanked the company."

She turned the phone around so everyone could read the screen. The headline said: *Disgraced Company Founder Finds New Home.*

Marcus focused on the Sophie aspect. "Bet you're glad Sophie's out of the country. At least you won't have to face both of them."

"We can't prove that." Renee looked up from her phone. "International flights don't happen at the drop a hat. She might be *planning* to go overseas, but she could be in Dallas or Atlanta twiddling her thumbs. But enough of that, I've got an A.I. singing my latest song. You ready for it?"

"You've given up on doing your own? I thought people's lack of appreciation for your skill meant you were the only good musician in the city." Alex was caught up in the banter. This was what he needed, and the companionship of friends who could be off-the-wall and unselfconscious about it grounded him like nothing else did.

"I'm no corporate buffoon." She frowned and sat up. "No offense intended, Alex and Marcus. I'm my own person." She relaxed and smiled. "Once I hear the A.I. version, I can make corrections on the fly. Besides, this helps me to hear the nuance in how the lyrics and music integrate. Everyone ready?"

The song came out as biker rock, with heavy guitar and drums. After the intro, a pretty soprano sang the wistful words: *Following woe isn't my day / My angel gives me a better way / Sometimes in a dream, at other times real / My midnight guardian is the ultimate deal.*

"That's it?" Marcus chuckled. "I expected a chorus."

"Shush it. She said she's still working on it. I liked it. That part was clearly about Alex. Maybe the next verse is about me." Priya smiled.

Alex noticed that Renee was already back on her phone, tapping and whispering, unaware that her work was already being revised by those about her.

He wished for that self-assurance, for focusing on his dreams without letting others distract him or pull him away.

We're working on it.

He smiled. Somehow, together, he expected it would get done.

2

Two Down, Two to Go

AS LUNCH wound down, Alex's phone vibrated. He frowned, pulled it from a pocket, and frowned again when he glanced at the screen.

"You need to take it?" Renee and Marcus had their phones linked up with a game, and it flickered mutely between them. She whispered, "No you don't," and she drove her thumb into the screen three times in succession.

"Not again," Marcus grumbled. "Ok, I give. You know the game better than I do. Well, Alex, who needs you on your phone?"

"It was a text—" His voice faltered.

"People get texts all the time. Who was it?"

"Eliot."

Renee looked up from her phone. "You done pretending all this is fine? If you walked away tomorrow, they wouldn't miss you. Your desk would be filled with someone new in two weeks."

"I'm figuring that out, and I've retired from pretending," Alex said. "Especially when I'm not on the clock. It doesn't pay overtime."

Marcus eyed him. "You quitting the firm?"

"I haven't yet. With Eliot texting me, maybe it's

time."

They both waited, expecting a joke to diffuse the weight of his declaration, but Alex didn't have any way to diffuse the text he'd received.

"Can you tell us, or it is proprietary company stuff?" Renee pulled her guitar from its case, and she strummed it once. "I'm ready."

"For what?"

"To make a song for whatever that text was about. I told you I'm sourcing material for an album. The drama at your company is giving me all the material I need."

"Eliot wants to meet." His sigh told his opinion. He thought, *No. Just no. Don't do this to me, Eliot.*

"He's supposed to be in Spokane, isn't he?" Renee strummed her instrument and hummed before testing some potential lyrics for her song. "The big man flew away / His company refused to pay / They held him on a string / In case they needed a scapegoat again."

"Catchy." Marcus was scrolling his phone, and he stopped and double tapped. Then he held it up for Alex to read. "This is a post by one of my fav podcasts, *DontTrustTheMan*. Here's what he says," and he turned the phone back to read it to his friends.

"I know the story." Alex had read half of it and recognized a version of it from the previous year.

"I haven't even read it."

"I did. It's about a snake, that if it sheds its skin and says, 'Look at the new me!', well, it's still a snake except it's now bigger and stronger. Don't trust the snake."

"Nah, this is about a scorpion. Let me read it—"

"You don't need to. The scorpion asks the frog for

a ride across the river, and the frog makes him promise not to sting him. In the middle of the river, the scorpion stings the frog. As they both go under, the frog asks, 'Why?' The scorpion shrugs and says, 'I'm a scorpion, and that's what I do.'"

"It's not a frog, it's a butterfly, but you clearly know the story." Marcus' shoulders dropped, and he looked deflated. He brightened and said, "But that's the point. You know Eliot hasn't changed, and from what you've said, meeting him might not be a good idea."

"Who said I'm meeting him?" Alex had his phone back out and studied the message.

Renee snickered. She wasn't watching them but was whispering into her phone. She looked up and said, "The way you're holding your phone. It's a corporate thing. You think we can't read you, but corporates are an open book to the rest of us."

"Besides, at the meeting, Mr. Sutter said we weren't to bother Eliot with company matters, only pop in to congratulate him, or whatever people might want to say to him. Maybe you should ask before you agree—"

Instead, Alex said quietly, "This is something I need to finish."

Renee tilted her head. "Finish or start?"

He didn't answer. He wasn't sure, but if he had to start a confrontation to end one, maybe that's what it took.

You're learning.

The air around him warmed a degree, starting at the base of his neck. It was enough that Marcus noticed.

"Dude, where's the extra heat coming from? Do

you feel it, too?"

Alex smiled faintly. "Sort of."

"COME IN, hero." Eliot Kane's smile looked professionally reattached. Sophie Verden reclined on the couch behind him, all charm and unreadable calm.

Eliot had requested Alex to meet him in his old office. He was collecting his personal things, but he hadn't said anything about Sophie tagging along.

"You didn't say this was a ménage à trois. Why bring Sophie?"

"We've had an interesting week, haven't we?" Eliot smiled, and it looked effortless. "Certain discrepancies ... ones we've asked you to handle, but all fixable—if you cooperate."

"I won't falsify data."

"You misunderstand." Both Eliot and Sophie spoke at once, and their tone synched so perfectly it chilled him. Eliot spoke, Sophie echoed, with dovetailing syllables. "We only rewrite perception."

Sophie stood, as flexible and fluid as a great cat. "Before I left the country, I wanted to give Kane & Sutter a second chance. You can help with that, Alex. You can save Eliot's career with the company and secure yours, also." She almost purred.

Alex felt heat crawl up his spine. "You're not exactly human, are you?"

Sophie laughed softly. "I once was, but then, neither are you, not entirely. Not anymore."

For a moment, he pictured the man from behind the mirror pulling the crack wider to step through. He hadn't seen him since, although he was certain he'd heard his voice, one that sounded so much like his own. Then her eyes stole his attention. Her pupils shimmered like copper medallions. Light drained from the room as if obeying her. And the interesting thing was that she kept looking over and behind him, as if she were looking for or at someone besides him.

Eliot's grin widened. "Tell me, Alex, when that voice in your head talks, does it love you—or own you?"

He wanted to run but couldn't move. Somewhere inside, a force pressed his feet against the floor. The heat inside him grew, and he felt he would explode. Not knowing why but only that it was the thing to do, he balled his hands into fists and tightened his torso as he flexed his upper body. In the flex, he released something that flew through and from him, like a giant raptor—or an angel on the attack.

The walls and ceiling vibrated, and Alex thought, *Oh, no! I've seen this before.*

The heat and pressure grew, with the objects in the room outlined in brilliant gold. In and through the shape of the Eliot that Alex knew, an angry cobra swayed and hissed, darting in Alex's direction but blocked by an unseen hand. Sophie was equally hideous as a harem dancer wearing scarves that scarcely covered her and glittering jewels decorating her skin. She held out a hand and blew him a kiss.

The real, once-human Eliot hissed—an actual hiss—and slammed a palm against the desk, sending a pressure wave through the air. Alex stood, planted, as his clothing whipped against him and the things in the room slammed backwards into the walls. Without warning, Eliot and Sophie were flung backwards, away from Alex, as if they had been battling the wind, and it suddenly became a tornado.

Then, just as suddenly, the office lights returned to reveal the entire space in disarray. Eliot stumbled to one knee, drained and whimpering. He looked like a lost, defeated little boy rather than the successful businessman who co-owned a major corporation.

Sophie was even worse. Whatever Alex had released had stolen her beauty from her. Her hair was brittle and in disarray, and lines and liver spots painted her with age. She took in her hands and touched her face before looking at Alex with pleading in her voice. She held out her arm like a supplicant or a beggar beside the road.

"Please, I need my beauty back. Please, don't leave me like this."

Alex was sickened, and a voice—*the voice*—whispered in his ear.

Two down. Two to go.

He wasn't sure he wanted to take on two more like this, but he had a pretty good idea his angel wasn't giving him a choice.

This was a battle he must win.

3

The Return of Dr. Milt

ALEX DIDN'T text anyone to get together that evening. He was in full recovery mode, and he needed his time alone.

He didn't even stop by the Kaffe Shop. He walked on the opposite side of the street with his fists thrust deep into the pockets of his cashmere coat. Through the glass, the place was buzzing. If he'd decided to stop, would the people have vacated the establishment just for him?

How did that happen?

And if he changed his mind now and decided he *would* go to Joey's, would the people inside become lemmings, scrambling through the door en masse, and over the cliff we go?

He wouldn't do that to them, or to Joey. And maybe that's the reason Joey still had a full house, because his ... angel? ... lived inside him and knew what he would and wouldn't do.

After all, he'd seen what lived inside Eliot and Sophie ... or *had* lived in them. He suspected they were just themselves again, that whatever had controlled them had abandoned them.

Or been driven out.

He suspected their possessors *were* driven out, but he was also certain they had *abandoned* them. Once the illusion was stripped away, the magic was gone. No one would ever envy them again.

The "whatever" that had driven them out was easy. His angel had confirmed that pride was what gave Eliot his power. It had been real, and it had captivated Alex. The man's confidence, his way of slicing and dicing people with a word. His ability to express assurance and to garner praise in everything he did.

And Sophie? She had deceived him, and it would have worked except that she let her inner voice leak out before she had him fully hooked. Now he knew her beauty was an exterior trapping, a payment of sorts for the thing that lived inside her. He was certain she must have been beautiful at one point, and she had traded whatever made her *her* in exchange for her eternal beauty and prestige.

As he walked, he was wandering aimlessly, or so he thought. Then he noticed the streetlamps. When he approached them, sometimes they brightened—not much, just enough to notice—or darkened. He found himself taking the brighter path each time, and he understood that he was being guided.

By his angel, he was certain. At one point, he would have fought giving up control to someone—or something—else, but tonight, he was glad he wasn't alone. His decisions hadn't gone so well for him, had they? It was nice just for a short time to let someone else take the lead.

He began to recognize the buildings surrounding Nicolette Mall and wondered why the mirror-Alex had led him this way, when he found himself standing before the old stone church. The stained glass grabbed his attention first, then he noted the band of rectangular light leading from the street to the building. The front door was open, and he headed up the steps and inside.

The interior felt clean, vast, and spare. Lights hung from long chains, and the pierce work in the metal shades scattered dancing patterns of shadows across the stone walls. The nave was crisscrossed with shadowy beams, and above the altar, Jesus hung suspended on a cross.

From Marcus' descriptions, this wasn't the Lutheran church he'd grown up in, although some Lutheran buildings might well look like this. Jesus above the altar was the same, draped in a loincloth with bloody nails in his hands and feet, and a crown of thorns forcing blood from his scalp. It was horrific and beautiful at the same time.

He slipped into a pew and breathed in the ancient aromas of stone and dust and incense. There was peace in the old stone walls. Should he genuflect? He chuckled.

If you want.

A soft glow filled the pew around him, and he knew he wasn't alone.

"When will I see you again?"

Every time you look into a mirror.

"Yeah, right." He barely whispered the words. "You're me, but I don't see how I'm you."

Sincerity is belief. When you begin to trust in yourself, you will begin to believe in me.

"And we have two more opponents to vanquish. I was listening. I don't know that I want to fight them."

That is why you have me. Trust in yourself, and I will be there when you need me.

He remained where he was for a time. When worshippers began to gather, he excused himself and returned to his walk. This time, however, he no longer felt the need to wander. His home was within an easy stroll, and he soon found himself at his door.

He was barely inside, when his phone vibrated, an email from Dr. Julian Milt.

He opened it to read: *We should talk. One last session. Tomorrow, 9 PM, my office.*

No signature. Only a shimmering line beneath the text.

Nothing about it sounded appealing. Their last visit had literally been an entrance to the underworld, as close to a Lutheran hell as you could get. Marcus had described it often enough.

And nine at night? In an empty building? There was no way anything good was happening in an empty building in the dark.

He tossed his phone on the couch and flipped on the coffee maker. When he placed his steaming cup on the coffee table and leaned his head back, he could just see the blank phone accusing him.

You have to do this. You know you do. Don't give up now.

Was it his phone talking to him, or his angel ... or was he simply talking to himself now? He no longer knew.

His stomach churned. Yet something told him the end waited there.

He forwarded the message to Marcus: *What do you think?*

He read the reply and smiled: *But you know I love you. Why would you do this? Haven't you had enough?*

And Marcus didn't even know about the meeting with Eliot and Sophie.

He replied: *If I don't text by 11, and you're still up, maybe call an exorcist. Or the police. Whichever you find first.*

Marcus replied with a thumbs-up emoji and: *bring holy water and sarcasm.*

He was glad he had a good Lutheran demon-caster to back him up. If the meeting went anything like the one with Eliot and Sophie, he would need one.

The whisper warmed his ear: *Don't forget. I've got your back.*

"Right. I'll try to remember that." He powered down his phone and tossed it on the coffee table. He stood, emptied his cup, and headed to the shower.

Tomorrow would be a long day ... and possibly a longer night. He needed all the rest he could get.

4

A Floor of Fire

THE FOLLOWING day at the Kane and Sutter tower, life was weird.

There were no flashing lights, no ghostly figures wandering the corridors, nothing like that. The weird was in his head: passing the newly refurbished conference room and remembering opening his eyes to find his boss and their client whisked away with only an imprint on the wall to reveal they had been there; Eliot's office—now with the door closed and locked, of course—but the memory of the broken people he'd left there still resonated; the strange light by the stairwell, only now connected in his mind; and the copy room, shooting out paper at him as he walked by, perhaps warning him to run, run, run.

He refused to walk towards the backside of the building where the therapist's office hunkered among the doors lining the corridor. Were there two Dr. Milts, one with purple snake eyes that twisted and swirled with otherworldly evil, and the other a normal, helpful man who treated his assistant with respect and helped Alex's co-workers with marital problems? He had seen the man destroyed, then almost immediately he'd walked out of a restroom on the other side of the office. How did anyone explain that?

Lunch with Renee avoided any mention of the dreaded visit to Dr. Milt's. He trusted that Marcus hadn't said, and he refused to. He needed her sharp and sometimes piercing observations about life and him to keep him grounded in the real world, otherwise, he wouldn't make it through the day.

Their plates were empty, with only scattered crumbs and wadded napkins to tell the story of their meal. He had ordered black coffee as a chaser, ostensibly to calm his nerves but equally for something to do with his hands.

He tore open a creamer package and swirled it into the cup. His spoon created a mesmerizing design that was eerily like Dr. Milt being sucked into a wall ...

He pushed the cup away and sat back. "Do you remember the lady with the kid?"

"From that project? Sure. She was a hard woman." She was tearing the tops off sugar packets and taking them like shots. Four empties littered her plate.

"Except with her kid. With him, she wore kid gloves." Talking was easy with a shared past. He liked that. It was part of his comfort level around Renee.

"Yeah, I remember. He looked at her with love. Were you there when he was being bullied by that red-headed kid, and when his mother came around the corner, he didn't have to cower any longer? I would liked to have had a mother like that."

Alex did. Sure, she didn't punch anyone in the face for him ... and the realization hit him. She had done exactly that. That argument with his father all those years ago. He hadn't abandoned them; he had been sent packing.

He saw his mother through new eyes ... and with new respect.

Was his protector from the mirror the same as that mother from their college volunteer project? A thing—no, a person—filled with love for the child in her care, but able to bring to bear incredible presence and power when the bullies appeared?

Was he that boy, sometimes getting in over his head and being taken advantage of by bullies bigger than him, and then his "mother" steps in with the big guns and says, "Not this one; not this time."

He watched Renee toss back her sixth sugar packet and smiled. "That red-headed kid's face turned from gloat to panic in a heartbeat."

The same as Sophie's face when the light appeared from behind him. As Eliot's did when the mirror-Alex took over.

He thought, *Is that who you are to me? Both loving protector and guard dog when an enemy appears?*

The whisper surrounded him: *I wouldn't refer to myself as a guard dog, but yes.*

He chuckled and stood. "I'm covering the lunch. Thank you for your support."

Renee looked surprised. "Thanks. I don't know what I did, but I'm glad I did it."

"You were you, and that's what I needed." He almost felt he could face Milt, especially as he suspected he wouldn't be doing it alone.

MILT'S OFFICE looked identical to before—same beige décor, same faint music. But the air stank of copper. Marjorie was nowhere to be seen, but that wasn't a surprise. It was nine o'clock, and the midnight cleaning crew would be arriving soon.

"You came," said the therapist. He emerged from a shadowed corner, but his calm, professional mask was gone. In its place simmered something as old as rust. "You've carried their mark a long time."

Alex's throat tightened. "Whose mark?"

"Those from the light." Milt's mouth twisted. Even in the dimness and shadows, his pupils danced. "Those that make the mistake to resist perfection."

The floor whooshed the way a gas grill sounds when being lighted. Beneath them, pale blue flames whipped across the carpet and sent up coils of black residue. From it rose the faceless Commuter, with his immaculate, creaseless coat flickering like it was no more than smoke rising from the destruction underfoot.

In that moment, time fractured. Paper whipped from surfaces and froze in mid-air. The laptop on the desk was levitated by an unseen force. Even the flames stopped their dance and waited with gleeful expectancy.

At the center of the fracture stood the shape from every dream Alex had experienced: tall, radiant, and with eyes both his and not-his.

"I am Cael," the angel-like creature announced, his voice entwined with both thunder and heartbeat. The walls vibrated with his proclamation, and Alex was pushed to the limit to hold his place in the room. "I command you to stand down. This one is not yours to claim."

The flames whipped once more as they encircled them, but nothing burned. Behind Dr. Milt, a ghostly vision of Eliot's face contorted—beautiful and horrifying simultaneously—as his tailored suit smoked at the seams. On the other side, Sophie as a beautiful seductress stepped backward into shadow that swallowed her like water. Only her voice remained, calm and lilting.

"He's yours, then. See how long his goodness survives."

They vanished.

Alex turned toward the light. "So, you're real."

"I am what remains when the real stops hiding," Cael replied in a voice of thunder and tender touch. "You want this world to be tidy. It isn't. But it's still loved."

"I didn't call you."

Cael nodded. "You remembered me."

Milt bowed slightly to the winged being. "The circle completes. Faith is delusion, Alex. This creature comes to you when it wills. You cannot control it. To place your trust in a creature of light is to give up your true purpose. Give in to your true nature of despair. It is who you are. When you give in to despair, there's nothing left for anyone to take from you."

Alex stepped back—but there was nowhere left to go. Cael vanished, the walls turned to glass, and inside each pane his own face stared back, frightened, multiplied a hundredfold. Himself in bed, listening to his father walk out the door. At a party while trying to understand why he was the only one not laughing. Walking by the old stone church and finding the door locked again and again. The feelings welled inside him, and he felt the emotions for what they were.

Despair. He had lived it. He had fought it, but he

had never truly beaten it. At times, especially when he wrote letters to his father that he refused to mail, it returned, overwhelming him once more.

"Why me?" he whispered into the shadows.

The Commuter provided the answer: "Because you have failed to choose. And chaos always leads to despair."

Then Cael's light poured from every glass pane—first faint, then roaring. The panes of glass around the room became mirrors as they fractured outward. Through the broken reflections poured Cael's presence—the image shaped in Alex's own likeness, radiant and calm, with crystalline eyes gleaming like the rising sun.

5

The Revelation

MILT YELLED, "No! I defeated you!"

He held an opened palm toward each shattered mirror, and one by one, they slowly began to reform into solid panes of glass. It was as if the surface melted at the pressure of his power and once more became what he demanded of it.

It wasn't to be, though. As his hand moved from mirror to mirror, his repairs refused to hold. He turned slowly, repairing pane after pane, only to have them shatter once more.

"This can't be. This is my domain. I rule this world. Humanity is mine to control!" Milt's face turned truly evil.

Cael's voice vibrated with authority: "Where my power of protection is released becomes *my* domain. Again, Alex is not yours to claim."

With a shriek—a sound not of pain but defiance—the blue flames encased Milt's legs and leapt for his torso. He began to swat them away faster and faster until he dissolved into a puff of black ash that vanished before hitting the floor.

From behind them, smoke condensed once more into the Commuter, the faceless man from the train, holding an unlit lantern.

"Indifference," Cael murmured. "The final test. Beware. It can be banished but never vanquished. Its seed will regrow if you choose to water it."

"Is there any hope?"

"Yes. Chaos can be overcome but only by will."

The angel-like being bowed his head and knelt, his hands on the pommel of his light sword, with the tip against the flames covering the floor. His wings flexed slowly in and out, his only sign of life.

"By my will," Alex muttered. "Okay, so that's how it is. I'm on my own."

He'd hoped to hear the familiar voice in reply: I've got your back. All he heard was silence.

The Commuter bore more transparency than before, as if Dr. Milt had provided extra strength. The black smoke from the burning floor drew to him, darkening his presence before dissipating, only to be replaced by fresh smoke.

He must be weaker, as he now spoke through vibration rather than speech. The words appeared in Alex's head and were felt in his feet, shins, and calves.

"There is no need to continue fighting, Alex. I've ridden the train with you for months and watched you search the faces around you for truth and meaning. There is no truth and meaning. You don't have to choose, just hold out your hand and I will give you what you desire: rest. The world is noise. Walk off the track. Nothing needs saving. Only rest is there for you in the end."

For a heartbeat Alex wanted that ease. No expectations, no fear of failing others. Just drift. He saw images—his father in the birchwood walking alone, his mother's empty teacup, a home tidied of emotion and of his father.

His choices became clouded, as though his vision narrowed, and all he could see was the slender path directly before him.

Then another memory cut through the morass of banality: childhood Alex freeing a thrush from the fallen branch.

The small kindness that changed gravity.

He faced the faceless figure. "No. Some things deserve to keep beating."

Light burst from his chest—white without heat. The Commuter staggered. The Commuter's face formed a mouth, and it opened. Alex felt his cry in his bones and heard it in his head.

"He is not ready. He has doubts. Give him to me." His face became featureless once more, even as he battled the light.

"He is ready," Cael murmured, with his head still bowed. "Because he chose to look past what was and to see what is."

Alex understood that Cael was not bowing in submission to the Commuter but to him. He was giving him permission to do what must be done.

The faceless man tilted his head. The light continued to batter him, and his suit whipped against him, revealing him to be nothing more than sticks and wire. "Then finish what reflection began."

Cael turned to Alex, this time raising his head and opening his eyes. "You've fought the choices you thought you'd already made. You knew there was more. You've chosen to fight against the dark. Here is your final test. Only you can dispel the darkness that tries to consume each of us."

Alex remembered flexing his torso before and what had happened. He gripped his hands into fists, lifted them to shoulder height, then flexed. This time, what poured from him was not only light but heat. The smoke that made up the Commuter couldn't replenish itself fast enough, and eventually, the final whisp released its hold on the day and dispersed into the air.

Only the lantern remained. It tumbled to the floor, and inside its glass a single gold feather slowly turned, alive but no longer free.

Cael stood, and he began to beat his wings faster and faster. Light flowed from them in pulses of fractured crystals until Milt's office vanished in the brilliance. The three of them stood on the frozen lake again, Cael with his wings unfurled, Alex holding the lantern, and the feather alive but trapped inside.

The stars overhead observed, silent judges to the outcome of a battle Alex was never intended to win.

"Each of them was a piece of your own forgetting," Cael said, his voice now one of care and understanding. "Pride that wanted control. Deception that feared truth. Despair that mocked faith. And this last—indifference—is eternity's rust. It is trapped but can break free to live and grow again."

Alex's breath misted in bright curls. "If I destroy him, do I destroy part of myself?"

"Each of these has taken a part of you. Would you rather that you kept them, harbored them in your heart, and perhaps set them free to grow once again?"

"Never!"

The feather twisted violently, showing its desire to be free. Alex cringed at the thing he held in his hand.

Cael offered encouragement. “Some endings are mercy.”

“You said he can’t be killed.”

“For a time. You must never water the seed of indecision and chaos that’s left behind. If you do, he will return to life once more.”

6

The Decision

HE KNELT with the lantern in his hand, watching the feather flutter in the cage, so alive and oddly alluring at the same time.

"It is what it does, draws you in even as you despise it." Cael stood over him, his wings held wide, a covering over both Alex and the decision he must make.

"The others, they wished to hurt me. Their undoing didn't feel like it was me. You were my intercessor, the help I needed."

"I cannot help you in this. Indecision and chaos are part of every man's life throughout each day. This is an evil you must vanquish each day you live."

There was that word again, vanquish. If an enemy couldn't be killed, how was it possible to vanquish it every day?

"It is by choice." Cael replied to the unvoiced question.

"You know my questions, even when I don't say them aloud."

"I am you. Your thoughts are my thoughts."

"But yet I can't read yours."

"I was created in your thoughts. Your need for what

you didn't have brought me into existence. Every thought I think is from you."

"Just not right now."

"We are no longer one, but we can be again."

He wondered if Cael had always been inside him, and if everyone had a similar twin. "Are you my guardian angel?"

"I am what you need me to be. I am what every human holds deep inside."

"Most don't discover it, do they?"

"The divine is a mysterious realm, and not all the answers come to everyone." Cael paused, held out his hand to Alex, and brushed his temple. "Not everyone searches as you did."

"Okay. I'll take that as a compliment, I guess. What about this guy? What do I need to do?"

"You have made up your mind?"

"I've made my decision, yes. People count. They are what matter."

"Then you must release him from his cage."

"What?!?" He fell back on his buttocks. "Ouch, warn me next time. I thought we caged him to keep him from being released."

"The cage protects him from you as well as you from him. You cannot do what needs to be done without setting him free."

"I just break it?" He lifted the lantern to peer inside, and the feather danced crazily.

"Think it, and it will be done. It is the decision that breaks the prison, not physical action."

He set it on the ice and backed away. He looked into Cael's face, studied his features, so much like his own, and took in the set of his eyes. It was odd seeing a man so like him, very like a mirror, but not replicating his actions like a mirror. A twin might feel something like this, but it could be unnerving.

Cael nodded at him, and Alex released the Commuter in his thoughts.

Nothing happened to the lantern. It was unchanged, but inside, the feather dissolved into gray smoke and evaporated from the metal-and-glass container. It resolved into a grayer and washed-out version of the man from the train.

The Commuter extended a hand. “No pain, no calling, no burden. Step onto my track, and you rest at last.”

For a heartbeat Alex felt the pull back into his old life. He was overwhelmed with the loss of family and friends, the nights he’d cried for his father, and how broken he’d felt when he gave up love for perfection. The imagined relief flooded over him. No more visions, no half-lived double life.

Just sleep. Rest. Letting a job and money and possessions fill his days, with no purpose except for filling his life with a good time.

Then he remembered Marcus’ relentless jokes keeping the dark at bay. The sound of Renee’s voice singing *“our mirrored hands refusing night”* rang in his ears. Priya’s astonished gasp at the sight of light in her apartment grounded him back to people he knew really cared about him.

He looked up. “Rest isn’t the goal.”

Cael’s eyes softened. “Then indecision and chaos must burn.” He held out his sword to Alex.

Alex stepped forward with the sword in his hand. Fire blossomed from the end—but it didn’t consume.

It clarified. The faceless man staggered, his edges unraveling into smoke and cold rain.

When it cleared, Alex stood alone on ice so clear it reflected both sky and self without distortion.

Cael watched him, smiling. "You understand now," the angel said.

"Not perfectly."

"No human does. But you finally believe you're more than an accident."

Cael raised his hand, and light poured from his palm and surrounded Alex until the world around them vanished.

When the light faded, they stood inside Alex's apartment.

Every mirror—from bathroom to hallway—reflected multiple angles of him, each carrying a different expression: pride, fear, apathy, hope. Some revealed him at work, frustrated by Eliot, or as a boy crying as he missed his father, or with Renee working with their volunteer group in college and seeing how their successes brought joy to those they helped.

Each was a fragment of who he had been.

"Will I always have these as part of me?"

"Every fragment of your life is still a part of you." Cael touched the cracked bathroom mirror. "Fragments only hurt if you forget they still belong to the same glass."

Alex stood beside the angel, their twin reflections making the two into four. "What happens now?"

"You choose whether to keep seeing yourself as two."

He thought of his joke rules: Say thank you. Notice one good thing. Don't let cynicism finish a sentence.

Those rules had always been thin shields but honest ones. He smiled. "I'd rather have you as part of me if it means staying true to myself."

Cael nodded once. "Then integration, not escape. We become one once more."

"I won't lose you, will I?" A small hesitation told him he would miss the winged creature if he never saw him again.

"You have me now. I am always you. Together or apart, we are one."

"Okay. My decision is made. I'm ready."

With those words, their reflections merged until only one version of Alex looked back—calm, unhurried, carrying light in his eyes but no halo.

He felt an ache inside, but it was a good feeling ... like forgiveness for the man he once was and a hope that he could be better in the future.

7

The Aftermath

HE WOKE in his apartment, with the morning sun casting blue streaks on the floor.

No ashes. No scorch marks. Just the faint smell of rain and cedar. He threw back the bedding to find his legs in sleeping pants and his stomach a cavernous hollow, meaning he was gnawingly hungry. Food would be on the agenda and soon, but he had another station to visit first.

He swung one leg off the bed, then the next, and finally sitting, glanced around the familiar space. He looked at his palm, then rustled through the bedding, and yes, it was still there. The scorched fabric proved that the past year had been his reality, and not a dream he was just now coming out of.

He stifled a yawn as he entered the bathroom. His towel hung over the shower door, and the lights gleamed on the porcelain throne. That wasn't his interest. The mirror was.

He could see himself, nearly to his knees, his chest and stomach, as familiar as yesterday's coffee. He twisted around and worked an arm up his back. He could just touch where his wings would be if he had them.

Nothing, not even a ripple in the skin to suggest they had ever been there.

On the bathroom mirror, the crack still glowed softly. He leaned in, ran a fingernail across the glass to feel for the indentation and it was perfectly smooth, although still visible on the back side. It had to have been a divine event to so perfectly damage the back of the mirror and leave the front solid and smooth as though a strange, winged man had never stepped through.

Coffee found him in the kitchen, and a bowl of instant oats joined him at the kitchen bar. His phone buzzed, and he tapped the reminder and headed to his closet to dress. Shirt, socks, pants, and shoes ... then his fingers through his hair and he was headed out the door.

The sun seemed especially bright, and the city smelled especially good today. Was it the changing weather, or that he was just paying attention again? It was like he'd been half awake for the last decade, and he was seeing everything like it was new.

He paused as he approached the office building where he'd worked the past two years. The sign over the door was changed. He glanced across the street, located familiar buildings, and then up to the windows that fronted his section of the tower. This was it, the place he worked.

It no longer said Kane & Sutter above the door. And the new name, Sutter One West, seemed as weathered as the old one. There was no telling what building it came from, perhaps even having spent the past few years in this building's basement.

"Good morning, Stacie," he remarked as he

walked up to her desk. “I like the new name outside.”

“What new name is that?” She worked her pen like a seesaw, and it also said Sutter One West on the side.

He took a second look at her pen. The name ... perhaps the sign *was* as old as it looked. He wondered if he’d find Kane & Sutter or Sutter One West on his notepads in his office.

“Never mind. I like your pen.”

“Thank you.” She smiled brightly. “This is our six-month anniversary together. Best pen ever.”

One anomaly he did discover was “a localized power fluctuation” reported on the twenty-second floor. The internal report didn’t mention Eliot or Sophie, but that wasn’t as surprising as the omission of Dr. Milt. Eliot and Sophie were only back to tie up loose ends, but Milt had worked at the tower up to the day before. Surely someone would miss him.

On his morning break, he took a stroll past the elevators towards the therapist’s office. He walked directly to his door and twisted the handle to find it locked. He glanced at the name plate beside the door, only to read STOREROOM.

A glance to either side confused him more. Jerry from Records turned the corner pushing a cart with a pile of folders inside, and Alex asked, “Jerry, I can’t locate Dr. Milt. His office should be right here.”

“Milt, Milt.” He appeared to be thinking, and he finally shrugged. “Can’t help you there, man. What does he do here?”

“The company therapist. His office was through this door. I was here last night.”

“Hey, man, I don’t think so.”

“Are you certain?” Alex was truly spinning his

wheels.

"Pretty sure." He pulled out a set of keys, located one, and slipped it into the lock. He removed the key and pulled the door open. Inside was a tight closet with shelves on both sides stacked with cleaning supplies. A mop bucket took up much of the floor space, leaving no room for Marjorie's desk and certainly no room for a door into another office.

"Okay, sure. I must have been on another floor." Alex excused himself. On the way to his desk, he circled by Eliot's office, only to find it scrubbed clean with a blank name plate on the wall. Really weird when the man made a special trip from Spokane to clean it out yesterday.

BACK AT HIS desk, he spent hours prowling through the company's computer files, marveling at bureaucracy's ability to memorialize miracles as maintenance. The Verden accounts, nowhere to be found. No record for salary payouts for Eliot, and as he expected, the building didn't record offices for Dr. Julian Milt. Even Alex's office phone records didn't show any of the calls he'd made to either of them.

And he had made them. He remembered marking them on his daily log, something he always did as good record-keeping. He opened his log, scrolled back through two weeks, and found nothing.

Yet he remembered each one. He closed the file and muttered, "Guess even angels have to wade through HR."

Inside him, laughter, so much like his own, but doubled. He could feel the angel inside, but Cael's presence was smaller now. He was already missing him, and he wondered if the winged man's presence would eventually dissolve into something like intuition. He hoped not. He liked having him around.

His phone buzzed.

MARCUS: You alive? I didn't hear last night. If yes, brunch. If no, still brunch.

ALEX: Alive enough. Thank you for checking up on me.

MARCUS: Sorry. Fell asleep.

Renee added a group message: *Dream rent now due, pay up.*

He laughed—real laughter this time—and for one instant saw a bright silhouette reflected in the phone screen beside his own, grinning.

"You're still here. I'm glad."

Of course I am. I really do have your back.

THAT WEEK he finally wrote to his father, a real, honest son-to-father heart to heart.

Dad,

I used to think goodness was a hobby for people without deadlines. Now I know it's the only job that matters. You don't have to understand, but I need you to know I'm okay. I'm trying to live honestly, even when that honesty aches.

Your son,

Alex.

He didn't mail it. He had a better plan.

He kept the letter folded behind a photo of his mother watering daisies—a private covenant with her to always place the people in his life first.

8

The Sword of Light

SUMMER SLID back over Minneapolis without apology.

The morning sun hit Alex's windows earlier, and the crickets chirruped longer into the evenings. And with his new attitude towards life, his evenings expanded into exploring the small universe that gave his city so much character.

The warmth of summer showcased the city's best side. Sidewalk cafés spilled laughter, cyclists thrummed by the lakes, and every bus stop carried the warmth of small talk.

He stood at a small bridge in the park and watched a mother with two children and a dog. It wasn't the people that interested him but the dog. The children, both under ten, had different dog toys, and they each tried to keep the dog's attention. The dog was happy to share, bouncing from one child to the other—and the two children shared with equal happiness. They didn't get angry when the dog chose one over the other. There was no jealousy. They understood the truth in the situation: The dog loved them both and would share its time and attention equally. Its joy wasn't in the toys, it was in the people who shared the toys.

He stood and watched long after they moved on, soaking in the life that he had almost overlooked. It wasn't the birchwood, but it was Minnesota, and he could live with that.

For once, he wasn't in a hurry to be anywhere ahead of schedule.

THE NEXT morning began with an old habit reborn: coffee, an open window, and gratitude for what life offered.

He was aware of his mirror, but it no longer centered his life. It just was. The crack in the silvering? Background ... proof of concept ... a gentle reminder that a person's life didn't have to continue down the same spiral. When things began to close in, there was always a way forward.

Placing his coffee cup in the sink, he moved toward his closet to change. His phone was on the bedside table—it no longer centered every waking moment—and the screen flashed. When he tapped it, a series of messages appeared.

REN: Don't know if you have the time, but the music's on. Doing a set at Nicolette Mall. Open air, noon.

Another one said:

PRIYA: Mom's scheduled lunch today. Please say we're meeting for lunch. Anywhere.

And finally:

MARCUS: Dude, where's my brunch? Still waiting. Thinking of starting my own podcast to fill the time at this rate.

He smiled. Friends. In a group chat, he replied:

Renee, there. Look for me. Priya, tell your mother your friend's future depends on you. Marcus, will lunch do? We're heading over to see Renee's performance.

In the hallway, he locked his door, noted his neighbor's morning trash bagged and outside the door, and picked it up as he walked and dropped it in the chute at the end of the hall.

Outside, he noted things he hadn't before. Drivers choosing electric vehicles that slipped by soundlessly. Cats on windowsills watching him as he walked by. A man in a suit and tie pausing to retrieve a paper cup from the sidewalk to drop it in a bin.

The city's hum had changed in texture—still businesslike but threaded with small kindnesses he hadn't noticed before. A couple he'd spoken to twice had a sign on their recycling bin that said, "Extra recycling space available." The crossing guard by the local school sang to the children instead of shouting at them.

He suspected the world had always been that kind; he simply matched frequencies now. Or his inner self did, the one who'd come to save him and now resided back where he'd been all along: inside of his thoughts, dreams, and plans for the future.

He still checked mirrors by instinct, and every so often, the line of light through the bathroom crack brightened just enough to answer, *I'm still here*.

THE INITIAL turnout for Renee's performance was thin. She sang under a banner touting her name, with the logo for Radio K—the alt music station on the University of Minnesota campus—a mic on a stand, and a speaker hooked to her guitar. To the side, a table held flyers manned by a thin college boy in a headband and a tee, also emblazoned with the Radio K logo.

The crowd didn't stay thin for long. It was lunch, and The Nicolette Diner offered boxed specials at a discount for the duration of the presentation—likely subsidized by Radio K. The words in the songs were familiar to Alex, because many of them painted the story of the past year of his life. It was a tale of challenges, transition, and just a slice of metaphysical hijinks here and there. It told an entrancing tale of fantasy and derring-do to those who hadn't lived it.

It was just his life to him.

When the crowd began to swell, and Renee was between sets, he made his way to congratulate her and let her know they were there but wanted to allow room for others to enjoy her music. The gratitude in her eyes warmed him, making his day.

ON ONE SUNDAY morning, he walked by the old stone church. The doors were open again, and he stepped inside just to see the stained glass from the inside. They stunned from outside when the moon slipped behind the clouds and darkness was the backdrop for the old building; he was certain they would be equally fabulous from inside. He could see the colors as he approached the building, and they did not disappoint. Fire and sky in the glass flashed and churned, sweeping him along. The church was empty except for the echoes of light spilling across the pews. He glanced at his hands to find sunlight slashing across his palm.

A sword of light through the stained glass, except this time painting his hands in color.

He knelt—not because of any ritual, but because his gratitude for awakening to what his life could be outweighed the oppressive gravity that had bound him to things that didn't matter.

"I won't forget this time," he whispered.

Somewhere above the altar, air shimmered. The voice was gentle.

You never forgot. You only needed to rediscover what was there all along.

His eyes were moist, and he smiled through the tears. "Then help me remember better."

He didn't hear Cael's reply, but the familiar warmth at his neck assured him that he would.

9

Time Among Friends

HIS INTEREST in his work at the newly renamed Sutter One West waned. Who could care about databases when the world was out there waiting to be discovered?

Each time he opened a new spreadsheet on his laptop, he rewound back to the Verden accounts and his dinner with Sophie at The Capital Grille. That wasn't a film he needed in his mind's projector, and he had to break the pattern.

HR offered him a sabbatical, without pay, of course, but he would remain in the employee directory. When did he intend to return? A few weeks, he didn't know. If they could give him a call when things backed up? He was sure he would be ready by then.

Weeks passed. Sutter One West never called.

MARCUS JOINED him one evening with a bag of take-out and two canned drinks.

"Because I know you're broke. You've not been at the office in weeks. I can't have my best friend starving, even if he is a pudzo for turning belly up on the best position in the Twin Cities."

"I don't know about that. HR seemed relieved my

sabbatical was without pay. Cross your fingers you still have a job in another year."

"Still, I'm the one with a paycheck." He began laying out small containers of Chinese food, opening them, and filling the apartment with delectable aromas.

"I have a little reserve tucked away." He opened one of the drinks and walked to the window. He didn't dodge windows and mirrors any longer. His reflection was just him, and if he did see something that wasn't quite what he expected, he knew Cael now, and he accepted it as a reminder that he didn't have to face life alone.

"Are you just going to wait, or have you applied somewhere else?"

"We'll see. Whatever I do, I want it to matter, and not just to a company's bottom line."

Marcus spooned a portion of rice into his mouth, and he thought as he chewed. "The company's bottom line is my bottom line, too, so I'm good with that. Oh, I can't forget this."

He turned his phone screen up and tapped it several times. Marcus' voice played through the speaker.

"This is Marcus Havel bringing you *Faith with Wi-Fi*, your daily connection to a life lived better. Today's topic is—"

He tapped the phone to shut it down.

"Hey, bro. I want to hear the rest. I didn't know you'd gone live."

"I haven't." Marcus seemed pleased. "I'm thinking about it. I want your feedback on the title and my intro."

"Not too bad. I like it. Are you quitting Sutter to do this? Do it if you want, but how are your finances?" Alex already had that on his mind. He had funds in reserve, but that would go quickly without any income, and he was having to be careful.

"I'm not rich like you. I need my job. Hey, pudzo, did you take all the rice balls? I wanted seconds."

Alex passed him the ones he hadn't eaten, and Marcus eagerly swept them onto his plate.

WITHOUT FEEDBACK from HR at Sutter One West, he began looking for what was available. When he was with Renee or Priya, he mentioned that if they heard of anything to let him know. Until then, he wanted to reach out to the community and perhaps volunteer. It might be a good way to determine his next move.

"Like that volunteer project in college." Renee reminded him of how he'd seemed to lose himself in the work. "I was surprised to see you in corporate after that, but you knew what you wanted, I guess. Personally, I think you'd be great at working with people to improve their lives."

"That's exactly what I'm searching for." He felt a surge of hope, and from inside, the warmth of agreement.

"I know of a few. I'll get the word around."

THE SUMMER stumbled on, becoming a financial scramble, and he took on part-time work with Joey. It was enjoyable, he liked meeting the people, and it almost provided enough to pay the rent. Then one morning brought an email—a rejection as usual, he first thought—from a community organization Renee mentioned months earlier, seeking volunteers for youth mentorship.

He hovered over Reply a long time, then typed two words: *I'm in.*

That decision felt larger than any corporate promotion. In it lived every small kindness he'd once dismissed as outside his strategic plan to make his mark in the corporate world.

He realized his childhood rule had never changed: Leave places kinder. He finally understood it wasn't just an instruction for how to live—it was the identity he wanted to take on.

His volunteer gig at Minne-Apple Youth Center soon turned into a full-time role with a civic-renewal project promoted by the youth center's founders. Instead of algorithms and deadlines, his days circled around neighborhood meetings to work out compromises on small irritations before they became large ones; residency permits for unwed mothers and international climate refugees; and constructive focus projects for teenagers testing the patience of the city.

At first, he worried the paycheck wouldn't stretch. It didn't—no surprise there—but the meaning in the work was exactly what he was searching for. He kept his job at Joey's.

With his new co-workers, he caught himself laughing from the belly, an unplanned sound, and realized that at one time, it would have embarrassed him. Now, the people he spent time with did similar things regularly, and they still enjoyed their lives to the fullest. He was once more reminded: Perfection wasn't the end goal. People were.

When exhaustion came, he fell into it. Taking time to rest was no longer a crime against progress.

An old nonprofit client reached out, telling him they'd seen his name on the project promoted by Minne-Apple's founders. Would he be interested in consulting on a different civic-renewal project under a Main Street Grant? It would be pro bono, of course, but it would be a positive mark on his record.

He accepted. Less money, more meaning. The offices were in a rehabbed warehouse—and smelled of sawdust and coffee instead of corrosion.

He invited his friends to come visit the project, and afterward, they made their way to the Honeycomb. It was a slow night, and they were able to banter without yelling.

Renee remarked, "You look ... lighter. Less haunted, still charmingly weird."

Marcus studied him. "I think I see a glow around you. Enlightenment or burnout? Whichever, when I get my podcast up and running, this will be part of it."

"Bit of both," Alex said. "Call it hybrid energy."

"Podcast?" Renee leaned in, and she probed Marcus. "How do I not know about this? I've got songs to write, and this might be my hit number."

They laughed until the bartender told them to lower the existential decibels. For Alex, laughter registered differently now—not defense, just resonance—and he enjoyed having it around.

When Marcus joked, "If your angel's freelancing, tell him the IT department at the company could use a few moral upgrades," Alex nearly spit his drink.

He thought, *Humor is humanity's proof of trust.*

Priya appeared at the door, and as she headed in

their direction, Alex glanced from Renee to Marcus, puzzled.

"I texted her," Renee volunteered. "She promised she would be here after class."

As she pulled up a chair, she quipped, "From spreadsheets to saving the city. It's a miracle. I'm so proud of you, Alex."

He shrugged. "I prefer more human goals now."

Marcus hooted and slapped his leg. "He's gone full saint. His angel still won't pay the rent on time, though."

Renee pulled out her guitar. She glanced at the bartender, and when he nodded, she said, "I wrote something for you."

It was the best part of the evening, a time spent among friends.

10

The Song

RENEE'S NEXT concert was amid blueprints and dust. The Main Street Grant project was in its final push for funds, and Alex had recommended his friend for the event, titled *An Evening on Main*.

The event was to commemorate the city's founders, Franklin Steele and John Stevens, a combined free birthday party on the street with cake and ice cream for attendees. Of course, the big donors were inside, with the largest room—intended for a youth games area—draped with cloth and polished to a tee. Behind the cloth, the walls were rough block, and sawdust filtered from the ceiling.

Naming rights were up for auction, and when finished, the winners would have plaques on the interior doors to reflect their contribution to the project.

Renee began with a slow, clear melody:

"Light glimmers on the Isles of Minneapolis / Where we walk, but we are never alone / The mirror reveals who we are inside / The fire burns bright and draws us home."

When the last chord faded, warmth enveloped the room. The bulbs in the portable lighting fixtures shifted spectrums to gentle gold. One person began to tentatively clap, then it spread to everyone. Renee stood and took a bow, and that's when the clapping became a standing ovation.

When the friends gathered afterwards, Alex said, "I especially liked where the light glimmers on the Isles. Have you been there at night?"

"I've listened to you describe it enough." She laughed. "I feel like I have. Are we eating here or meeting somewhere else?"

"Cake and ice cream outside." Priya grinned. "My mother would approve."

"Can we do this?" Marcus hungrily eyed the lobster tails being served to the high donors. "Lobster might be my thing."

"Only if you're donating," Alex teased. "I think we can find you food cheaper."

AT HOME later that evening, he fell back onto the couch, satisfied with his day. He clicked on the television, and on the news, cameras panned the Main Street events and showed the masses of Minneapolitans who had turned up for free cake and ice cream. At the bottom of the screen, an added banner said: Recorded Earlier. A drone shot revealed secluded parking for the elite with valets and hired security patrolling the gleaming works of mobile, motorized art.

His phone vibrated. He saw Marcus' name, and he clicked to answer.

"Turn on your TV. Like now. I see us."

"Already there. The news is on. Do I need to change the channel?"

"Are you watching the event coverage? We're walking off at the bottom of the screen, but those cars, I mean, that Bugatti is three million. And I see two Rollses and a Ferrari."

"I see 'em. What about 'em?" He also saw the four of them as they walked away from the event, just four people strolling along the street, joking and very much comfortable with one another. He liked what he saw.

"I would've put more effort into shaking hands if I'd known they were that loaded."

"Would you really?"

Marcus laughed. "I like to think I would, but no. Besides, I was happy with our burgers at Foodz. I can order lobster tail any time. I can only have you guys at Foodz."

Alex chuckled. "I don't know about Foodz, but you're right about those cars. Just one of those could finish the entire project."

"When will you know? You know, how much you got from them."

"I'm just a consultant, and it's been pro bono, remember. My knowledge in this comes in sideways, but I'll likely know something tomorrow."

"Sweet moneymakers. I figured the project spent a ton setting up that event, but I'm starting to understand why they say it takes money to make money. Those people expect kid gloves, but if it goes right, it'll all come back and more."

"They're hoping so. I won't be able to give you details, but I'll let you know if it was a success when I hear."

They disconnected. He was aware that's what he'd turned down. He could have been one of those donors someday. The corporate world would have carried him that far, that was if he was willing to pay the price.

He pictured the Commuter. Indifference to the plight of the less fortunate wasn't his path any longer. He had plans, this time the right ones, and he hoped Cael supported him all the way.

I've told you: I've got your back. We're in this together.

Alex smiled. He expected nothing less.

THE NEXT evening, he met up with Marcus outside Sutter One West. He was early, so he scanned the list of the building's occupants. The firm rented space in the tower, but so did others, including the once-respected Dr. Milt. Where the therapist's name once proclaimed him to be a verified and respected occupant of the building, now, the tag had changed: LEASE AVAILABLE.

He backed up and stood under the dark windows, remembering the office where he had spoken with Marjorie Breakwater and met Dr. Milt. Then Jerry showed him inside the storeroom that had been Milt's office, and it was just that, a storeroom. It was the same as the name on the building, Stacie's ink pen, and the conference room's sudden transformation. Even Eliot's office, his no longer.

The sad thing was, each time he sat in Milt's office, he emerged more dissolute than before. He understood that his life's choices, from age nine to today, had wiped the joy from him.

"Thank you for teaching me how despair dresses," he whispered.

The city lights blinked once, giving him polite

acknowledgment, and Alex was startled when Marcus burst through the door with a skateboard in hand.

"Hey, pudzo, you ever ridden one of these? I bought this from Rick. He said his ex, that's Rebecca, told him to keep it. I think her actual words might have been to shove it, but I don't track that sort of thing. You wanna have a go?"

"They're divorced now?" Alex scratched the top of his head. "The last I heard, Dr. Milt had worked out their problems, and they were back together again."

"Who's Dr. Milt?"

Alex glanced at the list of renters in the building and stopped at LEASE AVAILABLE.

"Ah, no one," he said. "Just someone I used to know. Did Rick include the pads?"

"Pads? What are you talking about?"

"Protection for when you fall. You know, knee pads, elbow pads, a helmet, maybe?"

He sent a silent thought to Cael: *Does Marcus have one of you? If so, now's a good time.*

When he needs him, he will be there.

That was the best he could do, and he looked away when his friend decided to give his newly purchased skateboard a try.

11

Feeding the Five Thousand

A YEAR SINCE the weirdness of his journey started, and once again, he faced the mirror where it all started.

The line down the center glowed faintly like a healed scar under transparent skin.

He knew he was different. He felt it inside, yet in the mirror, the hair, the nose, the eyes were all the same. His chin was as pronounced, and the full lips he'd hated as a teen, still there no matter how often he'd wished them away.

It was as if his four adversaries never existed. When he mentioned them, even his friends gave him a puzzled look, as if they wanted to accommodate his memory, but they had no idea who he was referencing.

Eliot Kane had been Marcus' boss too, and yet, a blank gaze, laughter, and an elbow in the ribs was his response when he mentioned the man whose name had been on the building.

On the building, then magically gone.

He had tempted him with pride, and Alex had nearly fallen into the well. Would he have ever climbed out? That was not an answer he had to give, but he thought not.

And Sophie Verden, so mysterious, so beautiful.

Her very beauty was the source of her deception, and it failed her in the end. She offered him exactly what he dreamed of: companionship and admiration. His time with her left him drained and unable to tell what was important anymore.

Dr. Milt had robbed him of his sense of hope, even as he gave him platitudes to guide him to success. He hadn't offered him the attainment of a promising future but had attempted to strip his faith by painting it as a delusion. The man's smooth appearance had been tailored to hide the despair he wrapped around him.

"Are you still there?" he asked the mirror. He was treading unfamiliar territory, and reassurance was important.

Always, the soft internal echo: *I was here before, and I will be here after. Call it conscience if you wish, but I've always spoken when you needed me*.

"Will you show yourself if I need reassurance?" He remembered his fourth spiritual enemy in human skin, the Commuter, who showed him a future of chaos, one he wanted to avoid at all costs.

The mirror began to glow, and out of the brightness, he saw Cael standing behind him. The angel spread his wings, and from each feather tip, light shattered across the room in a kaleidoscope of refractive color. He placed a glowing hand on Alex's shoulder, and then he faded back into the mirror. Alex's shoulder continued to glow, attesting to the handprint of the divine.

He breathed out. For the first time in years, the

room's silence felt full.

THAT EVENING Alex lingered by the warehouse window, taking in the city lights rippling across the river. The double panes of the insulated glass blurred his reflection, one of him slightly offset from the other. Then a third image appeared surrounded by great masses of quivering feathers that slowly flexed back and forth. For a moment he saw the three outlines in the glass as him, and he knew it for what it was.

"I don't have wings," Alex said softly. "That's you, keeping me company. You are my reassurance, right?" Alex asked softly.

Always, said his inner voice. *Until you no longer need to ask.*

The reflection merged into Alex's, leaving only him and the city lights in the distance. Outside, snowflakes began to drift in front of the glass—quiet, luminous, ordinary. He pulled out his phone and checked the forecast. Tomorrow was September 24, and the predicted snowfall had begun. They were beating the old record by a day.

He watched it for a long time, then whispered a single thank you. His breath fogged the glass, the proof of his humanity. As he turned away to gather his things, the moisture hung there like a signature that he had come so far in so little time.

We have come so far, he thought, and he smiled that he would never feel alone again.

ON SATURDAY he finally mailed the letter to his father. Then he went on with his day. The snow was light, and two days later summer returned with sunshine and shirtsleeve weather. This Saturday was set aside for a picnic in the park.

His old friends were there plus more he'd gained at the non-profit. A game of touch football brought howls of laughter from the onlookers, but when the softball game started, knees turned green; and a few bruises began to blacken arms and legs.

The meal was more food than they could pack away.

Marcus said jokingly, "Now I know how Jesus' disciples felt when they finished feeding the five thousand."

"Oh?" Priya wiped her mouth and dropped a chicken bone in the trash. "I don't know that story."

"With the five loaves and two fishes? How can you not know this?"

"It's a Bible story, right? I am from India. What's the point of it?" She smiled prettily.

"Only that there was more food at the end than at the beginning. Look at all that." He pointed to the bowls and containers of uneaten food.

When the leftovers were divided among those who wanted some, they could barely carry them home, truly a Jesus feast of biblical proportions.

WEEKS LATER, a reply to the letter arrived—terse but warm in its own way.

Proud of you. Didn't expect different roads to lead to peace, but maybe that's the point.

He thought of Marcus' story of Jesus feeding the five thousand, with more left over than what there was at the beginning. His father's terse words were the same: a handful of letters offering even more in meaning. He framed the note beside his mother's photograph in the location the letter had once filled, two halves of a legacy—skepticism and wonder—settled peacefully under one pane of glass.

In his imagination, he listened to echoes of their voices, the disagreements mellowed by time into something that resembled love.

He imagined them laughing that their son had required divine intervention just to learn the balance between skepticism and wonder, one that in his mind they had now achieved.

Later that week he walked the river in twilight. Snowmelt in the shadows glittered like veins of flowing mercury in the dark. He paused at railings where he'd once doubted everything and said simply, "Thank you," to the water, to the shimmer, to the invisible network of grace that was threaded through the noise that had almost consumed him.

In the reflection he saw only himself, smiling easily. For a heartbeat another outline overlapped—wings half-folded—then the water rippled, and when it settled, only he was there.

He stepped away, reassured without having to ask.

Epilogue

Light on the Isles

1

Morning Rhythm

WINTER WAS a fist pounding the city with repeated bouts of snow. January recorded the second-highest snowfall in one storm at over two feet, and even critical services were curtailed for all but the most vital situations. For the unlucky (or unprepared), broken water pipes brought both inconvenience and a bucket list of future renovations.

A few weeks in early March promised hope, but true spring came late that year, tentative and forgiving. Snow remained for weeks in alleyways, on empty lots, and in shaded areas that languished on the north sides of buildings. It bled out in rivulets of tears that refroze night after night.

Finally, the ice slowly began releasing the sidewalks, sunny side first, and the lakes cracked with the snapping release of tension, as if breathing again after months of forced inactivity.

Alex woke early to the first glow of sunrise held back by the blinds. The room was cool, and he nested more tightly under the bedding. He dared one arm to tap the face of his phone to reveal the time: 6:37.

He could rarely sleep past his arbitrary wake-up time, even though he no longer needed to. He shifted position in the bed and smiled. The habit might remain, but the anxiety was gone. The pressure to perform, to show up early, to be the last to leave the office, the drive for perfection ... the change of direction in his life was taking a breath after nearly pulling him into an ocean of self-inflicted misery, and he was living a better life for it.

He now understood the old story about being gifted a human at birth. Each person on earth receives a human we are required to look after. We must ensure it is given the best chance for a good life. Our human must be protected, watched over, and loved, and we can't allow our human to come to harm. We can't trade it in if it gets damaged or broken. It's the only one we get.

That human is us.

He was now caring for his human in the best way possible.

"And that means coffee."

He tossed the bedding aside and felt his legs prickle. Spring might be in the air, but winter still owned the nights. The bathroom mirror revealed his face, chest, and arms, but it had become just a mirror. He pulled out a tee and slipped it over his head. His sleeping pants would do just fine, as he had nowhere to go and no schedule to get there.

He padded into the kitchen, hit the switch on the coffee machine, and heard the almost instant feedback of warming water. A cup appeared from an overhead cabinet, and he placed it on the counter.

A twist of the blinds slashed sunlight all the way across the room, painting the walls yellow and orange.

The coffee maker signaled, and he poured a

steaming cup, pulled half a bagel from a bag, and stepped to his balcony door. A twist of the handle, and the sound of the just-waking city slipped inside: car horns, the cycling of heating systems, steam from underground boilers, and best of all, birdsong.

Cold air, also, and he shivered as he shut it away.

Some mornings he thought he felt someone standing behind him, and this was one of those. A warmth on his back, the feeling of someone looking over his shoulder, the gentle comfort that meant he wasn't alone.

He smiled. "Good morning, partner."

Then he stepped into his day.

HE DID have to work. He might have changed, and his life's goals might have readjusted, but his landlord still expected him to hand over a rent check each month.

Then there were food and travel into the city center, some of which he could offset, and much that he couldn't. He learned to economize, to lower the thermostat, to walk except in the most brutal weather, and to order meals in a critical way. One for the road took on a new meaning when he could stretch a take-home portion into another meal or two.

Before leaving—he was still filling in at Joey's—he turned off every light except for one over the bar. A thin journal lay open with a pen resting on a blank page. It was his reminder that every day was a gift for him to use as he chose.

He also accepted that the results were on him. He could do nothing, lay around, and fall into indecision—and chaos—or he could make a plan—for whatever—and end the day successfully.

He no longer pegged each moment of his day to some future goal. He liked the analogy that yesterday was a film set broken down at midnight, with the actors off to other productions, and even the scripts recycled. By the time he woke, yesterday was edited and in the can, and reshoots? No one got those. Only today was in current production, so this was the important one.

He put two items on his list for the day:

- Smile back.
- Keep noticing.

He placed the pen back on the journal. Smile at what? It didn't matter. At the crossing guard, to a child, when he ordered lunch. Just smile.

And what should he notice? Everything but especially the good things. Sunshine. Birdsong.

The sound of laughter.

From down the hall, someone with a private treadmill thumped in a repeated fashion as they completed their morning run. Outside, traffic pulsed, the sound of life sharing the day with him.

The apartment smelled faintly of cedar and coffee—which to him was the present tense of grace.

Somewhere behind the glass curtains positioned throughout the city hovered a reflection, perfectly aligned, one he was certain he would see today, wearing the same quiet smile as he found in his mirror.

All he had to do was look, and it would be there.

2

Friends in Orbit

A FEW WEEKS later was the first time he flipped through the local radio stations and caught Renee on the air. She was now taking inspiration from across the city and had been to both Duluth and Minnetonka for radio show interviews.

Her face was everywhere now, it seemed, including posters at Nicolette Mall and one billboard near the old stone church promoting her for an upcoming event.

She would be headlining, and that was exciting.

But to hear her in rotation on the airwaves? He sent her a text.

ALEX: Guess what I just heard? Live and on the air?

He set his phone aside. It would notify him of her reply. A few minutes later, it did.

REN: Not live. I'm in my bathrobe.

ALEX: But on the air! Congrats!

REN: THX. A late lunch today? Haven't gotten together in a while.

ALEX: Regular place? 1:30?

REN: Or be square.

ALEX: I'll take that as a yes. Looking forward to it.

He didn't expect a reply. If he was off the mark, she

wouldn't hesitate to let him know. He returned to the radio and located Marcus' new podcast. He had a seven AM timeslot, and Alex wouldn't miss it.

"Good morning, Minneapolis! Marcus Havel here, bringing you today's *Faith with Wi-Fi* Morning Edition, and today I want to start off with a nod to an old friend. Buddy, if you've listening, and you'd better be, don't forget that every window can be a mirror, and two of you are better than one any day. Now, to today's talk. I have a newly minted lawyer at my side who's learned to balance the American dream and her family's inherited tradition, Priya Kapoor. Priya, what was your first time experiencing inescapable faith?"

Alex let the podcast play itself out as he prepared breakfast. Even that was healthier. A more relaxed morning schedule allowed him that. Steel-cut oats, a pat of butter, and granola topping along with almond milk was his choice for today.

His phone vibrated.

REN: Was it "Light on the Isles"?

ALEX: Something new. I didn't recognize it except for the beautiful voice.

REN: You schmoozer. Can I call? If you have time, that is.

ALEX: All the time you need.

When he answered, he wasn't surprised when she leapt directly into dialogue.

"Okay, you don't know this because it hasn't aired, but it will, so I'll tell you now."

"I'm listening." He trusted her and didn't think she would say anything that should concern him.

"In Minnetonka, the interviewer wanted to probe my life, the romantic side, particularly. Do you understand what I mean?"

He laughed. "I understand that he doesn't know you at all."

"Yeah, that's what I thought. You and me, right? Why would he think we have a thing together? It was crazy."

"Crazy." Not what he'd expected.

"I told him that if we had a 'thing' together, you would be asking me on dates, and we'd hang out together, you know, stuff like that, but I spend all my time writing songs, you know?"

He realized that was exactly what had been happening, without the romantic part. He imagined his bodyguard, his guardian angel, and he wondered why Cael had missed this.

You weren't ready until you saw it yourself.

"Anyway," she continued, "that's why I told you."

"Okay, told me why?" Did he want to hear this part?

"So if it comes out on the radio? These podcasters say whatever's in their heads, and I don't know what might come out of this one's."

"Like what?"

"What if he says I find inspiration in you, you know, because I love you or something?"

"I would be okay with that. It's not the worst that could happen." He pictured Sophie at the restaurant touching him under the table, and him pulling away and leaving without her.

"Then that's cleared up. We're still on for lunch? I've missed being your conscience, now that you have one of your own." She laughed.

"Still on. See you then."

He looked forward to her next song on the radio, her raw and hopeful voice reminding him of how much she'd meant to him when he was at his lowest. He remembered the Nicolette concert when someone in the audience asked who *Light on the Isles* was about, and she just said, "A friend who figured out how to exist twice and still pay rent once."

A new text vibrated his phone:

MARCUS: Did you catch my podcast? I interviewed Priya. If my buddy's angel ever needs a tech upgrade, call me—he owes consulting hours. See you, pudzo.

PRIYA'S CELEBRATION dinner was delayed, as her parents insisted on flying her back to the old country to show off their newly minted lawyer daughter to their family. After all, she had graduated top of her law class. They were less excited that she joined a legal-aid collective, but the title of lawyer allowed them to ignore that.

At their celebration dinner, she told stories of her time in India.

"You would have to be there, but they took me to my mother's family who live in a rural area. They told everyone that now I would be able to support them in their old age. Me, I thought, how? I can barely support me."

They laughed, and Marcus said, "At least your parents want to show you off. Mine? When I left the Lutheran Church, they sent me flying via my father's boot."

That brought another round of laughter.

Priya continued, "My father's family is from the city, and they understood. My amma, my father's mother, told me to never marry a man who earns less than me, and never give him my paycheck. He must earn what he gets from me, and she was proud of me."

"Hear, hear!" Alex lifted his bottle and clinked with hers. "I'm with your amma all the way."

"Proof," she said, "that reason and revelation can share a table and even split dessert."

He held up his bottle in solidarity. "Amen to compatible data sets."

3

Echoes Across the City

OFTEN, FOR weeks at a time, he wondered if Cael had been a figment of stress, and that Priya was correct. Repressed anxiety relieves itself however it must, and if that means seeing angelic beings in his mirror, then that's what happens.

His current situation supported that. He was sleeping better, his circle of acquaintances from work seemed more like friends than the people he'd rubbed shoulders with at Sutter One West, and the beautiful moments in each day stood out to him as never before.

He'd known flowers bloomed around the city, but for the first time, they were what he saw, not the curbing scarred by too many impacts with tires. At Joey's, the smiles when he greeted patrons stood out more than their weary looks when they walked in.

Please and thank you. He heard them all the time.

Cillie Rothenberger with the podcast *Taking Time for Life* said: *The beauty in life is there, alongside the ugly things. How we see life is through what we focus on.*

Marcus shared with him a verse from Philippians he'd been forced to memorize as a boy. "Fill your minds with things that are good and deserve praise, things that are true, noble, right, pure, lovely, and honorable."

Like please, thank you, and flowers in the city.

Occasionally he caught news clips of things that seemed too impossible to ignore.

One told of a bus driver who found himself dozing off. A streetlight flared, or so he claimed, jarring him awake, and he narrowly avoided a car slowing for a right turn.

In another clip, a distracted mother plunged into a lake. She was able to escape, but her baby was in a car seat and disappeared underwater with the car. A stranger appeared, dove in, and carried the child to safety before disappearing.

And on cool evenings, strangers at the station or waiting to cross the street moved his direction, telling him it was warmer where he stood.

During fundraising for a new project, dinner was set up at a rooftop restaurant overlooking the city. A mix of high society and regular folks sampled the buffets and carried sparkling stemware under the gathering sky, and in the west, thin clouds burned with reds and oranges. A slim, older woman found him and tapped her glass to his.

"I remember you. You were at that Kane building, weren't you? Rising executive, or something like that?"

"Kane & Sutter." He said it like his words were confirmation. It was a long time since he'd heard those names used in the same sentence.

"It is you." She smiled. "I worked there. Oh, it's been decades now, but I remember being asked to move on when I wouldn't do what they asked."

"Do I want to know?" He wasn't sure he did, but his own experiences there dangled temptation before him, and he took the risk.

"Likely the reason you are no longer there. I kept my integrity. The job? My life is better now, and I don't have to apologize for what I am."

"It's interesting that you remember them. No one else does."

"We always remember what changes us. It's when we forget that we no longer remember who we were. I'm expecting great things from you."

He stared into the night, incorporating her words. When he turned to ask her name, she was gone. No one remembered seeing her, and he had to let it go. However, the fundraiser did double the expected donations, surprising everyone except him.

As his face became better known in the non-profit sector, news reporters began to ring him, asking about the mysterious hero who looked so much like him.

He brushed it off, saying it couldn't be him. "Coincidence," he'd tell reporters whenever the rumors were too close to home. And yet ... when he noted Cael's absences, they coincided almost exactly with the incidents he'd denied.

And when he was alone? He sometimes traced the glowing crack that still ran through his bathroom mirror and felt an answering stir of warmth across his shoulder blades.

4

Return to the Lake

ON THE FIRST true summer weekend, the gang gathered at the park for the day.

The group included Marcus, of course, and Priya, who was now attached more than ever, after returning from her intrusive trip back to the old world. She was spending more time with them than ever as she put acceptable boundaries around her life.

Priya brought with her a new tagalong, Ayaan Sharma. He was one good thing about her visit with her parents. She hadn't known him before, but his parents were excited to hear that she was from Minneapolis, and surely she knew their boy, Ayaan.

How could she, she thought, as more than 400,000 people called the city home? Yet, a week after returning, she got an unsolicited email from an A. Sharma. The last name seemed familiar, she opened it, and he was now a part-time companion who would tell anyone who asked that he hoped it would be more one day.

From his non-profit, Alex invited anyone who had the day free, bringing on board Freida Erricksen, Lance Abbot, Jim Lancer, and several others. They arrived in various styles of summer dress, but all were ready to have a good time.

Renee, of course, found every reason to be close to Alex whatever he was doing that day, which meant that when he walked to Lake of the Isles that evening, she was at his side.

"This is my first time. Mystery meets mirror." She wrapped her fingers with his, and they fell into an easy rhythm.

"The mystery makes sense, but I don't know about the mirrors. That's part of the appeal. Outdoors, only trees, no glass. I can't see myself anywhere." He wanted to tease: *except in your eyes*, but that was too much too soon, and he wasn't ready for that.

When they arrived, contrary to his words, the air was perfectly still, and the water mirrored the skyline.

Dragonflies shimmered over the water, just touching the surface and causing occasional disturbances where ice once held him firmly affixed to its glassy surface. As soon as they touched, the water created small ripples that stilled almost immediately.

"If I spent time here, I'd dream of it too." She smiled and took in the greens and blues under the late day sun. The water would darken soon, and then anything under the surface would disappear.

"I love it here, too." Her words resonated in him, and he loved her for that.

"Corporate continuum or nature as nurture?" She rocked her hands as if weighing one against the other.

"I'll take nature, thank you. Corporate almost had me, and I was fortunate to break away."

He knelt at the edge and smiled at the reflection looking back—unbroken now, casually human.

"What do you see?" She knelt beside him and

reached her finger towards the water.

"Don't." He touched her wrist.

"What then?" She studied the water, then turned to him.

"You don't see it, do you?" He stood. He wasn't disappointed, just aware that he'd always see in the lake things and events no one else ever would.

"I see that it's special to you."

She stood to get her bearings, and he whispered, "Still here?"

A ripple crossed the surface, catching the final rays of the sun until it flashed gold.

"Oh, Alex, did you see that? It's beautiful. Where did it come from? There's no wind."

He wanted to respond to her, but he was listening to the answer he'd asked of his angel. He heard it not in words but in laughter: the chirruping of a cricket, a bird's song as it readied for its nighttime ministrations, and through the soft and repetitive sound of the ripples as they reached the shore.

The lake remembered everything. He remembered everything. This place would always be a part of him.

"Let's make a ripple of our own." He lifted a small stone from at his feet, grinned at Renee, and tossed it. It hit far out into the water, and circles raced outward in perfect symmetry.

Ripples never vanish, he realized. They just widen until the eye can't follow them, affecting everything in their path.

The two young people held hands all the way home.

WHEN AUTUMN bowed in again, Alex walked to

Lake of the Isles at dusk. This time he was alone.

The city reflected on the surface like a constellation of low-hanging stars.

He watched a kid toss pebbles, and he counted the ripples spreading outward, a silent hymn of cause and effect, with only the plunk of the stones as a percussion accompaniment.

He closed his eyes, breathing the cool air until his thoughts slowed to the rhythm of his heart.

His memories blurred: the trembling bird in the birchwood, his mother's voice about invisible helpers, the day the mirror cracked.

He whispered into the wind, "I see you," unsure if he was speaking to Cael, his distant childhood, or his conscience itself.

The breeze rose, playful, folding around him like unseen wings.

5

Evening at Renee's Show

DURING THE first full thrust of winter, with an Alberta Clipper howling against the apartment windows, he was waiting on a frozen pasta tray in the oven. His bank accounts were still tight, and it was another way to economize. He rested on the couch with his head back and his eyes closed, listening to a podcast about why non-profits were the answer to America's inner-city woes.

His phone vibrated, and he held it up to check it. It was a text notification, and he clicked it.

REN: U home? Best news EVR!! May I come over?

ALEX: In this? Must B outstanding?

He added the abbreviated B to copy her style and the question mark to show she had his support but didn't know if this was the time to be out.

REN: YES & YES. On my way

If he was having company, things needed done. He was in his tee from earlier in the day, and his outer shirt had only made it as far as the arm of the couch. He shook it out, shoved one arm through and then the other, and began to button it. His socks were likely okay, as the floor was warm, and he was at home. He hung his cashmere on his coat rack and kicked a magazine under the couch. The pasta was ten minutes from coming out, so he set the timer for that length and put out a hot pad for when it emerged.

She was as tangled as he expected when he opened the door.

"Renee, come in and get yourself sorted. Let me take your coat."

He helped her peel it away and added it to the coat rack. When he turned around, she had her hands in her hair, organizing it from windblown to slightly disorganized. Her face with bright with excitement.

"So?" He felt his face copying hers.

"It's happening!" She balled her fists and shook them in a silent cheer. "It's finally real!"

When she began a victory dance, he grasped her upper arms and looked into her face. "Okay, what's real?"

"My tour. The radio station is owned by a company, which is how things are done, and my records are so hot, they want me to do a regional tour."

"During an Alberta Clipper? They must be really happy with how well your records are doing." He pulled her into his arms and hugged her before releasing her to look back into her face. "Congratulations."

"I wish you could go with me."

"So do I. Listen—" His timer went off, and he held up a finger. "I'm sorry. That's pasta. It's got to come out. It serves four. Do you want some?"

She frowned for a second as if deciding, then smiled. "Yes. How can I help?"

Before the meal was over, they had a get-together organized at Foodz so that she could perform one last set for all her friends. He assured her that everyone would be there.

HIS FAVORITE tune used the same line that had followed him for years, rewritten slightly:

"We walk the glass / We learn the flame / What once was fear / Now signs its name."

Afterward she hugged him tight. "See? You inspired a tax-deductible miracle."

He laughed. "Song royalties count as hope, right?"

"That's the only currency left."

The Foodz event was indeed to be the final hurrah for Renee's time in Minneapolis. She was headed to Nashville next, where she would be staying on the station's dime while they worked on a recording contract. She was on her way to the airport as soon as she left the eatery, and her Uber waited for her at the door.

"I'll miss you, Alex." She had a small bag and her guitar already over her shoulder.

"And me, you. You've been my conscience, at times wrapped in sarcasm, but my foundation, anyway. I wish you the best."

"And me, you." She tiptoed to give him a light kiss on the cheek before waving and calling out to everyone else who'd come to see her perform.

When she stepped out into the night, the streetlights turned her breath to gold, and Alex allowed that maybe some people carried their own magic inside.

Back in the restaurant, he joined his friends. The place smelled of cedar, liquid refreshment, and possibility; and he was glad for everyone who'd joined Renee to wish her their best on her new voyage into life.

He called to them, "I want to join in and sing one of Renee's songs before we leave. We don't have her guitar—"

"Or her musical ability," someone in the crowd called.

"Right, right." He laughed and found it difficult to wipe the grin from his face. "Still, I'll start."

He began, and the song rose in volume until everyone had joined in.

"We walk the glass / We learn the flame / We lose the fear / We keep the name."

It was the old version they remembered, and when they finished, applause rolled like tidewater. Marcus whistled; Priya wiped one discreet tear; and Alex clapped with a full heart.

He caught a flicker at the corner of his eye, and when he turned, two wings with translucent feathers folded in contentment behind the stage.

Then the light shifted, and the scene settled back into the ordinary Foodz stand-up comedy corner.

The lights hummed softly as if they, too, breathed out the words of the song.

6

Storefront Reflection

HE WAS SURPRISED when Marcus first asked him to join him on his podcast.

"What, I'm an expert now? On what? You're the one with the stable job history. I bounce from non-profit to non-profit. My longest running job at this point is barista at Joey's."

"Well, Priya's done it, and there's no reason you can't, too. Besides, I've already been announcing you." Marcus grinned mischievously. Now that he had his own podcast where he blended theology with troubleshooting tips, he was willing to take spiritual risks. "Spiritual tech support," he called it. "I've made you the muse of my broadcasts. You can be uncredited if you want, but then when I go national, I'll have to decide whether to share any of the profits."

He grinned and clapped his shoulder, which Alex tolerated because Marcus' jokes were solid.

Priya agreed that he should do it, declaring that she had paid her dues, and he needed to step up and be a man. Ayaan was now her constant companion, and with his support and her fiercely logical mind, she had gone from the legal-aid collective to a position as a public defender. With her evaluation of Alex's experiences, she had stopped insisting that faith was just neural misfire.

"I don't pretend to understand what you went through," she admitted during one discussion, "but my logic finally met its match. In my head, logic and humility are finally getting along."

They vowed to meet monthly, at the same table, and to never lose the same easy rhythm.

Alex was certain no one would need to mention angels again to believe.

LATER HE walked home alone along the river. City lights stitched gold into the flowing black water, glowing in the same way as the crack in his mirror.

He paused at a storefront window. The glass showed his reflection exactly as it should: a man in his twenties, shoulders relaxed, with his eyes clear. No second self. No halo.

Just as he turned away, the reflection lifted one eyebrow—the small half-smile he used to give himself years ago, before he knew why it mattered.

He laughed under his breath. "All right, Cael. I see you."

7

Closing Light

LIFE WENT ON, new non-profits needed his services, and spring returned. Occasionally he caught Renee's songs on a new station. He and his friends met up at Foodz, the laughter was still bright, and he even contacted his father once or twice.

It was everyday Minneapolis, the City of Lakes, the best place in Minnesota to live.

Yet, small signs still happened. A mug fell from the counter and didn't shatter. A streetlight flared brighter as he helped an old man across Nicollet.

Once, during a blackout, his apartment alone was faintly lighted—not enough to boast about, just enough to find candles.

He called them "grace glitches," laughed, and tucked them into the place in his mind were all things unexplained went. Miracles, he decided, were feedback rather than spectacle.

Occasionally, as the arrival of the midnight hour brought sleep to the city, the voice arrived like the exhaled breath of a dream:

Goodness persists, Alex. You've just learned to speak its language.

He mumbled, "Got that memo."

A soft chuckle—his own, doubled—answered.

The final time, the aftermath left nothing but the slow percussion of rain, the steady music of an ordinary, luminous world falling on the roof and trees and sidewalks of the city.

Dawn came pale and pink while painting the clouds. In the distance, church bells rang, for once on key with the city's early sirens and warming hum.

Alex stepped out of his apartment, keys jangling with a discordant sound, a mundane noise that was perfectly beautiful in its ordinariness. He looked east, where the light grew stronger with every breath.

Somewhere above and within, he felt the words inside: *Keep walking. Your future is one step away.*

He did—and every step left a faint shimmer on wet pavement, too brief for anyone else to notice, but exactly long enough to prove that faith had left its imprint on a young man's soul.

www.ingramcontent.com/pod-product-compliance
Lightning Source LLC
LaVergne TN
LVHW020700110826
845149LV00012B/2062
* 9 7 8 1 9 5 7 1 7 3 5 3 5 *